DON'T BLAME ME

TIME TO FORGIVE?

JOANNA WARRINGTON

1

AUSTRALIA, EARLY MARCH 2020

I can't wait to share my news with my partner, Glen. I've just been promoted. When I go back to work on Monday, I'll be deputy manager of the Orange Tree Café. I feel in my pocket for the red badge with my new title emblazoned in gold. 'Go and celebrate,' Josh, my boss had commanded, letting me out early. I pop into Dan Murphy's on my way home for a bottle of bubbly. Glen and I haven't spent much time together lately. We've both been working long hours. We'll crack open the bottle and drink it on the balcony. Already I'm really looking forward to the evening ahead.

My phone is ringing. Tucking the champagne under one arm I pull the phone from my pocket. It's my brother Andrew calling from England.

'Dad's dying,' he blurts. 'Dee, you need to come back,' he says with urgency. 'They've said he's got weeks, maybe a month or two at the most.'

Although I have been expecting this news and been in touch with Andrew each day for an update on Dad, I'm unprepared. There's a pause while I gulp. Shock takes hold and I lean against the shop window.

'You still there, sis?'

'Andrew, I've just been promoted. My new job starts on Monday.' It's the first excuse that springs into my head, but it's a feeble one and I immediately feel dreadful for sounding so cold-hearted. But the fact is, I'm scared to go back to England even though I want to spend time with poor Dad. I'm scared to confront the past.

'Dad needs you. I need you.'

I want to hide and pretend this is not happening. Like I did when Mum died five years ago.

'Let me talk to Glen.' This will buy me time. In my heart I know that I have a duty. Poor Andrew is dealing with everything on his own. What's wrong with me? I try to shake myself. I've let what happened to me all those years ago turn me into a sour, bitter woman and despite all the counselling in the world, it feels as if I'll never be able to snap out of the permanent state that I'm in.

'Dee, you didn't come back when Mum was dying, and I doubt you'd trouble yourself to step on a plane if I was terminally ill either. You've got a short memory. When you needed us, we bent over backwards to help.'

'That was different.'

'You left us to pick up the pieces. You have no idea what Mum and Dad went through after you left.'

'Andrew,' I pause. My heart is hammering. I'm so upset I can barely get the words out. 'Nobody, I repeat, nobody was there for me.' This isn't true but I'm ranting and can't control myself. 'I'm not blaming you, it's just how things were. You all rallied round in a practical sense, yes, and I'm grateful for that, but I was living through hell and I had to escape. Why can't you understand that?'

I ran away to Australia in my early thirties to be as far away from England as possible. It was the only way to cope. But twenty-five years have now passed. I can't believe I'll soon be fifty-five. And I can't believe it's 2020. Where has the time gone? If I don't go back now, I never will. And if I can't go back now, a bigger reason won't come along to make me. Psychologically it's become harder and harder for me to return to England as time has gone on. Deep down I know, and I've been told by Helen, my therapist, the only way to purge my soul is to return, confront what happened, then put things to rest.

Being in Australia isn't practical when there's a crisis. You can't get any further away than here. If I'd chosen to start a new life in France or Spain, I could easily hop on a plane, be back in England in a couple of hours and all for around fifty quid if I searched for a cheap flight. I'm so cut off here. But it was my choice.

What am I to do now? My new job starts Monday. I want to see Dad. I want to be with him in those last weeks. I've not seen him in ten years. I must be there to help Andrew. It's not fair to leave everything to him. And yet, something deep inside my gut is stopping me.

I reach the apartment where Glen and I live, fumble for my keys and unlock the door.

Inside, I'm frozen to the spot. Something is going on, upstairs. I drop my keys and the bottle on the carpet, my hand shaking as I reach for the banister to steady myself. Shock slices through me with the realisation that Glen is upstairs having sex with another woman. This can't be happening. My mind is playing tricks. Please God, wake me up, let this be a horrible nightmare.

Who is she? And do I know her? Why didn't I see this coming?

I climb the stairs, careful to avoid the step that creaks, and by the time I've reached the top, inches from the bedroom, my legs are like jelly and a fist has tightened around my heart.

Anger wells to the surface as the sounds grow louder. All I want to do is claw his eyes out. I turn the handle and step inside. They are wrapped together like a pair of climbing plants. Glen stares at me, his jaw dropping open and his face tightening. There's terror in his eyes. It's stark and primeval.

It's as if a nuclear bomb has just decimated my entire world. Everything happens in slow motion.

'Dee...' He jolts, pulling the doona over his naked body.

'How long has this being going on?' I spit the words at him.

Her fragrance mingles with the smell of sweaty bodies and catches in my throat. There are drinks either side of the bed and she is occupying my side. Her drink is on my bedside table next to the Hilary Boyd novel I'm reading. I reach to grab his beer and chuck it over him.

'Calm down, Dee,' he screams. 'Go downstairs. Give me five minutes. We'll talk.' He sits up and reaches for his underpants without disturbing the sheets still covering him.

'Talk? What is there to talk about? You've treated me like a dirty rag to be trampled on. You need to get over your mid-life crisis. Most men buy a sports car, but not you, you have to find a cheap tart to screw.'

'I should go,' the woman mutters.

'I'm sorry, all right?' he screams at me.

'Get out of my bed, you slut,' I shout at the woman. She's sitting up, reaching for her knickers. I lurch towards her, grabbing her clothes, in a heap by the bed. With my shaking hand I toss them at her. 'Go,' I shout. My insides crumble. She's everything I'm not – young and blonde, and I resist the urge to dig my nails into her pretty face.

I RUN down the stairs and out into the cool night air leaving the front door wide open. I only stop when I'm out of breath and wheezing. On the beach, the sand is soft under my feet and the inky sea is my solace. The lacy waves curling to shore soothe me and the breeze blows the tensions out of my muscles. I collapse onto a rock and loneliness kicks in. The ocean makes me think of the many miles I am from home. Home - the word jars in my head. I've not used that word to describe England for such a long time. I've lived in Australia for over twenty-five years – this has become home. The moon is high tonight edging the tops of the waves with silver and as I gaze across the ocean stretched out to infinity I feel strangely cut off from the rest of the world, as if I'm hanging off the globe by my fingertips.

I struggle to my feet. There's a barbecue party going on further along the beach. Bare footed and dressed in shorts, couples sway to music drifting softly from the speakers wedged in the sand. They are happy couples in love and having fun. Like Glen and I used to be. We met at a beach barbie five years ago and shortly after we moved in together. Following a string of relationships ever since I left England, lasting anything from a month to a few years - all ending in disaster - it finally felt as if I'd met the one. Is it just me or does this keep happening to other women too? Is this how I'm going to spend the rest of my life? Hopping from one person's bed to the next, it all ending in disaster, never quite achieving long-term stability.

I drop to my knees, forming hollows in the sand and let out a sob. My world is tilting on its axis. What am I going to do? I can't stay and listen to his excuses and justifications. There has to be a pre-existing script for people who find out their partner is cheating and a set of storylines that could go in either direction – split or stick. But what is my storyline? I don't know where to go from here. I need to find strength to carry on but right now it feels as if my heart has been ripped out of my chest. My life is starting over again, I must accept that fact, but

I'm not ready to move on. I get up, crying and stagger towards the jetty. At the end of the planking I stop to lean over the railings. And then a thought occurs to me, like a slap across the cheek. I'm not enough for him and never will be. A quarter of a mile out to sea on the jetty the water stretches to the earth's edge and out of sight. I could haul myself over and nobody would know. 'Fuck you, Glen,' I scream into the night air.

I turn and head back to the beach, not quite knowing what I'm going to do next. So many recent events and memories that seemed insignificant now add up. Glen had been shifty lately, as if he felt guilty about something. It had been bothering me but when I asked him, he said there was nothing wrong. On Valentine's Day he gave me cheap garage forecourt flowers but no card. He doesn't hold my hand anymore and we've not made love in weeks. The writing has been on the wall for some time and I've not seen it. I've been a dumb puppet on a string in this relationship.

I switch my phone back on, and it starts ringing. It's Andrew again. I toy with the idea of hitting the ignore call button. I can't go back to England to look after our sick father. I'll lose my job at the café if I swan off for a few weeks, and in any case where does he think I'm going to find the air fare on my shitty wages? And there's zero chance of borrowing money from Glen, especially not now. But I need to get away, I can't stay here, not with this going on. Andrew rings off and my decision is postponed.

England seems so far away, not just in terms of the journey time but in decades too. I haven't been back to the country of my youth. The thought of returning to Heatherly, the house in Rivermead, the small village in Kent where I grew up leaves me feeling unsettled, especially after what happened all those years ago. I came to Australia to forget.

I wouldn't know what to expect if I went back. It would be like travelling in a time machine, stepping back into my old self and I'm not sure how I'd cope. With Mum gone and Dad so ill, it would be sad to return only to watch Dad slip away and having to say goodbye to the house and all of the memories. And then I realise that my later memories of Mum and Dad aren't in England, but abroad because they used to either come over here for several weeks at a time, or we would meet halfway, in places like Thailand or Hong Kong.

Yet, if I returned to England, it wouldn't have to be for long. It's beautiful here. I have the type of lifestyle people crave. Miles of golden sand and blue sky. It's all sea and surfers and hip cafes like the one I work in. It was Glen's suggestion to come here to the east coast, mainly because he loves surfing. I was settled over in Perth where we met, but my friends have now moved on from there and I'm not sure I would want to go back to Perth.

Andrew has left a message. 'Hi, sis, please, I know it's not easy for you, but it isn't for me either. I'll pay for your flight. You always said you'd come back if anything happened to either of them. You couldn't come for Mum, please, at least be here for Dad. Café jobs are ten-a-penny. I'm sure you'll find another one when you get back to Oz.'

Under normal circumstances, I'd be incensed by his last comment, but tonight I let it wash over me and all I hear are the words 'I'll pay for your flight.' On impulse I call him back.

'How's Dad?'

'He's still got Ruth, the carer living in, but she's finding it hard looking after him. I go over as much as I can but it's getting tough. Yesterday he was doubly incontinent. Ruth washed six pairs of trousers, not to mention washing him as well. He's been referred to the memory clinic and the continence clinic. He can remember how to use the remote control, when he wants to, but sometimes he doesn't recognise people. I don't think he'll have long from what the doctors have told me.

He's so frail. He's lost a lot of weight. He's done well to get this far.'

My heart slams in my chest on hearing this news. Dad was diagnosed with prostate cancer four years ago and has received hormone therapy. But it has travelled to the bones. He's also recently been diagnosed with vascular dementia.

'He's had some tests. The tests show that the cancer is spreading to other organs. It's metastasized. And his PSA level is through the roof.'

'How can I help?'

'I think you should get back here. I wouldn't be truthful if I didn't say that everything about him is worrying me at the moment.' There's a sense of urgency and authority in his voice. 'I'm asking you to. There's a lot you can help with.' He sighs. There's tiredness and a note of frustration in his tone. He's shouldering it all and clearly finding it overwhelming. 'Like I said, I'll pay for your flight. We can take it out of Dad's account. I've got power of attorney. I'm at the house now but I can only stay a few days then I need to go back to work.'

'Will you take down all the photo frames and any pictures on the walls before I arrive?' The thought of walking into a shrine fills me with dread.

'Of course,' he replies. 'He knows which pictures I'm referring to. He knows the effect they will have on me.

Rivermead, the small village where we grew up and where Dad still lives, is too far away for Andrew to drop in every day. He's a busy man, working as an accountant up in the City. He lives with his wife, Tracy and their two children, Izzy and Emily in a detached house in Surrey with a swimming pool and a tennis court. His life has followed an orderly fashion. University, marriage, kids. He's done very well for himself. I last saw his family six months ago when they came to Australia.

I clamber onto the pavement and stop to perch on a bench to shake the sand from my shoes. Happy memories of Rivermead from long ago fill my head, but then a dark cloud descends to wash those memories away, and is replaced by a shot of anxiety. An ominous feeling sits somewhere deep inside me. If I go back to England will I find a direction, or will I have to confront my painful past?

2

Back from the beach, I spot Glen standing by his car watching as I approach, his overnight bag slung over his shoulder. He has that post-coital dishevelled look about him, his hair is messy and his shirt is untucked. Something in me constricts. My first instinct is to shout and scream and demand answers. The tendons in my neck feel like guitar strings stretched to breaking point, a sure sign that the mother of all headaches is on its way.

He hangs his head wretchedly and stares at the ground. A hard, sour nut wedges itself in my throat. 'Too ashamed to look at me?' I grit my teeth and wait for his pathetic apology but there isn't one.

'I'll move out,' he mutters, raising his head like a naughty schoolboy. There's no emotion in his eyes and I wonder how long he's been preparing this speech.

'Leaving me to pay the rent?' I screech.

'You don't want me. You won't talk about things.'

'What is there to talk about? I don't sleep with other men. You've got zero respect for me.' I don't want him back, only a weak woman would do that. I just want to slap him, but I restrain myself.

'She doesn't mean a thing to me, Dee, I swear. You have to believe me.' He drops the bag on the ground as if he thinks he's in with a chance of winning me back.

'Oh please, do you think I'm a complete idiot?' I'm inches from him. I just want to poke my fingers into his eyes.

'My head's been all over the place lately.'

I let out a laugh. 'It's all about you. You don't give a damn about me.'

'You're always working. I never see you.'

'Don't you dare pass the buck.'

'Well when did we last make love?'

I sweep my hand through my hair, too flabbergasted to speak.

'See, you can't remember.'

'You're despicable. I'm not to blame for any of this. How long has it been going on, this thing with her?'

'It was only...'

'Just the once? Please, credit me with some intelligence. Just admit you've been sleeping with her for ages. That's why you've been behaving weirdly lately.'

'I expect you've got a few little secrets of your own tucked away.' He sniffs. 'I've seen the way your boss looks at you.'

'For Christ's sake. I'm not listening to this crap. I'm going back to England. I've no idea how long I'll be gone.' I walk towards the outside steps that lead up to the door of the flat and before opening the door I turn to him. 'I'll take my stuff with me. I'll be gone tomorrow. Then you can do what the hell you like. You can move her in for all I care. She seemed to like my side of the bed.'

He rushes towards me. 'Please, Dee. You can't just walk out on me. Not before we've talked.'

'Oh yes I can and that's exactly what I'm going to do.'

'The past five years meant nothing to you?'
'Apparently not,' I snap.
'But England? You can't go back there.'
'It's got piss all to do with you. But for your information, my dad's ill. I've got no choice.'
'Aren't you going to speak to Helen?'
'Why?'
'Because she's your therapist. To see what she thinks?'
'Don't pretend you care.'
'It's a bad idea, Dee. Don't go.'

I tap down the unchecked emotions swirling in my stomach.

'We've been together for five years. Of course, I care. I cared enough to pay for your therapy sessions.'

'Oh, how very big of you, Glen. So, it all comes down to money? I'll pay every penny back if that's what's bothering you.'

'Don't be stupid. That's not what I meant. I'm just worried about you.'

'Well don't be. Get out my way. I'll be gone tomorrow. You can sort this place out.' I march into the flat to pack, knowing that he's right, I should speak to Helen first, but there's no time, I've a flight to book.

GLEN DOESN'T FOLLOW me into the apartment, he knows me well enough not to try to change my mind when it's made up. I can hear him outside deliberately grinding the gears of the car, revving the engine, sweeping away at speed. Enraged and without stopping to consider the consequences, I race to the bedroom and rifle through his wardrobe, pulling shirts and trousers from their hangers, grabbing his trainers and the line of smart shoes he wears for business meetings. I only stop when the cupboard is bare, gathering everything up, opening the window and hurling it all out. His shoes and trainers splash into the communal swimming pool below, floating like driftwood. His shirts balloon into small tents, to immerse in chlorine. With the help of tomorrow's sun, I'm hoping they will fade.

I walk from room to room. We've lived in this small block of apartments close to the sea for two years now. We'd fallen in love with it the moment we'd seen it. There are five apartments in a row close to the shops. We liked the fact that the garages are on the ground floor and the property above. It's not a big apartment, but somehow we've acquired lots of possessions. Apart from my clothes, the emerald ring and Georg Jensen silver bracelet I inherited from my mother, none of it matters and is replaceable. I head into the lounge, collapsing onto the settee, pulling my legs into a fetal position, welcoming some wallow time. I'd love to devour a bar of chocolate and a bottle of wine right now. It's every broken-hearted person's rescue remedy, but I must book my flight. Before I head into the study, a shard of light from the table lamp catches the crystal fruit bowl on the coffee table making rainbow diamonds that dance across the ceiling. I pick it up and throw it at the wall. It makes a dent in the paintwork and pieces of plaster crumble. Good. I feel better already. Now that his clothes are gone and the expensive gift from his mother scattered across the carpet, I turn my attention to booking the flight. I go into the study to turn on the computer. Glen's face stares smugly at me from a picture on the desk. I smash the frame against the desk, pull out the photo, ripping it into tiny pieces and scattering them across the carpet. I grind my foot into a fragment of Glen's grin. This is what that bastard has done to me - torn my dreams apart.

When the flight's booked and I'm packed, I hurl myself onto the bed, pummelling the bedding, biting the doona, until my teeth hurt. The temperature inside me is rising; I feel as if I'm going to boil over any second. I so badly want to punch him in the face. I fling the doona off; I will sleep on the sheet. But it's useless. How can I sleep where he's shagged her? I roll onto the floor, pulling my legs up to my chest, fury coursing through my body. How dare he treat me like this?

The following morning, there's a dull ache across my chest as yesterday's events float through my waking mind. Despite what's he done; I'll miss Glen. He was my soul mate and I still love him even though I'm hurting. I don't want to start all over again and meet someone new. I'm too old to join the dating scene. Deep inside I think I've always known that Glen and I wouldn't last. He oozes charisma and a certain charm that women love. Not to mention his rugged looks. In a room full of people Glen has a way of making each person he talks to feel special and important, as if nobody else matters. Physically I do not match up to him. I have varicose veins like Japanese Knotweed, my grandpa's nose and my auntie's fried-egg boobs. But the one good thing about my nose is that my sense of smell in uncommonly acute and my fried-egg boobs mean that I can go jogging without the discomfort some women experience. Glen used to tell me he loved my dark glossy hair and that I looked like Miranda Hart, his favourite actress. I think I'm too tall and most men don't like tall women. It has its advantages though. I can reach for top-shelf items in the supermarket. But most of all I loathe my feet. They're so big they look like barges on a canal and make slow dancing at a disco difficult. And I have to stand sideways at the kitchen sink to wash-up.

I can't turn my love for Glen on and off like a light switch, even though what he's done is appalling. Maybe I'm in shock. I need to build a steel wall around my emotions in order to recover and move on. I close my eyes and try to push the rosy bits to one side, focusing on his bad points. His morning post-kebab breath, his addiction to cheese-and-onion crisp sandwiches and his horrible habits – cutting toenails in bed and eating lettuce with his fingers.

I open my eyes. I'm going to need time to adjust to the new state I'm in – having to get over the relationship. You don't get over a five-year relationship in a hurry. I must take one day at a time.

I get up, make coffee and pack. Tipping things into my suitcase I almost forget – the letter from New York I keep between two books in my bedside cupboard. I received the letter years ago. Making me wait and worry was unforgivable.

I put the letter into my handbag. Few people write letters these days. It's all email and What's App and Facebook, but I'm not on Facebook. I'm a private person and don't want my life spilled across a computer screen. If people want to stay in touch with me, they can make the effort. Not being on social media it's hard for people to keep up with me because I've moved so many times to different places within Australia.

I thought about binning the letter. Helen said that it would be cathartic, a way to move on, but I can't.

3

With the first leg of the journey over, we land in Dubai. The doors of the jumbo-jet open into a blast of desert heat. It feels as if I'm trapped in a hairdryer on full power. It's early March and the Middle East is always hot.

Down a flight of steps, I pass water flowing down a granite wall and ahead a queue snakes around the immigration hall. I nearly join the queue for veiled women, chuckling to myself when I realise my mistake. Wearing a low-cut top and short skirt, I definitely don't qualify for that queue.

A line of white-gowned Arab men with red-checked t-towels on their heads who look as if they are Opec board members, sit in booths. One of them calls me forward, scrutinising my passport with a fearsome frown. I'm looking forward to resting in the airport and enjoying the wonderful shopping experience before heading for my connecting flight to London Heathrow.

I loiter in the duty-free trying on lipsticks, when the Islamic call to prayer begins. It's haunting, melodic tune makes me smile. It feels so out of place as it rings through the busy mall.

The urge to go on a frenzied shopping bender in the duty-free is strong but I restrain myself after one lipstick and an eyeliner, and head to a shop devoted to my favourite spread, Nutella. Nutella is the reason for the extra pounds around my middle. To hell with the diet. Glen's cheated on me. It's time for me to cheat on myself. I'm inspecting the various jars and Nutella products on display with fancy packaging, baulking at the inflated prices when a high-pitched voice calling my name, cuts through my thoughts. I turn. Standing there, unbelievably are Lyn and Pandora - two friends I was at school with. They are my closest English friends and I've known them ever since we were in nappies. They've been over to Australia to stay with me several times.

'Dee, I thought it was you,' Lyn shrieks. 'Oh my God, fancy bumping into you here.'

They reach forward and hug me in turn.

'Let me guess, you've been trying on perfume? You smell like a brothel,' I tell them, laughing.

'So where are you off to, Dee?' Pandora asks. 'We've just had a week here. Dubai is such an amazing place, although we're both dying to get back to England for a drop of alcohol.'

'I'm flying to Heathrow. Dad's ill. Not sure how long I'm back for or what my plans are. It's a long story.'

As we chat, Lyn turns to glance at the departure board. 'Pandora, it's time to board. Shame we're not on the same flight as you, Dee.'

'I've got ages to wait,' I tell them.

'We need to get together,' Pandora says excitedly. 'A proper catch-up.' We hurriedly exchange phone numbers. 'There's a primary school reunion on the 27th. Please say you'll come.'

A lump forms in my throat at the thought of a school reunion. 'I'll have to think about that.'

Lyn, seeing my apprehension puts her hand on mine. 'I know, I keep telling her, what's the point in going to a reunion?

If you want to catch up with old school friends, why not chat on-line in your comfy leggings, instead of squeezing into a brand-new outfit?'

'It'll be fun,' Pandora gushes. 'And not everybody will be there.'

I flinch. 'Not everyone?'

'Yes Dee, I don't think you-know-who will be there. He wasn't at the last one.'

'Well... in that case I guess I could come.'

We say goodbye. Still cradling a Nutella jar, I watch them head towards the moving walkway. Middle age has firmly slugged into the picture for Pandora who has put on a shedload of weight and looks clown-like. She used to be so slim, but she's always loved her coffee-and-walnut cake and is now paying the price for all the moments on the lips. Back in our early twenties when we went clubbing she could get away with it. She has grown an enormous bottom which wiggles and jiggles and is articulated in such a way that it seems to move separately from the rest of her body. The years have been kinder to Lyn, by comparison, whose recent obsession with cycling and running - an escape from being dragged into a hide with her bird-watching husband, Ray - has helped her stay trim.

I consider the primary school reunion. The absence of a significant other, at the grand old age of fifty-five makes me feel disinclined to rock up at what I feel to be too like one of Mrs Hancock's, 'let's all gather in a circle on the rug' session, clutching our half pints of milk and chewing on bogies, sharing our thoughts for the day, or - in the world of today's children - the 'show and tell.' Do I really want to expose myself to a social gathering which has the potential to feel like a kind of beauty pageant of who has achieved what in the past three decades? I know that the occasion will be fraught with awkward tension, mainly because I will have to account for myself and portray the person I now am. The truth is, I'm not sure who I am, and it doesn't feel as if I've achieved very much in the intervening years.

But despite my nerves about the evening, a part of me is curious and even mildly excited to find out how the lives of my fellow classmates have turned out. They were there at the beginning of my life, the formative years when I learned to tie my shoelaces and made everybody laugh with my poo and wee jokes. A part of me feels a wave of nostalgia, but with the passage of time we are now strangers and we are going to be introducing ourselves all over again. As I'm not on Facebook there will be no sneak previews. In the absence of any trailers, I have no idea what to expect. Some of us will remember each other with crystal clarity, while others like me have brain fog and can only remember a small handful of names.

THE SEAT BELT signs go on and the plane prepares to descend into London Heathrow. Now that I'm here I'll be with my brother soon, and with mixed feeling about that I make my way through security to the baggage reclaim. We last met up six months ago, when he and his family came to Australia. When there's a crisis we are there for each other at the end of a phone line and we do get on, but sometimes we clash because our opinions and outlook are very different.

Wheeling my case behind me, I scan the sea of faces waiting as passengers spill into the terminal. Just when I think he's not here, Andrew slips through the crowd to greet me. He's three years older than me and if I am to compare him to a film star, I'd say he is most like Robin Williams in looks.

Andrew's hair is thin and no longer dark and glossy like a newly polished pair of shoes. He has a receding hairline and there are wisps of grey. He's physique is more apple-shaped than I remember and he's squeezed into jeans that look too tight and is also wearing a supermarket t-shirt with a tea stain down the middle. I've never understood why he doesn't wear dark t-shirts; he can never manage to drink a cuppa without spilling it. He's definitely put on weight. He has a saggy belly. Too many beers I reckon.

Andrew breaks into a smile under the harsh lighting and rushes towards me, planting an awkward kiss on my cheek and grabbing my case. I catch a whiff of the smell I remember, mothballs. My brother has never worn after-shave. Says it makes his nose wrinkle and brings on hayfever. Suddenly feeling emotional I want to hug him, but we aren't a tactile family and it wouldn't be natural, so I rub his arm instead and we break the tension with laughter.

'Good flight?'

'Legs are killing me. I'm going to sleep like a log tonight.'

The truth is I feel as if I've been awake for days.

We battle through the crowds, careful not to trip over cases on wheels coming from all directions like missiles, and head towards the moving walkway. I turn to look at Andrew. 'Am I going to be shocked when I see Dad? You need to prepare me.'

He makes a pock-pock noise with his lips. It's what he does when he's contemplating the most diplomatic answer. 'How long's it been since you saw the old bugger?'

'Ten years ago, when we met up in Sydney. I can't believe it's been that long.'

'Bloody hell, that long?' He gives me a withering look and shakes his head. I stare down at the metal runners. I have no excuse.

'I know, it's mad,' I mutter. 'But please don't make me feel any more guilty than I already am.' Tears threaten, and I sniff them back. After the long flight I suddenly feel emotional.

'You'll notice a big change. Four years ago, the only thing he had wrong with him was his dodgy knees. Then he started suffering with stomach pain and after tests they diagnosed prostate cancer. He's going downhill. Yes, you'll be in for a shock I'm afraid. And, he's in the early stages of dementia. He will make conversation but sometimes he gets completely confused.'

'We chat on the phone once a week, but he gets very muddled and I never know what to say about his illness. It's men's stuff.'

'He's been quite open with me, which surprised me. The thing is, sis, prostate problems strike directly at any man's self-image, pride and enjoyment of life. You women bond together in distress – men retreat into their caves.'

We reach his car, a black Audi A4 and he flicks open the boot to put my cases in.

'It sounds as if you're getting on better with Dad these days,' I say.

'Since his illness I guess I've mellowed towards him. I feel sorry for the old bugger stuck at the bottom of that lane, all alone, Mum gone. Whatever I thought of their sham marriage, he does miss her.'

I frown at him. 'Their marriage wasn't a sham.' We get in the car and I pull my seatbelt over me, clunking it in harder than normal. What's the matter with my brother? 'Their relationship was next to near perfect. They were lucky to find each other. He told me that when Mum died. He was very tearful. Her death knocked him for six.'

'Huh huh.'

'Don't just say huh huh. Explain yourself.'

'That's just your opinion, sis. You didn't always see what went on.'

'Tell me then. What did go on?'

'It doesn't matter,' he snaps. 'Let's just concentrate on making Dad's last days comfortable ones.' A sense of awkwardness settles over us as we drive out of the multi-storey carpark and head onto the M25. Peering up at the thick bank of cloud crawling across the sky, I smooth away the lingering awkwardness by talking about the weather.

'I miss the rain and the English summers. They're pleasant and uplifting. Our summers are oppressive and it's difficult to breath. It's as if you're in an old person's house and their heating is whacked up so high but they don't realise how uncomfortable it is. But it's weird because twenty degrees feels cold and we need a jumper.'

'The weather here's been ghastly since about August. It just hasn't stopped raining. Hundreds of homes have been flooded. One evening Tracy went out and had to turn back because the roads were like lakes. It's never been as bad as this in my whole lifetime.'

'That's global warming for you.'

'Maybe. It gets everybody down. A few days of this and you'll be looking forward to getting back to Oz. The other day we had hailstones as big as Imperial Mints.'

'I bet that was refreshing.'

'Ha ha.'

We're silent for a few moments and I consider his comment about my returning to Oz. I still don't know what I'm going to do. I think I'm going to stay in England a while, but I don't know how long that will be.

Andrew breaks the silence by switching the midday news on. He prefers Radio Four but give me Radio One any day with its all-day nonsense and hip tunes.

'Ministers are considering their next steps in dealing with the coronavirus... Many supermarket shelves are stripped bare of essentials... Prime Minister, Boris Johnson, is urging people not to panic...'

Something catches my eye in the storage tray in front of the automatic gear lever, sitting between a packet of chewing gum and a tin of lip salve. A box of Valium, Diazepam. Shit. Didn't I read somewhere that it's more addictive than heroin? Maybe it's

Tracy's. But I'm sure Andrew mentioned the other week that she had just bought a new car, a Hyundai. I'm worried now. Why's he taking Valium? Something's wrong, but I don't know if I should pry. It's not my place and it doesn't feel right. Andrew notices me looking at the packet, and probably anticipating my questions he quickly asks, 'So, how's Glen? I bet he'll miss you.'

'We're over.'

'What are you like? You get through more relationships than I have hot dinners.'

His flippant comment hits me like a punch in the gut. 'Glen was cheating on me, Andrew. I caught him in bed with someone.'

'Shit, I'm sorry. But you have to admit sis, you do pick 'em.' He slaps my leg and smiles. 'Every time we meet up there's a different one.' He chuckles, oblivious to my feelings.

His insensitive comment is the type of ill-considered remark our mother would have made. I'm not going to rise to it. And it's just not true. 'We were together a long time. Five years,' I tell him forcefully, hoping to elicit some kindness.

'Now that you're back, shouldn't you see a solicitor about…?'

I interrupt him before he can finish. 'Just leave it, Andrew. I don't want to have to think about all that, not yet anyway.'

'It's been twenty-five years for Christ's sake. Surely you want closure?'

I don't want to continue the conversation. Andrew shouldn't have brought it up. It's my business and I'll do what I want. I've managed well enough burying the past and becoming someone new, but the past always lurks in the shadows. And now it is time to revisit it, to unravel it, straighten it out so that I'll be able to move on. But I don't want to admit that to my brother. I'll do things my way, in my own time.

4

We turn off the M23 at Haywards Heath, where Pandora lives and head along the A272, bypassing Tunbridge Wells and heading out on the Maidstone road towards Rivermead.

We reach the brow of the hill and I gasp as I glimpse the village laid below like a freshly painted Constable.

'Pull over,' I say. It's been so long. I just want to take in the view for a few moments. Andrew huffs with irritation but he pulls onto the verge, leaving the engine idling. I climb out and drink in the scene before me, taking in deep breaths to fill my lungs with the clean, sweet air. The freshness of grass, with a whiff of manure, are in sharp contrast to the arid smells of dried-up Australia. The clouds swirling above are brush strokes on a canvas. The church and castle stand proud over the village. Everybody wants to live in Rivermead. It always used to be the case, and probably still is, that when a house is photographed for sale in *Country Life*, the caption reads, 'in much sought-after village.' Lush fields full of cows and sheep sweep down to the River Liss which wends its way through the valley. Beyond I can see a row of timber-framed buildings. Oh -

and there's the pub. The King's Head had been the setting for so many happy evenings, relaxing with family and friends. New Year's Eve parties with a huge free buffet, summer evenings outside with a jug of Pimms. But there were some evenings that were less peaceful, like the time when I caught Dad and Andrew arguing by the bins.

I'm gazing round now to see how things have changed, but it's just as I left it - all those years ago - and yet everything will have changed. Time has moved on, but I haven't. I wipe the tears that spring to my eyes. It's been twenty-five years, but the memories hit me hard in the chest.

My mother's words come back to me. 'You can hide in Australia and pretend it didn't happen, or you can return to the village and confront your demons.'

Being in Australia seems so long ago and yet it's only twenty-four hours since I left it. It's a world away. We drive through the village, passing the pub covered in Virginia Creeper, the doctor's surgery, and timber-framed buildings set in Sussex stone. A comforting feeling wraps around me. This is home, where I spent the first thirty years of my life. It was the starting place for all of my hopes and dreams. But it's also where the nightmares began. For many years I woke screaming, re-living what happened, my body drenched in sweat. This village has lived in a cloud in my head, formidable from a distance. Nearing the café, a chill snakes through me, and my chest constricts.

'Not much has changed. The village shop manages to keep going, and the café, The Black Kettle, is still open. A miracle really. The only people that can run cafes these days are chains,' Andrews says matter-of-factly. When I don't answer he sails blithely on, oblivious to how I must be feeling. It's as if he's forgotten, but how can I ever forget? Does he imagine that I've healed and moved on? 'Poor woman, I think she struggles,' he continues. 'Rents are high, but the locals are determined to keep it going, even though the tea is as weak as dishwater. She's added a sewing and craft section in an adjacent room. You should nip in there sometime, say hello. She gets busy in the summer when the tourists flock to the village.'

He glances over at me and frowns. 'You okay? You're very quiet. I guess you must be nodding off?'

'I'm all right, Andrew,' I say stiffly, even though I'm not.

'John Le Carre once said, home's where you go when you run out of homes. That's what's happening to you I reckon, now that you and Glen have split up.'

It's a crass comment. He's thinking I might stay for good.

The buildings trickle away. We pass an old cricket pitch and more fields with the river running along the bottom. The car slows and we turn into the narrow private lane under a canopy of trees leading down to the house, Heatherly. Andrew applies the brakes as the car jolts and rattles over potholes and loose gravel, brushing past nettles and a riot of other weeds lining both sides of the track. Bumping over the speed hump, I remember the reason why my dad had it built.

'Do you remember the accident you had right here?' Andrews asks.

I was five when we moved to Heatherly. Not long afterwards, Dad and I were in the Mini Clubman and we hit a Volvo coming towards us up the lane. We weren't protected by seatbelts because back then it wasn't compulsory to wear one. I was flung forward and pieces of glass from the shattered windscreen flew into my face. I needed twenty-odd stitches to my forehead. I touch the scar and remember how frightened I was to see so much blood pouring down my face and the panic in Dad's eyes as he picked me up and ran with me in his arms to a nearby house to call for an ambulance.

We drive under a bridge with a track connecting a farm to its cottage, passing more dwellings which once housed farm workers many years ago. We reach the bottom of the lane and there it is, beyond a short hedge, in all its glory. Heatherly. The sight of it takes my breath away. It's more beautiful than I remembered. Andrew stops the car and for a few moments we drink it, in silence. We both know that this treasure will soon slip from our family's hands. There could be a For Sale board staked into the ground, in a matter of weeks, and everything wrapped up with a solicitor. My heart sinks at the thought.

Our family have lived here for half a century, but the house has stood for nearly five hundred years and there are no visible signs that it won't be still standing five hundred years from now. I remember Mum telling me that it was built in 1300 by a yeoman. For years I wondered what a yeoman was but as a teenager I became interested in history and looked it up, discovering that yeoman were farmers who owned land and could afford to build themselves a house.

'It's easily worth a couple of million,' Andrew says.

'I hope you're not thinking about your inheritance. Dad's still very much alive.'

I want to freeze time. I cast my teary eyes over the lawn. The flowerbeds are bare, the perennial plants having been cut down for their winter rest but there are low shrubs. Over the years my parents experimented with different garden styles and were always busy with a spade and a fork. They transformed the front garden from its former neglected Victorian vegetable patch into a riot of colour. Rose beds were carefully tended from June through to September, their heavenly fragrance wafting up to my bedroom throughout the growing season. In the centre of the garden, taking pride of place is Dad's apple tree, the jewel of the garden. The way Dad planned it we would be drinking in the aromas of the early summer blooms and sinking our teeth into the delicate skin of homegrown apples in the autumn. But as the years went by, the neglected tree was in no fit state to be the jewel of anything. It bore apples but they all had brown spots. The gardening programmes Dad watched made it all look so simple.

'Come on,' Andrew says, putting his foot on the accelerator, 'let's go and see Dad. Ruth will be glad of a break.'

'So, what's the situation with carers?'

'Ruth is living in but it's hard for her. She needs help. Sometimes she doesn't get much sleep because Dad gets up frequently in the night. I've been coming in for a few hours a day to help out. But I can't keep it up. It's exhausting. I've been working from here. All I need is a phone line, my laptop and WIFI. I want you to have a good night's sleep but please if you can work something out with Ruth, see how you can help so that she gets a few hours break each day.'

'Anything to avoid him going into a care home. I'll muck in. It's much better he stays in his own home. Less disruptive for him.'

We enter the house through the back entrance into the utility room. When we were young this was where we kept shoes, boots and trainers creating a bed of dusty mud, lying not in pairs but often far apart, kicked off in random directions. This was not a room where housework mattered. Piles of washing was often dumped next to the machine waiting to go in. For any visitor this chaos was a warning of what to expect inside, but ironically everywhere else in the house was immaculate. The room is tidy now. Dad's wellies and an old pair of garden shoes sit neatly against the wall waiting for an expedition across the fields. But I get the feeling they've not been worn in a while. There's a familiar smell of damp which trails through the adjoining stone hallway. Immediately I'm hit by memories. There were bad storms one night and we woke to find the utility room, hallway and kitchen two feet deep in water. And another memory hits: the utility floor lined with newspaper; when Flaxen, our dog, now long dead, was being toilet-trained.

The utility walls are woven with hairline cracks and the grubby pattern of fingerprints. Are my fingerprints among them? There's a dog barking. Pippin, Dad's Jack Russell, rushes to greet us, her tail wagging. As we walk through the hallway to the kitchen at the front of the house, I glance at a familiar oil painting on the wall, noticing a filigree of cobwebs above. Suddenly I feel all soppy and sentimental. I used to stand and stare at the scene; a bridge over the river in Bruges and imagine myself in the picture, eating ice cream on the bridge. I wonder if my brother will grab this painting for himself. Or maybe he won't be soft and sentimental like me. I have a strong feeling that nostalgia will hit me in every room. It's going to be a trip down memory lane.

In the kitchen, Pippin rushes towards us, her tail wagging and I bend to stroke her coarse fur. Who will take her on when Dad dies? I guess Andrew will, but he's hardly a dog lover.

We chat with Ruth. Dad, we are told, is in the lounge. It seems odd that he's in the grandest room in the house when there's a leather armchair and television in the alcove here, with a view over the front garden. The lounge is what they called an open hall, when the house was built in medieval times. There would have been a central hearth. I used to love staring up at the criss-crossed beams, but the room, being so high, was always hard to heat. I used to help Dad chop wood to feed the fire, but we always needed the addition of a Calor gas heater to warm the room.

Ruth bombards me with the details of all the medication Dad's on and tells us that he must have a glass of Movicol for his constipation as soon as he wakes. I stare at the boxes of Movicol. They look like bricks stacked up.

'Your dad's really struggling to go,' Ruth says. Woo. Steady on woman. Too much information. I don't want to hear about my father's bowel movements thank you very much. I was feeling peckish until now. I nod politely.

'Poor sausage. He hasn't been in days. Although we'll have a problem if he goes the other way and has diarrhoea. We're nearly out of loo rolls and the shops are clean out of them. I went to Sainsburys and Tesco yesterday. Shelves are bare. It's all this panic buying. Nasty virus, I hope it goes away soon,' Ruth says.

'The world's gone mad,' I say. 'People can be so selfish.' The only thing I stock up on is gin and coffee. I can't bear to be out of either. I can't understand all this panic-buying; maybe it's the brain's survival mode overriding any rational thinking.

'And when you give him his meds, please take his teeth out first.' She puts her hand on my arm. 'The tablets get stuck under his dental plate otherwise, ending up as a chewy mess on the roof of his mouth.' She smiles. 'He'll be very pleased to see you.'

I'm dreading it. I'm going to be shocked, I know I am. I mustn't cry, I must act normal. But what is normal? It's going to be awkward; I'm going to be gauche because I won't know what to say or how to act, how to get back to the way we were years ago. It's unforgivable that I didn't come back for Mum's funeral five years ago. I hope he doesn't bring that up.

We go through to the lounge with its artfully chosen soft furnishings and its duck egg blue walls. Dad is slumped on the velvet settee. When he sees us, he hauls himself into a sitting position.

'Hello,' he says casually, as if I'm the neighbour popping by for a cuppa.

I look at him and feel my heart breaking. Oh my God! What's happened to him? Words leave me. I'm too shocked to speak. His once bright blue eyes are now cloudy. He looks so much older. I can't believe how frail he is. He could easily pass as ninety, but he's eighty. Ravished by the curse of cancer he's lost so much weight. It's gone on his arms and shoulders. His neck is scrawny like a turkey's neck and his skin is as thin as onion peel. It's obvious looking at him that he's not long for this world. I can't help it, my eyes are watering. I sniff back the tears.

'Dad, who's this come to see you?' Andrew asks in a loud voice, near Dad's ear.

In a softer voice than I remember, Dad says, 'I've had lots of visitors today.' He smiles up at us. 'The lady's been. Where is she?' He chuckles. 'I've asked her to marry me so that she can have all my money.'

Andrew throws me a look of despair. 'Dad, Dee's come all the way from Australia to see you.'

Dad reaches for a scrunched tissue sitting on the coffee table and dabs at his nose. His face is tinged yellow and is a spider's web of thread veins. 'Don't be silly Andrew,' he reprimands, in a crackly voice. 'I keep telling you not to be so silly.'

I feel a sharp stab of rejection and swallow hard.

'Don't you remember your daughter? You haven't seen her for a few years, but she's the same old Dee. In all the time she's lived in Australia she's kept her English accent.' Andrew waves his hand in my direction as if he's presenting me to the Queen.

'Is the lane muddy?' Dad asks. 'You did wear your wellies I hope, because that lady - whatever her name is - won't be happy.'

'Dad, it's me, Dee, you remember me, your daughter.' I lean down and kiss him lightly on the forehead, trying hard not to get upset.

'Where shall I put this?' Dad asks me, waving the tissue in his hand.

Andrew picks up a bin and tilts it towards Dad, waiting for him to drop the tissue in. Andrew's face is taut, his posture stiff – he looks at breaking point. Dad makes a fist around the tissue, pulling his hand away, not wanting to part with it.

'Put the telly back on,' Dad orders and in that moment something inside me twists. My dad doesn't recognise me anymore. There's a hint of something in his eyes that he vaguely knows me, as he watches me pick up the remote control. He recognises me as somebody he knows well, that is all. Who does he imagine I am? A neighbour, another carer? It's hard to tell. All I know is that I am the stranger in the house I grew up in, the only house I could ever call home. I'm not the little princess I used to be all those years ago floating around him in my pretty pink dress, asking him to pick me up and read a chapter from Winnie the Pooh. And he is no longer the wise owl I used to go to for advice and support. Dad was a civil engineer and had dozens of people working for him. As I flick through the channels on the telly, Dad in his hoarse voice demanding the snooker, I remember the time he told me that when I grew up, life wouldn't always be easy. He was right. It isn't. His steadying hand on my shoulder as we stood by the graveside on that March day twenty-five years ago confirmed those words. Seeing him in this pitiful state is breaking my heart.

5

When it's time to go to bed, Andrew lets Pippin out for a wee, then shows me to my room. I don't know why, but he's chosen the worst room in the house. It's not my bedroom - the one I had while I was growing up, with its green nineteen-seventies Laura Ashley décor. I want to ask him if I can sleep in my room, but something stops me. He's stressed, he's still got to put Dad to bed because Ruth is about to have a break, but it's also that feeling that I'm a guest and guests don't get a choice.

Stepping over the threshold into the bedroom, I feel the walls close in on me. It's the one room Mum and Dad never got around to redecorating. I'd forgotten how hideous it is, and yet there's a comforting feel within these walls because it's a time-warp. It's steeped in a bygone era; a chintz nightmare of frills and flowers – pink and green everywhere. There's a single bed and beside it a table with a yellowing doily and alarm clock. Even the single bed is a throwback, covered in a shimmery satin eiderdown.

Alone for the first time since seeing Dad, Andrew asks,

'How do you feel, sis?' Tucked in his voice is a note of compassion, the first I've seen today. 'Don't take it personally.'

'It's hard to come to terms with the way he is.' There's a sad inevitability about what is happening to Dad because it's the natural progression of life. This is another bereavement journey. When I left here to go to Australia, a part of us, as a family died. I thought I would be prepared for Dad going, but now I realise, I'm not prepared at all. 'On the phone he sounded okay. He was just Dad. Rambling on about life in the village.' I pause, a sudden thought popping into my head. 'But now I come to think of it, he never asked much about me and what I was doing. I could have been anybody. In the last couple of weeks he's been a bit gibberish, but there were lucid moments.'

'He never did ask many questions. He's always been self-centred,' Andrew says sniffing and drawing the curtains for me.

'It's hard to tell what's the dementia and what is the old Dad,' I say dumping my bag on the bed.

'But he was also probably trying to be diplomatic, sis. We all were.'

'Avoiding the subject?' Raising my voice, I turn to look at him. 'I hate that coldness about this family. The stiff upper lip. Everybody stepping around me, hoping I'd recover. Well I've got news for you.' I put my hands on my hips. 'It's taken bloody years to get over what I went through.'

'Whatever I say, you flare up. You're probably just tired. Get some sleep, I'll see you in the morning.' Andrew sweeps out of the room, a wounded expression on his face, leaving me to unpack.

I glance in the mirror on the dressing table. My eyelids have locked in a half-shut position, like a stuck Venetian blind. I'm about to get into bed when a text pings through from Glen. 'Hope you got there safely. I still love you. Miss you.' Without bothering to answer, I block his number and switch my phone off. The need for sleep hits me like an oncoming train - urgent, insistent, out of control. Nothing like normal sleepiness. It's more like being given a general anaesthetic. I don't know how I've struggled through the day. It was like some surreal torture deprivation scene.

The following morning sunlight streams into the kitchen illuminating all the grubby surfaces. Dad is sitting in his armchair by the window staring out over the front garden and Ruth is preparing his breakfast. With the weather looking promising, I want to take a walk down the lane and reacquaint myself with the village.

'Morning,' Dad says, turning to acknowledge my presence. Now that he's slept, maybe he'll recognise who I am. But when I smile at him, his eyes have a vacant faraway look about them. He eases himself out of the chair, plods around the kitchen, hunched over, each step seeming to be a massive effort, as if his legs are dead weights. He won't let either of us help him. He stands at the kitchen sink and turns the tap on to wash up the dirty dishes next to the sink.

'I'm all right,' he says, waving us out of the way with a tea towel as he slops dishwater onto the floor.

'Dad, please, sit down, let me wash up.'

He mumbles something and carries on. I watch him lay a bowl on the draining board with the slow deliberation of a person who realises they aren't quite in control of their faculties. He turns, wipes his wet fingers down his trousers and leans against the side for support.

'Come on Dad,' I coax, taking his arm and guiding him back to his armchair. 'Have you had your tablets this morning?' Sitting down, he glances at the pile of packets on the worktop. 'I don't want them today, stop fussing.'

Ruth catches my attention, nods, mouthing to me that she's already given them to him.

I make myself some coffee and we sit in silence for a few minutes. Just as I'm starting to feel like a spare part, Andrew arrives back from the supermarket. He dumps the shopping bags on the worktop, looking flustered. 'Bloody people. No loo rolls again. And not much of anything else.'

'They'll start handing out ration cards soon. It's the only way to beat Hitler, pull together,' Dad says in a weak voice.

'I thought I'd get in there early to beat the queues,' Andrew says, ignoring Dad. 'God knows who all these bog roll hoarders are. They should be buying condoms, not loo rolls, to stop the idiots breeding.'

'Churchill will sort it all out soon,' Dad says.

'They're saying that up to a fifth of the workforce might be off work with this coronavirus. That's why people are panicking,' Ruth says.

'I'd really like to walk down to the village. Is that okay?' I ask Andrew. 'I won't be long.' I give Dad a peck on his cheek, but he doesn't respond.

SUCKING IN THE FRESH AIR, I adjust to the cool temperature of the English weather, light-headed with the sense of release from the confines of the house. I love being outdoors - even as a child I roamed the fields at every opportunity, running up and down each row of hops in the late summer mist, breathing in the aroma of beer, playing on the tree swing that hung over the river and scrumping apples from the orchard.

In the distance, in a cottage garden, is a magnificent blossom. It has a dreamy appearance and I realise - with a sudden pang - how much I've missed the changing seasons. Today's wind is flirting with the petals which will be blotting paper choking the drains after rain. The rhythm of nature goes on.

I join the footpath leading down the hill to the village. Daffodils and lush grass line the track, nodding in the chilly breeze. There's mud underfoot, squelching, pulling at my trainers, threatening to claim them, but I don't care, I just want to get to the churchyard.

The footpath connects with the road for the last leg of my walk. There's no pavement, only a damp verge. Years ago, when there was just a trickle of cars, I could have sauntered down the road quite merrily, without so much as a backwards glance, but now I must stick to the edge. There are many more cars around.

I stop for a moment, looking across the fields, as I consider my mission this morning. I must face this. I must summon up the courage to visit the churchyard. The place where my two children, Sophie and Poppy, are buried.

In the village I head straight through the archway and into the churchyard, following the brick pathway to the church entrance. Taking the rusty latch in my hand I'm surprised to find the church is unlocked. My heart is thumping. I need to sit down first, to collect myself, before visiting the grave. Pushing through the heavy door the cool air wraps around me and my eyes adjust to the gloom. There's a smell of beeswax and musty hymn books. Light filters through the stained-glass windows, creating a rainbow across the pews. Such beauty and yet this place is filled with sad memories.

My squeaky trainers on the flagstones break the silence and I slip into a pew. I picture the two small white coffins sitting next to each other. How the hell did I get through that funeral service? Twenty-five years later it's still hard to fathom. Burying my own children. It's the one thing, that remote possibility you dread, no parent wants to think about. It creeps into your thoughts and your nightmares, catching you unawares, making you shudder. Those terrible what-ifs, you tell yourself will never happen, because it can't, it just can't, you'd never survive, you wouldn't know how. But sometimes it does happen. It happened to us. I can't understand how I functioned for weeks, months after. My body ticked along but my mind had frozen over. I think I just went through the motions, like a robot aided by strong tablets that turned me into a zombie.

We didn't want a big funeral, just our immediate families, but Mum had other plans. I think she thought that it would be comforting surrounded by lots of people who cared. 'It's going to be a smashing day. I've invited your Auntie Hilda and my cousin Ralph, who never leaves Bournemouth, but is coming by train if he can get a cheap ticket. And your Uncle Reg and Auntie Edna are coming all the way down from Leicester.' *Smashing.* The word still jars. Dad was horrified. The look on his face when she said it.

I picture Mum, arriving with me and Dad in the limousine, clapping eyes on all of Jay's mother's family who'd journeyed down from Essex. 'What a hideous motley crew of in-breds,' Mum had said. 'Whatever did you marry into?' And Jay's mother, Eileen, complaining all day that her 'pins' were hurting.

I've no idea how I survived it all, how I didn't give up. I wanted to, many times. What did I have to live for? I'd lost my entire family, including Jay, my husband. Hours before the funeral Jay disappeared. I didn't know what had happened. My first thought was that he'd taken his own life. You hear about that happening. God knows, I wanted to myself. I rang the police and all the nearby hospitals. Nobody could track him down. Days later we found out that he was holed up at Mike's, a work colleague.

The day after the funeral, Jay called his parents. Told them he blamed me for everything. He didn't want any more to do with me. I was mortified. He said I was a bad mother. Those words really hit me, like a fist in the belly. He didn't have the guts to ring me, face me, tell me how he felt. Instead he told his mother that he needed to move on, start afresh. Move on? How the hell could either of us move on? After what we'd been through.

My eyes narrow, my hands ball into tight fists. The pain I felt when he left has gone, but I still feel a certain degree of anger. I've had one letter in all that time, to remind me he'll never forgive me. It's hard enough that I can't forgive myself. I never will. The guilt churns. It will never go away, worming around my inner being, eating my insides, tearing me apart. My hand reaches for my head, clamping, harder. I look up at the cross. If I believed in God then maybe I'd ask for forgiveness, but would I feel forgiven? Would prayer make any difference? Nothing will wash the guilt away. Perhaps there are times when guilt is meant to be permanent, like a tattoo.

In the days after the funeral I didn't know what to do with myself. Apart from cry. I saved the tears for when I was alone in the bath, or sitting on the loo, or curled up like a question mark in bed. I couldn't cry in front of Mum. She'd ignore me even when I was sobbing, my shoulders shaking. Maybe she didn't know how to console me. She was going through her own grief, but never outwardly showed it. I was barely aware of anything apart from the heavy weight of my own loss. A week after the funeral and with no more tears to shed, I went round to his mum's house to try to talk with Jay. I wanted to pummel his chest, slap him hard around the face, lash out at him. He was blaming me and that had to stop. I knew he'd be broken, diminished, a shred of the man he was, crippled and cowed by what had happened. Was I really going to lash out and hit him? I'd probably just have let out an inhuman howl, thrown my arms around his neck so tight that my knuckles turned white. But he wasn't there and his mum said he'd left the country.

Out on the brick pathway I step onto damp grass, weaving between the old crooked gravestones covered in lichen and trailing ivy. Many of the names are no longer legible and belong to a forgotten past. But as I reach the far corner of the graveyard where the more recent graves are, I hesitate, then take a few steps back. Adrenaline floods my body. I can't do this, but I have to. I know exactly where it is. It's burned on my brain. My heart is pounding in my chest, beads of sweat trickling down my brow. I need to, I must tackle all of the emotions that sit heavily inside me.

I take a deep breath, step through the grass, every part of my body resisting, railing against this. Fighting the urge to turn and go. A few more paces and I'm there in front of the stone. My children's names. It's so hard to accept that they died. The irony of the stone, permanent, to mark something so fleeting. Images hit, my children lying below in the cold wet mud.

They need me so much. I'm their mummy and I'm supposed to keep them close, warm, safe. I so wanted to be the type of mummy my own mum never was. My desperate need to prove myself, snatched from me. I sink to my knees, oblivious to the damp mud, imagining them in my arms. My eyes fill with tears, two hazy pools. The stone blurs. Great heaving desolate sobs rack my body, making me shudder and shiver. It's like a cleansing river because I've not cried like this in a while. I'm surprised that coming here is having this effect on me.

I stare at the epitaph and their engraved names. Poppy... just four months old when she died of complications in March 1995. Clammy hands cover my wet face. When Poppy was born so ill, I tied myself in knots agonising about all the things I could have done differently. Like breast-feed for longer and rest more in pregnancy. And if only I'd taken folic acid, eaten better, not rushed around. I pull a tissue from my pocket, wipe the trail of mucus running from my nose.

And Sophie, just three. Four days after Poppy. An accident.... a moment's lapse of concentration was all it took to snuff out my daughter's life. Standing here now, those last moments rush back to me. Letting go of Sophie's hand for a split-second. I'll never forgive myself.

No one understands what it's like to go through this amount of grief. Crushing, all-consuming, unrelenting, day-in-day-out and that routine of grief seems to go on for a long time. It's tiring. Waking up in the morning was the worst part. When it slammed into me. Over and over. Like *Groundhog Day*. Realising all over again that they were gone. And the silence, the emptiness. It was so palpable. The dull ache across the chest. Nobody really understood and even if they had, what difference would it have made? It wouldn't change anything. Wouldn't wash away the guilt that tugs and twists at my very core. They're still gone. A huge part of my life hollowed out. Leaving this massive gaping crater.

What's left of my life? That sense of loneliness, penetrating, like icy water, chills my insides. A life lived alone is a meaningless one. I want to share my deepest fears, anxieties and joys with another human being. I want to be loved unconditionally, no matter what. I thought that's what marriage could provide.

My head is pounding, feels as if it will explode. Helen spent years trying to convince me that it wasn't my fault, I must stop blaming myself, accidents happen. But how can I not blame myself?

Despite the damp grass I sit down next to the grave and touch the cold stone. 'How different my life would have been if you two treasures had...' I can't bring myself to finish the sentence. 'You would be twenty-nine and twenty-six now. What would you be doing? Would you have been clever like your daddy? I could even be a grandma by now. My life has had no real purpose to it without you sweet ones. I've travelled, I've partied, worked in bars, cafes...living the life of a twenty-year old.'

I stagger to my feet shakily, dazed, unable to move. I need a cup of tea with plenty of sugar. I can't see. I dab my eyes and pull myself together. I manage a few paces, turn, look back at the stone. A dull ache spreads across my chest because I don't want to leave them. I've been away too long. I'll come back, as soon as I can and as often as I can. I should never have been away. I belong here. I must mark each birthday with flowers. But flowers. Children are too young for flowers. They need so much more. I couldn't give them more. I couldn't give them a life. I stagger to a bench, slump down, head bowed, crying more.

I look up, feeling dizzy and put a hand on the bench to steady myself. I get up, disorientated and walk slowly away. Reaching the archway, I take out a pocket mirror from my bag and check my eyes.

Rounding the bend, the pub and an antique shop are on my left and just beyond I can make out the hanging sign of a black kettle above the cafe. And all at once I'm back there. Right under that sign chatting to a mother from Sophie's nursery school. Every detail of the conversation still there, tucked away. Mary had been wearing a red sou'wester, her boisterous Irish Setter straining on his lead.

The bell above the café door tinkles as I enter. It's like a doll's house inside and I stoop to avoid low beams. I'm greeted by the smell of sugar and milky tea. Along the wall is a pine dresser with rows of locally produced honey and other preserves and on the other wall are greetings cards. Behind the counter are shelves containing large retro sweetie jars. When Grandpa used to bring me here, I'd choose Shrimps, Aniseed Balls and Catherine Wheels and mint toffees that were probably responsible for all of the fillings and crowns I had in my twenties. They were innocent times. Little did I know what the future held. I want to close my eyes, be young again, with Grandpa's hand in mine. I'd like to wipe the slate and start again. A different life, a different me with hope on the horizon.

I smile at the woman serving a customer from behind the counter. I vaguely recognise her. I go through to the next room where pink gingham tablecloths cover round tables. I have the room to myself; the café is empty. Nothing has changed. It feels as if I'm in a time-warp, taken back to my youth.

The shop assistant pops her head round the doorway as I take a seat by the window.

'Do you know what you'd like, or shall I give you a few moments?'

I glance at the selection of cakes on the menu. 'I'm not sure.' It's hard to focus on the menu after being in the graveyard.

'I'll give you a moment,' she says, her notebook poised in midair. I'm definitely sure I recognise her from somewhere, but I'm not going to say anything. 'You don't mind if I just serve my other customer?' she asks, before returning to the counter.

'That's the woman I was telling you about,' the customer says to the shop assistant. 'Someone told me she was back. The one who let her child run into the road. Happened years ago.'

She thinks she's whispering but my hearing is razor-sharp. The menu is leather-bound and to make a point I snap it shut. With a racing heart I push my chair back, my big clumsy foot catching the table leg, nearly knocking it over. I rush past them, slamming the door behind me. This village is too small and in small villages memories don't fade.

Outside I'm shaking. A few paces from the café I stop to catch my breath. Looking down at the pavement I realise where I am...I'm standing in the exact spot where it happened. The cracked brick, it's still here. Where the police stuck the tape, marking where Sophie stepped out into the road. Talking to Mary right here, about Poppy's death was the last thing I did before my life imploded. Mary had stopped me to pass on her condolences. 'I'm really, really sorry,' she'd said. Sophie's hand was wriggling in mine. Why did I let go? It's a question I'll never stop asking myself. I want to reach back through time and stop the accident from happening, clutch her hand and this time I won't let go.

6

It's a couple of days after visiting the grave. I dress and head downstairs, the television is turned up so loudly that I can hear it clearly from the hallway. Dad is asleep in his chair in the kitchen, snoring. Donald Trump is making an announcement. I stand in the doorway listening. 'After consulting with our top health officials, I have decided to take several strong but necessary actions to protect the health and well-being of US citizens...we will be suspending all travel from Europe to the United States for the next thirty days.'

Ruth is draining some green beans in a colander, steam rising in the air. 'Is he blaming Europe for the virus?' she asks with a shake of her head. 'Sounds like it.'

I peer intently at the screen before picking up the remote from Dad's chair, stabbing randomly at buttons. 'We'll see the markets crash tomorrow after that announcement. Every day the news gets gloomier.'

'I suppose he's just taking necessary precautions. But what about people's holidays? I've got a trip to Florida in August,' Ruth says.

'It'll be all over by then,' I tell her, although I'm not convinced.

Dad stirs. 'Turn it on,' he says grumpily. 'I was listening to that.'

My mobile rings. It's my schoolfriend, Pandora, all in a fluster. 'Have you heard the news? Trump's suspending all flights to America from the EU. But not flights to America from Britain.'

'Only because he has golf courses here.'

'It's only a matter of time before he stops flights from the UK too. Spain and Italy are in lockdown. How long before our prime minister imposes a lockdown here? Which is why I'm calling...'

'I can't see that happening somehow.'

She's out of breath, talking at breakneck speed over me. 'We've been discussing the school reunion on social media. Some people think it should be cancelled and rescheduled to later in the year. A few people can't come because they're self-isolating with symptoms of the illness. Julia has a cough, Wendy's worried she's got it. What do you think Dee? Are you still up for it? We've decided to change the date to this Friday, the 13th, because world events are happening fast. I hope you're not superstitious. Who knows what will happen next with this nasty virus?'

My voice is flat. 'It depends *who's* going.'

Pandora pauses and I get the feeling there's something she's keeping from me. She knows exactly who I'm referring to.

'He lives in New York. Bit far to come,' she says in a soft voice. 'You're okay.'

'Mmm, I had a letter from him years ago.' I don't quite trust Pandora. What's to say that she hasn't told him about my coming back? 'Are you still in touch with him?'

'He sent me a friend request on Facebook years ago. His posts occasionally pop up on my newsfeed. Other than that, I don't have anything to do with him.'.

'Don't tell him anything about my life please,' I say.

'Maybe you should tell him you're back?'

'Why would I do that?'

'Because Dee, you're still married to him, to Jay.'

Her words jolt through me and whatever I'm about to say dies on my tongue.

Through the silence she asks, 'Are you still there? You okay? I'm sorry.'

'I haven't seen him for twenty-five years,' come my cold words. 'He sent me one letter, in all that time. He let me down, Pandora. Badly. Why can't you get that?'

The conversation moves back to the school reunion but there's a sense of unease between us. She doesn't refer to Jay again, leaving old wounds to reopen inside me.

There's a gush of excitement, the unease gone. 'We want this reunion to go ahead. There's a hard core of people who really don't want to cancel it.' There's despair in her voice. 'Well it's set now for Friday. Come if you can.'

'I'd love to come. If I'm staying here for a while, I don't want to be Billy-No-Mates.'

'That's the spirit. It'll do you good to reconnect with the people you grew up with.'

'It depends on Dad. I'm here to help out. I'll call you later and let you know.' I end the call.

'What was all that about?' Ruth asks as she puts the dishes away.

'A school reunion this Friday evening.'

'Go, I can look after your dad.'

'Are you sure? It's a lot to ask.'

'Go and enjoy yourself.'

'Ok...' I respond cautiously. 'If you don't mind looking after Dad. I won't be long. I'll just stay for an hour.'

'Stay for as long as you like,' she says with a smile.

Dad struggles to his feet. Egg stains congeal on his jumper

and tissues bulge from both his pockets. Hunched over, he heads for the fridge.

'You hungry, Dad?'

He grunts, opens the fridge door and peers inside, hesitating as if he can't remember what he wants. He takes out a block of Cheddar and cuts himself a piece. This is what I most remember about my Dad. Diving into the fridge, cutting a hunk of cheese, raiding the fridge of any goodies he can find - or desserts Mum was saving for visitors, then laughing when she gave him one of her stern tellings-off with a flick of the tea towel around his head. But Dad doesn't cram the cheese into his mouth like he used to. Instead he takes it to the sink, Ruth stepping aside, eying him with curiosity as he proceeds to turn on the tap and rub the cheese between his hands. He must think it's soap.

'Dad, what are you doing?'

Ruth takes his arm and turns off the tap.

'Get off me. We're at war and the enemy is invisible. Don't you know what's going on? We've all got to wash our hands. With plenty of soap.'

'I know Dad. The virus isn't in this house. I think you're safe.'

'Have you built an Anderson shelter? That's what we need.'

'You're perfectly safe, Ronnie love, come and sit down,' Ruth says.

Wanting to have a word with Ruth out of Dad's earshot I follow her into the utility room where she pulls wet clothes from the washing machine. 'Shall we work out a plan for Dad's care? What would work for you? I'm here to help in whatever way I can.'

She stands up and wipes her hands on her apron. 'What about if you looked after him every afternoon from two until six? I'm finding things hard at night. He goes to bed so late. His body clock is all over the place. He's prone to wandering. It can be exhausting. I can get him ready for bed but if I could have three nights off a week that would really help.'

'Yes of course. I wouldn't have the first clue about personal care, but I may as well admit to you, the thought of helping my own dad to the loo or in the bath fills me with horror.'

'I know, it's really not easy when it's your own parent. None of us imagine it will come to this. We just aren't prepared. But don't worry, I'll ease you into the role gradually and I'll be doing as much of the personal care as possible. It's what I'm trained to do.'

Her words don't stop me worrying about the challenges ahead: gaining his cooperation, will he resist my help? Will he be stubborn and awkward? I don't know my dad anymore. He's a different person. And I have no experience of dealing with elderly people.

7

With mixed emotions but mounting curiosity for the evening ahead, I get ready for the school reunion and head down the lane in Dad's old Jag wearing a smart pair of jeans and flouncy blouse. It's too far to walk to the school and I certainly wouldn't want to walk back in the dark. I'll have just one glass of wine, then go on to soft drinks. Andrew put me on the insurance a couple of days ago with stern words to 'take great care, it's Dad's pride and joy.' Dad was told a year ago by his doctor that he had to give up driving. He had only just bought a brand-new BMW sports car, but the gear box broke because he drove it in the wrong gears and then, according to Andrew, he couldn't remember how to start it.

I peer over the never-ending bonnet, brushing my hand across the walnut dashboard and beautiful tan leather upholstery with a tear in my eye. Dad loved his cars. Going to auctions was a regular day out; seeing what he could buy and marvelling at the polished motors on display. He has four classic cars in the garage, all covered in cobwebs and dust.

Mum called one of his cars a garden ornament because it never left the drive.

The Jag isn't an easy car to drive. The steering is heavy, and the clutch sticky. I can feel every ruck in the lane.

Pulling into the carpark next to the old Victorian school hall, I see a few women tottering on high heels are making their way through the entrance, drawn to the occasion by the mystique of their own past. I eye the women warily, trying to work out who they are. Will we all recognise each other? I conjure an image of what I looked like as a child. I was the tallest girl in the class and I'm probably going to be the tallest woman here tonight. I groan. For once I don't want to be tall, to be recognised because of my height. 'That's Dee Broomstick, remember her, the tallest in the class?' they'll whisper. I hated my nickname. I hope it's long-forgotten.

I sit for a moment waiting until more people arrive. When I look back to those innocent days at primary school, they were simple times. Even the worst days like when the older boys grabbed me, took me into the bushes and put red ants down my pants, were nothing compared to the horrors of adulthood. And even that horrible day at break time in the playground when the wind blew my skirt up, my knickers simultaneously falling down because the elastic had snapped, and everybody turning and roaring with laughter. It all pales into insignificance.

The biggest fear on my mind is whether they will ask, do you have any kids? I've got used to my stock answer. Why should I tell them the truth when they don't need to know? But I can't help feeling that the past is waiting in a box ready to jump out, because there are bound to be people here who know what happened. Doubt creeps through me. Why am I even here? Apart from a handful of people, there's been nobody I've wanted to stay in touch with in the intervening four decades.

Pandora and Lyn pull up beside me and I'm grateful for their timing - strength in numbers as we walk through the door. We greet each other, but without hugging because we are all a bit wary about the virus. Making our way across the playground we can hear Cat Stevens playing, *Remember The Days Of The Old School Yard*. Heads turn as we enter the hall - which looks peculiarly small now that I'm older and taller. There are whoops of recognition and the raising of glasses from several people. We wend our way to the makeshift bar; the counter where Mrs Eaton and Mrs Grove used to serve school dinners. Mrs Eaton was a plump woman bursting out of her frock and Mrs Grove had skin that looked like old leather. Someone I don't recognise serves us wine.

'School dinners.' Pandora winces.

My gut twists as images of sloppy mashed potato with grey lumps in, congealed gravy and beef as tough as old boots enters my head.

'Delicious,' Pandora gasps, rubbing her belly. 'Jam roly-poly and custard, chocolate swiss roll with lashings of chocolate custard.'

'And what about gypsy tart?' Pandora's eyes light up. 'They should have bought some for tonight.'

I used to think that gypsy tart – a pastry tart filled with a mixture containing evaporated milk and brown sugar - was served in every school up and down the country, but years later I discovered that it was in fact a Kentish delicacy, originating from the Isle of Sheppey.

I peer warily over my wine glass to survey the crowd, trying to work out who is who. A woman in a clingy dress raises her glass, and with a smile saunters towards me. 'Oh my God,' I whisper under my breath to Lyn and Pandora, 'It's The China Doll.' Karen Robinson. She still has dark glossy curls and a porcelain pale face with rosy cheeks just like Snow White. But she's carrying a little black bag, not a basket of polished apples.

'Karen, how lovely to see you,' I lie, stepping away from Lyn and Pandora who begin conversations with other people. How long will I have to endure her? I realise within minutes that I'm still reeling from her winning the fancy-dress parade in 1975, with her stunning red-and-gold kimono. I was so determined to win that blasted competition and Mum too was convinced that I would. She was the one who came up with the ridiculous idea that I should go dressed in Weetabix boxes stapled together. Only my mother could come up with such a daft idea and now, as I look back, I realise her cunning plan was to save money. And it was my naive ten-year-old self that thought it rather novel and worthy of first prize.

After the smiles and the perfunctory exchange of compliments, Karen asks, 'And what do you do for a living?'

'I've been in Australia for the past twenty-five years.'

'I thought I detected an Ozzy accent, but wasn't sure. Doing what?' There's a condescending tone to her voice. She hasn't changed. She always considered herself better than everyone else, even at ten years old. Just because her dresses were hand-crocheted and mine came from Tesco.

'Mainly working in cafes.'

She sniffs primly and I catch an air of disapproval. 'I went to Australia once, for four weeks,' she says. 'I know everybody raves about it, but my trip left unpleasant memories. I thought I saw a funnel-web spider in our apartment. I went mental, fell over and broke my ankle.'

Just as I'm about to ask more about her life, we are interrupted by Myra Brenchley, dressed in an all-in-one jumpsuit. Her hair is stunning; she's gone grey but looks as if she's aided the process with various different highlights. There are only two things I remember about Myra, other than the fact that she shares the same name as Britain's most notorious female serial killer. Myra was the first girl and the only girl in our final year of primary school to wear a bra. I always wondered whether she started her periods at primary school too. The other thing I remember is that she was a Rollermaniac, hardly surprising given that she was born in Glasgow. I have visions of her strutting along the changing room bench in her bra and knickers as we dressed for netball, singing the Bay City Roller's hit song, *Bye Bye Baby*. Myra was the most popular girl in the class. I'm not sure why because I wasn't keen on her. I think it was because she knew the pop charts so well and always knew what was number one. I hadn't a clue. For some bizarre reason I preferred classical music when I was at primary school. At home, Dad woke us to the 1812 Overture or a violin concerto. I only started to enjoy pop music at secondary school when the Bee Gees became big. But music only lived with me in those intense moments of falling in love in my early twenties, and when things became rocky music was my solace.

Oh God, I'm back to dwelling on the past. I must stop myself. I'm at a social event. I adjust my face, smile at Myra and we chat about our lives.

'Really nice catching up,' she beams, after we've covered the highlights of the past thirty years, leaving out, of course the biggest event of my life. I don't have kids, I tell her. After our chat I say, 'I'll see you later.' She breezes over to the bar to replenish her glass.

There's a man in a wheelchair by the buffet table. Finishing his conversation with a man I don't recognise, he looks around for someone else to chat to, and in that moment we catch each other's eye. His belly bulges over the top of his waistline and one of his eyebrows is pierced with a ring. He has a hoop in his ear and a tattoo weaving up his arm.

I feel my face drain of colour - an icy sensation crawling over my skin. My eyes narrow to slits. Am I seeing correctly? His right trouser leg is tied into a knot. Laurence Smith has lost his right leg. I adjust the expression of shock forming across my face as I head towards him, careful not to replace it with sickly sympathy. Relax I tell myself. This is Laurence and despite whatever has happened to him, he's still the first boy you ever kissed. In a pillbox by the river. I shudder at the thought. What a brazen hussy I was. Not just a peck on the cheek. A full-blown French snog, tongues down the throat jobby. I used to sit on his lap in his living room to watch Scooby Doo with him. Hell, we were only ten. What on earth was wrong with me? Not as if I was developed, like Myra at that age with her big tits encased in a bra, hormones raging.

'Laurence.' I rub his arm. 'Great to see you, but ...'

'Dee, you still look as stunning as ever, where has the time gone? I've not been so lucky as you can see. My body's fucked and I'm living in a residential home. My neighbours are all old folk. But hey, I'm alive and as they say,' he adopts a West Indian accent, 'shit happens.'

'I'm sorry. Can I ask...'

'I was crossing the road in the village late one night and a car hit me.'

'Shit.' My head is throbbing with each beat of the heart and I feel the first stirrings of panic in my stomach. 'Did they catch the driver?'

'Hit and run.' He sniffs. 'I was in hospital for a whole year. Broke my spine. Lost my leg. But I'm okay. I have a quiet life. Gone are my drunken evenings up the King's Head. This is the first time I've been out in, like ages.'

'I'm really sorry, Laurence. What was your life like before it happened?'

'It broke my marriage. She met someone else while I was in hospital and buggered off. I've found out who my friends are and who I can trust. My best mate borrowed a couple of grand off me - some of my compensation money - and never gave it back. I won't have anything to do with him no more.'

'I'm so sorry.'

'I'm okay. I've got a fridge full of chocolate, it's what I live on.

Not much else to live for. Anyway, enough of me.' He smiles brightly at me. 'What about you?'

I gulp. I'm tempted to tell him about my own horrors but too much time has passed between us and I don't know what his reaction would be. Now is not the time or the place. There are very few people I can open up to and Laurence is effectively a stranger. So instead I tell him all about life in Australia, glad to get off the subject of road accidents, instantly feeling happier. I show him pictures on my phone of kangaroos, beaches and various scenes and he asks lots of questions and makes comments about David Attenborough films he's watched.

A cluster of men with plates of food are soon gathered around us and we are all introducing ourselves, breaking off into new conversations. I move away from Pete The Puke. He's breathing fish paste down my neck and chewing in an ugly way. He became Pete The Puke when we were around eight years when he vomited on the ferry over to France on a day trip to Calais. I was merrily walking through the ship; the sea was choppy and everybody looked queasy, when I fell in Pete's vomit and ruined my school blazer. Everybody kept their distance for the entire day, pegging their noses and laughing at me.

Tiny Tim - the shortest boy in the class and still a shorty - beams at me, crumbs on his chin. 'If it isn't Deirdre Barlow,' he laughs. I'd clean forgotten that nickname, Deirdre Barlow from the soap opera, *Coronation Street*. It's coming back to me now. Silly really because my name is Dee. It's not short for Deirdre. In my mind's eye I can still see Tiny Tim and his cronies making glasses around their eyes with their fingers to mimic the glasses that Deirdre Barlow wears on *Coronation Street*.

'Don't do the impression with the goggle glasses please.' I laugh. The joke doesn't upset me like it did when we were at primary school.

I glimpse Pandora and Lyn chatting on their own by the toilets. I saunter over there. I can't wait to escape into the folds of my two closest friends.

'We haven't really had a proper catch-up, girls,' I say to both of them. 'What's been happening lately? Any gossip?'

'No man in my life,' Pandora says. 'But I guess you want the latest on Jules.' Jules is Pandora's brother and he's a compulsive gambler. After her sister-in-law's death, Pandora brought up their daughter, Ellie, as if she were her own daughter. A couple of years ago it looked as if Jules had turned a corner when his girlfriend Mandy fell pregnant.

'I thought he'd turned a leaf and was having treatment for his addiction. His daughter must be two now?'

'Has he heck?' Pandora tuts. 'Mandy kicked him out a few weeks ago. She'd had enough. A leopard doesn't change its spots.'

'Where's he living now?'

'No idea, probably homeless. We've all done so much for him. I've washed my hands of the bugger. He's brought it on himself. But Ellie is doing well. She's working on a ski resort in Italy at the moment.'

'And everything good with you Lyn since you married Ray? Is he still sneaking off to go bird-watching?'

Lyn's partner Ray is obsessed with birdwatching, even to the extent that he missed their daughter Felicity's birth.

'He's a lot more compromising of his time these days. We live between here and Norfolk. You'll be surprised to hear that he'll even come to Laura Ashley with me. In fact, he likes helping me choose new clothes.'

'Dee,' says Pandora. 'We were just saying, you really need to get connected. Join Facebook, stay in touch with people.'

'It's not my thing. I'd rather connect with people in the real world.'

'What's App and Messenger are great. You can send pictures

and articles to other people.'

I look blankly at them. They don't get it. All of these platforms are ways for Jay to get in touch with me or find out about my life. The last thing I want is for him to track me down. 'Sorry, you won't convince me. I'm a private person and unless the real world as we know it grinds to a halt, there's no way I'd entertain it.'

'Oh well, suit yourself,' Lyn says.

'They're a weird lot here, although I haven't spoken to everybody,' I whisper as I survey the crowd. 'Not sure I'd want to see any of them again. You two are the only friends I need right now.'

As I look out over the sea of faces, I realise that there's nobody here that I'd like to rekindle a friendship with. The thought leaves me despondent. I'm not sure what I was hoping by coming here but it was supposed to be fun. All I want is to reconnect with people, blend back into the community, maybe drop along to the pub. I left England the fastest way I could. And thought I'd never return. But I'm back and I need this to work. But how? I have Lyn and Pandora's friendship, but their lives have moved on. Here I am, at fifty-five with nobody and I just feel like a square peg in a round hole back here in Rivermead, with my Ozzy accent and surrounded by the guilt I've carried for the past twenty-five years.

I'm walking towards the bar for another drink, thinking some more wine will pull me from my gloom when the door opens. Heads turn to see who's arriving so late into the evening. My heart misses a beat. He was my gentle giant, I used to call him the BFG after Road Dahl's character. We used to be the tallest couple wherever we went. I would recognise that mop of hair in a crowd of people anywhere, despite the new salt and pepper look. That lean body in loose fitting jeans and wintry garb. The sharp jaw and the angular cheekbones. I stop in my tracks, mouth gaping open. Jay.

8

Shit.

My friends, Lyn and Pandora, are staring at Jay. I rush back to them. They turn to me, smiling apologetically.

'Both of you knew, didn't you? That he'd be here?'

Lyn stutters something and Pandora's mouth opens and closes like a fish.

'How could you?'

'We didn't know he was back, not till this morning,' Pandora says.

'You should be on Facebook,' Lyn says. 'Then you'd know what's going on.'

Jay makes a beeline for the bar. He either hasn't spotted me or is deliberately avoiding me. Several hands slap his back. He's caught in conversation. Stunned, I watch him. The healing strides I've made unravel in seconds.

'Why hasn't he come to see me?'

'I don't know,' Lyn mutters.

Pandora taps her glass and stares at the floor.

'I'll answer my own question then. Because he's a coward.

He's weak and pathetic and completely gutless.' My voice rises, taking on a belligerent tone. I can't control myself. I've held it all in for so long, I feel that angry. 'What sort of a husband would pack his suitcase and walk out on their grieving wife while she was at the funeral directors placing teddy bears in our children's coffins?'

'Dee, calm down, you're making a scene,' Lyn says touching my arm. Heads turn and stare at me.

'Don't tell me to calm down. I hate him. Not a single word in twenty-five years. How could he do that to me? All the pain he's put me through, and he just swaggers in as if nothing's happened. I want to rip his bloody eyes out.'

'Dee, please...' Lyn can see my fury building. 'Maybe we should all leave.'

I count to ten in my head. It's a meditative calming technique Helen taught me. But it's not working. I've dreamt of this moment, of seeing Jay again. Why should he get away with the pain he caused me? Trancelike, I circuit around the crowd, now a blur, like a poorly shot action photo. Colours swirl and blend. I need to do this. I've wanted to for so long. There's only one person in the room I focus on. The man I married. The man who let me down, so cruelly.

Reaching him, my heart hammering in my chest I tug his arm. He swings round, beer sloshing to the floor. I'm done with his crap. Not standing by me. Bailing out. It's time to...

'Dee...'

My hand cracks across his face. It's as loud as a clap and makes me feel better in a strange sort of way. He lets out a startled gasp. Dropping his beer glass, it shatters on the floor. He staggers backwards, clutching his face, eyes watering. The hall is silent. We're the centre of attention. Then the whispering begins. They don't know the pain he caused me. How much he deserved that slap. All they see is a mad woman. I look at Jay who has a mark on his face from the impact.

What have I done? My heart does a flip. I've purged something from my system, but I know I shouldn't have done that.

He looks shell-shocked and throws me a look of disgust.

'Nice to see you again too,' he snarls.

'Not a word from you in twenty-five bloody years.'

I turn to the gathered crowd and shout, 'Lovely to see you all again. Show's over.'

I can't wait to get out of here. I just want to disappear and never be seen again.

Through the gap in the curtains the sun cuts rough lines across the carpet. I've hardly slept. Tossing and turning all night, going over the evening. I couldn't help slapping him. I felt better for it. For a split second.

The bastard is back. I didn't know I'd feel this bitter. How could he just erase me from his life like that? Spend twenty-five years pretending I don't exist. They call it ghosting - ending a personal relationship with someone suddenly and without explanation, withdrawing from all communication. Deleting their phone number, blocking from social media. But that's different. I'm not just someone he's met online and we're not teenagers. We shared a life together. I'm his wife. He made promises to me in church in front of seventy-odd people. I gave him two children. Why did he just up-sticks leaving me to deal with it all alone? We could have grieved together and come through the other end. Such a selfish, insensitive thing to do. And at the time, why didn't I see it coming? How could I have been such a poor judge of character? I thought I knew my own husband. Oh Dee, what's wrong with you?

I pull my legs up, hugging them tightly. Tears flow down my cheeks. Seeing Jay again has completely winded me. All those raw emotions bubble to the surface. Everything I felt when he left me returned last night. I was used. Disposed of. I trusted him. Such a deep betrayal. The lack of closure was maddening, cruel beyond words. In fact, one of the cruelest forms of break-up I know of. It's emotional abuse. Yes, Dee, that's exactly what it is. He silenced you. You didn't matter. And last night you broke that silence. No wonder I slapped him. He deserved it. Didn't he? I'm trying hard to convince myself, but there's a tiny niggle worming around my head. I'm not comfortable with what I did.

I dress but linger in the bedroom. Another day to dwell and ponder. Smiling and pretending to be happy. Facing Ruth and her cheery questions about last night. What am I supposed to say? Lie and say I had a nice time? Even before Jay walked through the door, I wasn't enjoying the party, but his arrival made my world fall apart.

I switch my phone on, dreading the intrusion of the outside world but I want to call Pandora.

She gets a blasting from me. 'Did you tell him I was back?'

'I'm sorry.'

'Was he actually going to come over to talk to me? It didn't look like it.'

'I'm sure he would have.'

'I've got questions running through my head, all over again. Why? Why would he leave me like that?'

'Dee, he felt overwhelmed. He'd lost both his children. Try seeing things from his point of view.'

'Are you suggesting I don't then? It was humiliating. He was as good as dead. Seeing him last night brought all those feelings back. If I was in a happy relationship, then maybe I wouldn't be feeling so emotional about the past.'

'Darling, if you want answers, you're going to have to ask him yourself. He's here for a while. The virus has grounded him. He can't get a flight back to New York. Trump has just announced that the ban on flights into America is to include the UK, from Monday evening. If he wants to get back to New York he's going to have to be very quick about it.'

'Why's he even here?'

'He came back for a family wedding.'

'I'm not sure that I'm ready to talk to him. And having slapped him, I feel embarrassed.'

9

After spending the whole of Saturday cringing at the memory of myself at the party, Sunday arrives. Andrew said he would be coming over today but at the last minute he decides to spend the day with his family. I imagine them all sitting around their conservatory table eating croissants, reading the Sunday papers, topping their cups up with freshly brewed coffee. Then I look at Dad slumped in his chair by the kitchen window dribbling and staring at the Andrew Marr show on the tv. 'The government's scientific advisers are saying we need to reduce social contact to contain the virus,' someone is saying. What a terrible time for me to come back to England. I've not had the chance yet to see Andrew's new house and catch up with his family. They came to see me in Australia six months ago. I saw my nieces, Emily and Izzy, briefly the other day when they popped over with Andrew and it was lovely to see them again. Every time I see them, they've grown a few inches. Emily was a bit sulky, as if it was all too much effort to come and visit her grandad and Auntie Dee. I should get a move on and drive over to their house in Surrey. There's talk of the country going into lockdown. I might not get the chance if I leave it much longer.

I've got to escape from everything that's happening. Finishing my bowl of Rice Krispies and a mug of builder's tea, I head upstairs to the attic room, where my belongings are stored, leaving Dad with Ruth. I peer up at the vaulted ceiling, the beams meeting in a series of arches. Andrew, Mum and Dad helped me to clear my family home after Jay left. This is all that is left of our marriage. They fill a corner of the attic space. Just twelve boxes.

The attic is dark but a stream of light, almost divine, cascades in through a small window illuminating the exact place where my boxes are kept. It's odd that the boxes should be under the only light in the attic. Did Mum put them here deliberately to make things easy for me knowing this time would come? But as I look around, I notice a switch and a lamp.

Pulling a knife from my pocket, I slice open the boxes marked 'photo albums.' Inside the box, the albums have been neatly stacked and I know what each will contain. The navy one is filled with faded Polaroid images from my school days and 1970s' holidays to Spain and Italy. The years have taken their toll. The chemical adhesive has turned the pages yellow-brown and caused lines to appear across the photos trapped under the plastic. I put it to one side.

My fingers walk across each book, removing the pink-and-blue flowered album I bought shortly after our honeymoon in the Italian Lakes. Turning the pages, I pause and stare at Jay and me in exquisite gardens, the lakes as the backdrop. This is how I remember Jay, through the images that are indelibly printed in my memory. In one picture we are standing next to a fountain, with a statue behind us and Jay is looking adoringly at me. I peer closer. His smile extends to his eyes and there is pure love. My heart flips. Everything about us was innocent. Neither of us had any inkling of how our lives would unfold.

I'd forgotten the picture tucked into the back of the album - out of place having nothing to do with our honeymoon - it's a picture of me, mummy to be, in my bra and knickers, proudly displaying my bump. Overcome with an intense wave of sadness, my eyes fill with tears. I inch my bottom to the attic wall and stare at the photo, remembering how it all began. Somewhere, in one of the boxes is my journal.

It doesn't take me long to find it. I dust the cover with my sleeve, open the folder and read the first entries.

August 30th 1990

I've got a job! My first teaching post at a secondary school, teaching history. I was beginning to panic having applied for loads of jobs. Then this one came up, a week before the new academic year. It was either this or nothing. Jay turned his nose up when he saw the name of the school. 'You mean you haven't heard of it? It's one of the worst schools in the country. It'll be very challenging, can you cope?' Such a patronising comment. I'll show him, I'll prove him wrong. Of course, I'll bloody cope.

THE INTERVIEW WAS CONDUCTED *by a small panel, all a bit scary and because it was the school holiday - apart from the caretaker doing DIY - nobody else was around. The views overlooking the North Downs from the staffroom were stunning.*

JAY WASN'T AT ALL *happy for me when I told him my news. 'Don't say I didn't warn you,' he said in a sulk. Honestly, what would he rather? That I wasn't working at all?*

September 3rd 1990

My first day! One of the teachers took me aside at break and said, 'You see those tower blocks over there? Well that's where most of the kids come from.' He raised his eyebrow at me, a knowing smile on his face. Neither of us dared to admit what we were both thinking.

September 7th 1990

I wish I'd not taken this job. The kids are a bloody nightmare. I didn't want to admit to Jay that he was right. This is nothing like teaching practice. The kids wouldn't stop talking. They did the bare minimum and what they did was shoddy. They messed around the whole lesson, tilting their chairs back, laughing with each other, chewing gum. I'm getting a sore throat from shouting so much. I've given out so many detention slips, they're becoming like confetti. I've just found out that staff turnover here is high. Several teachers are on long-term sick leave after having nervous breakdowns. At this rate I'll be having a nervous breakdown too.

September 30th 1990

I can't control these kids. I feel as weak as dishwater. One child threw a chair out the window today and yesterday a child stood on the table and started singing. I've been eating my lunch in the cupboard at the back of my classroom, sitting on a pile of textbooks scoffing my Penguin biscuit and stifling tears.

1st October 1990

I don't want to tell Jay how awful my new job is, mainly because his teaching job seems to be going so well. But today it all poured out. I finally told him how much I wanted to leave and find something else. I got the impression that he thought I was exaggerating, with my dramatic descriptions of how obnoxious the kids are. He said, 'Stick with it until the end of the academic year. If you leave now, it won't look good on your cv.' It's okay for him. He's teaching in a grammar school in Tonbridge. There aren't many grammar schools left but they still exist in Kent and many teachers aspire to working in one. He did well to get the post. He doesn't have to worry about discipline. His students want to learn and are motivated to do well.

December 28th 1990

I don't think I'm cut out for teaching. I'm dreading returning to work after the Christmas holidays. I muddled through the first term but I've no idea how I'm going to get through the next. I've enjoyed the Christmas holidays so much, just being away from the place, watching films and forgetting about school. I can't stay at that dreadful place any longer. I've got to leave.

January 7th 1991

My friend Lyn is pregnant! I wish I was pregnant too. It would be my escape route from the hellhole. But I'm on the pill and we haven't been married long. We discussed having children just after we got married. Jay wants children at some point in the future, just not yet. But if it's left to Jay, it won't happen at all. The subject cropped up again today, when I told him about Lyn. He fobbed me off with a different excuse, but I'm conscious of the ticking body clock. 'You need to get stuck into your job first before we think of starting a family,' he told me. 'We'll lose our freedom if we rush into it. Those spontaneous weekend breaks we both enjoy, will have to go.' And, 'The mortgage on this place is massive, we need two incomes.'

January 2th 1991

Spoke to Lyn today. She's really excited about the baby. Wish I was her and pregnant. Life would be easier.

. . .

January 3rd 1991

Tonight, Jay and I tried a new curry restaurant. It was a very long wait but the prawn korma was well worth it. Really yummy!

January 4th 1991

Jeez, I've never felt so ill. I've been throwing my guts up for the past couple of days. We won't be going back to the Bengal Tiger.

February 28th 1991

I caught several of the buggers at school whispering about me. 'Mrs Frumpy looks as if she's got a spare tyre around her waist.' I do feel fatter than normal and kids notice these things quicker than adults. Nasty prats. My period is late. But that's not that unusual. Sometimes it can be. Could I be pregnant. Surely not? I'm on the pill.

And then I remembered, the curry.

8ND March

Plucked up the courage to see the doctor. He's sending a blood test to the hospital. I'll know in a few days whether I'm pregnant.

11TH March

Shit, I'm pregnant. I blame that dodgy curry!

10

I put the journal back in the box, grab our wedding album and carefully descend the narrow stairs. When I show Dad the pictures in the album it will jog his memory. He'll recognise me, I'm certain of that.

The gentle tapping of raindrops against the landing window makes me stop to look out over the sodden garden and beyond to the field which is full of sheep. Dad owns the field and a local farmer keeps his flock there. When I was young, rainy Saturdays were my favourite kind of days, when I didn't have to leave the house and we'd play board games around the kitchen table. Mum would make mugs of cocoa on the Aga and Dad would toast crumpets. Seeing the drops trickle down the window brings calmness and I realise something. I've missed the rain. I watch the water droplets make patterns on the glass. There is a laziness about them, as if they can't be bothered to conform to the laws of gravity.

I'm lost in the beauty and drama of the English weather when something catches my eye. I switch my focus from the raindrops to the field. There's a flash of colour. Somebody is out there, a woman dressed in a blue jacket. She's an older woman, nobody I know. She's holding flowers and kneels at the foot of the old oak tree, resting the bouquet against the bark. I can't make out who she is and why she's putting flowers there, but her actions remind me of when families place flowers at roadsides to remember the death of a loved one. Is the woman grieving and for whom?

I perch on Mum's antique chair and pull my phone from my pocket. I call Andrew and as I wait for him to answer, I can almost hear Mum berating me from above. 'Don't sit on that chair, it was Grandpa's.'

Andrew picks up just as I'm muttering to Mum that I'll be very careful with her precious chair. 'What's up? Coping okay?' Andrew asks.

'Sort of. My mission for today is to get him to recognise me.'

'Best of luck with that.'

'What are you up to?'

'I've just been in the garden centre. The supermarkets are low on basics but the garden centre is stocked up on gnomes. How mad is that? Never seen so many.'

I chuckle. 'Hope you took a picture. Where are you now?'

'Just coming out of my local store. The place has been mobbed, yet again. Shelves stripped of everything from pasta to eggs and of course bog roll. I sympathised with a check-out lady. It's awful what they're going through. Customers demanding things and being rude.'

'I wonder who these panic-buyers are. One of these days I'm going to arrive at the supermarket in my dressing gown at seven as they open, to find out.' I pause. 'Andrew, I need to ask you something. There's a woman in Dad's field, putting flowers by the oak tree. Any idea who she is?'

'Oh, her. We'll talk about it later.' I detect a wariness in his voice, a reticence as if he doesn't want to talk about the woman. 'On a more important note,' he says changing the subject quickly, 'we really need to look at Dad's finances. We can take three thousand pounds for this tax year, for ourselves out of his account. The tax year's coming to an end, so we need to do it soon.'

'No point in giving it all to the tax man is there?'

'We can also take another three thousand for the previous tax year.'

'That will really help me. I haven't got much left in my bank.'

'The stock markets are in freefall at the moment.'

'I wouldn't know. I don't own shares,' I say laughing.

'I suppose on the plus side, when Dad dies if his investments are worth less, we'll pay less in inheritance tax.'

'Yes. So, the woman in the field, who is she?'

I've just reached the car now, sis, got to go.'

'But Andrew...'

'I'll call you later.' He rings off. What's he hiding? Who died in Dad's field? I want to know.

I head downstairs and find Ruth and Dad in the kitchen. Dad is in his armchair by the window and the telly is blaring. Ruth is singing *Happy Birthday* as she washes her hands at the sink. The WHO and the NHS have been telling us to sing *Happy Birthday* twice while washing our hands, because that way we know we've washed them properly.

'You're really going for it this morning, Ruth.'

'They keep telling us to wash our hands. A flick of water is no good. There's a whole routine to it,' she says, scrubbing vigorously.

'How are you, Dad?' I ask brightly, boldly turning the television off and drawing up a wooden chair next to him. I open the photo album. Maybe his mind is clearer in the mornings and that thought fills me with hope. But as he turns his attention from the TV to me, I watch the shutters come down. He seems unable to smile. His face is like a mask and his eyes are dead.

As I open the photo album my heart plummets. Am I just torturing myself?

'Dad, who's this man? Recognise him?' I jab my finger at the photo of Dad at my wedding. In the photo he is standing next to me outside the church in a suit and an emerald green bow tie, chosen to match the bridesmaid's dresses.

'My daughter's wedding.'

'Yes, my wedding, Dad.' I stab myself with my finger. 'Me.' I jab the photo, then I jab my chest, but the message isn't getting through. He's like a five-year-old.

'My daughter's wedding,' he mumbles. 'She lives in...'

'Australia?'

'Does she? Why does she live there?' He frowns. I sigh and flick the page over. This is making me feel very frustrated and sad.

'Who is this, Dad?' I'm pointing to Jay's father, Bob.

His face changes like a storm cloud scudding across the sky. His eyes are full of anger and his body stiffens. 'It was his own fault.'

'What are you talking about, Dad? I don't understand.'

'That family. Nothing but trouble.' His finger moves over Jay's image. He pushes the album off my knee and waves me away. 'Put the snooker on,' he orders through pursed lips.

A headache is brewing. I desperately need air. What the hell is this all about?

11

The radio by my bed wakes me to Gloria Gaynor's 1978 hit, *I Will Survive*. Can't stand the record, takes me back to school days but it's become a sort of lyrical emblem in this Coronavirus pandemic, played across the radio stations, the words dramatic and hard-hitting. Gloria's even shared a video of herself singing the hit while washing her hands. 'It only takes twenty seconds to survive,' she says.

In the middle of the morning I decide to head down to the village to visit the children's grave. Through the fields I stop to enjoy the sight of young lambs. They stagger on wobbly legs, frolicking with one another, but staying close to their mothers. How I've missed these views and the joy and beauty of the changing seasons.

Random sounds sail in the breeze, birdsong and the rustle of leaves. I gaze up at the topaz sky, enjoying the big puffy clouds, so English and so welcome after the eerie orange haze created by the recent bushfires that ravaged the east coast of Australia.

I still haven't decided what I'm going to do long term. For now, I'm needed here.

As I continue my walk a thought occurs to me. How are we going to sell Dad's house in the current crisis? The pandemic is bound to affect the housing market. With the stock market falling, people will feel less secure about their financial situation.

I reach the road. I didn't notice the details of each cottage the other day when I walked to the village, but this time it is as though I'm consciously scrutinising every little feature. It's almost as if somewhere deep in my psyche, I'm trying to work out which country I belong to. Across the road the gardens, or backyards as my Ozzy friends would say, are a riot of straggly plants, herbs and brightly coloured annuals. Little brick pathways and rickety gates. Neatly tended hedges meet grass verges. So different to the suburban gardens Down Under with their swathes of sunburned lawn leading down to the road and usually no pavement to walk on. Do I miss those endless miles of sprawling suburbia, so characterless, so samey? Rows of identical brick bungalows that remind me of coffins, fast assembled flat-packs filled with aging Poms waiting to die under the sun. I could never imagine what was in those bungalows. But looking at this quaint row of cottages my mind is filled with all sorts of delightful images: farmhouse tables and pine Welsh dressers filled with jars of honey and homemade jam, and a cat curled up on an armchair. I'm liking it here, it's comforting being back. Damn it. I'll quit my job and stay for now. I'll email Josh later on and tell him of my decision.

When I'm in the village, I head for the path leading into the graveyard. I feel my soul being squeezed in a vice. It's as if I've entered an inner sanctum, as if there's my life out in the world, the one I struggle with and then there's this life, in the graveyard, the raw, private one where I am the bereaved mother of two. A soft breeze wafts around my shoulders. Reaching the grave my stomach tenses because even now it's still hard to believe and I ask the same questions: How can this be real? Did this really happen to me, that I buried two children? Who was that woman? Who am I now without them? I stare at the grave dazed and inert, crumbling to my knees in the wet grass as if I've been shot in the back. Right now, I wish I had been. I cry and listen to my logical mind tell me these are wasted emotions - they won't resurrect my precious babies. But my heart doesn't care. I will cry. It's been twenty-five years of anguish. How have I lived with this pain? It never goes away, it's all I will ever know. I sit under a tree looking at the grave until my grief abates and I am able to get up and leave this inner sanctum and enjoy the rest of my walk through the village.

Out of the graveyard and through the square I glimpse the pub, its walls overrun with the fresh spring leaves of Virginia creeper, and on a whim, feeling curious, I slip inside. I've never been a timid woman afraid to go in a pub alone. Pubs are like cafes, I'm comfortable going in both alone. And after the graveyard I need to be somewhere cheerful. I may even see someone I know.

There's a porch with a stone bench either side where a gaggle of people are smoking. There's familiarity underfoot as I walk across flagstones in the entrance hall, but it's clearly had a makeover. The walls are covered in silver-and-lilac wallpaper with a dramatic floral design and an antique gilt mirror hangs above an oak hall table with a carved galleried back. A waitress in a white apron is walking up the steps in front of me carrying plates of food in both hands. She smiles at me. The King's Head didn't serve food back then, I'm certain of that. Pushing through the same swing doors there is now a dining area to one side of the pub which appears to be quite busy. There are a few old men gathered around the bar, chatting to the barman as he polishes a pint glass.

I recognise one of the men. He was a regular in here back then and by the looks of it he's still part of the furniture.

'The missus and I are probably going to have to cancel our trip to Turkey in May,' one man says.

'Doesn't look like anybody will be going on holiday this year,' another man says.

'Every time I turn on the television there are people dressed in white protective gear and masks,' one man says.

'It's a hoax. Haven't you read? China's trying to destroy the West. Google 5G, tons of stuff about it,' says a young guy with tattoos weaving up his arm.

'Well, I wouldn't like to catch it. Not with my dodgy ticker. Probably finish me off,' an older man says.

'What can I get you?' the barman asks me.

I peer at the range of drinks on display. What did I used to drink in here? And then it comes to me. Southern Comfort and lemonade. That's what I'll have, for old time's sake.

'You new round here, not seen you in here before?' the barman asks.

We chat for a while then I take my drink to a table.

I'm just finishing my drink when I sense somebody is there and look up. Every part of me goes on pause and I am unable to speak. Jay. Standing in the doorway. I'd forgotten how good-looking and tall he is. He's the spitting image of an Australian-British actor, Hugh Jackman. His dark hair, streaked with grey, is even swept into the same style; short and neat at the sides but quiff-like on top. His hair line has hardly receded. The intervening years have been kind to him. I wish I could say the same about myself. I can tell he's still working out in a gym because his arm muscles are toned, and he's managed to fight off any creeping middle-aged spread. His arm is resting casually on the doorframe like a cowboy entering a saloon. Adrenaline floods my body and my hands tremble by my side. Did he follow me into the pub? He doesn't move. I get up and head towards him to leave.

'Are you going to let me through?' I ask him. I just want to get out of the pub, be alone. This is my chance to talk to Jay properly, but I'm not in the mood.

'Pandora said you were going to text me,' Jay says. There's an aroma of beer on his breath conjuring memories of post-pub snogs in his Ford Escort.

Why is Pandora interfering? She has no right. I never said that.

'I'm sorry, Jay, for slapping you. But you can hardly blame me.' I stop there, worried my anger will mount. But there's so much I want to say to him. We've got to sit down to talk but only when I'm ready to.

He lets out a big sigh and lifts his arm from the doorframe. 'I'm sorry too.' He raises his eyebrows in a pained expression and digging the tips of his fingers into his forehead he leaves red track marks. It's as if wants to tell me something but can't find the right words. 'We really *do* need to talk.'

'Yes, I know but I'm not ready. Just seeing you again is making me angry, after everything you put me through.'

He stares at the ground.

'I'll text you when I'm ready to talk. Give me your number,' I say in a cold tone. I punch his number into my contacts, my hands are shaking.

Outside the pub I realise the effect he's had on me. I'm sweating. My top is damp and clammy and there's a throbbing pain behind my eyes. I head to the churchyard to gather my thoughts before the walk home. Behind a large cedar I sink onto the sponge of moss.

It's going to be hard avoiding Jay. Rivermead is a small village. I don't want to worry about bumping into him every time I step out of the house. Seeing him has opened the wounds. Sophie was so like Jay and I could see her strong-willed streak in Jay just now in the pub. Was it the glint of defiance in his eyes as he blocked my path? Or the way he was standing in the doorway - the same stubbornness I had when Sophie stood in front of the Teletubbies dancing across the television screen when I wanted her to switch it off.

The expression 'time is a healer' is administered freely like paracetamol, but some wounds run too deep. When you have lost both your children, there is no way out of the tunnel of grief. Seeing Jay again is a painful reminder of what we went through. I get up and head back. It's nearly time for Ruth's break.

12

It's Wednesday the 18th of March and Ruth and Dad are in the kitchen. Dad is eating his breakfast and Ruth is cleaning the hob.

'Morning, Dee, sleep well?'

'Yes thanks. So, what's the plan for today?' Each morning, just after breakfast, Ruth and I plan Dad's care and support for the day, and the night ahead. She does most the personal care, thankfully, but I will have to help him wash and get ready for bed when Ruth goes home next week for a night. She's talked me through what I need to do and seems a bit anxious about leaving me with him. Dad is prone, on occasions, to getting up and dressing in the middle of the night and wandering round the house. I will need to be vigilant.

'Dee, could you just get him a clean jumper from his wardrobe? He's spilt egg down that one.'

I rush off to Dad's room and slide the mirrored door across, ruminating why my parents chose such an ugly modern wardrobe. It looks dreadful set against the oak beams. Inside, Dad's clothes are crammed along a crowded rail that dips in the middle. I stare at his dark-coloured Farah trousers, crew-neck sweaters and shirts. And then something catches my eye, a bundle of colourful items stuffed on the floor. I push the door further, careful to keep it on the runners and lean down to take them out. They are all women's dresses. Unsure what to make of them I lay them on the bed. I'll ask Andrew about these later. Dad must have been involved in amateur dramatics. How strange. Funny how I never knew this. And odd how Ruth hasn't asked me about the dresses. Maybe she doesn't consider it to be her place or is being tactful.

After putting the fresh jumper on Dad, I say to Ruth, 'I think I'll pop over to Tunbridge Wells, see what the shops are like these days and drop into a café. I'll be back to take over from you at around two, as usual.'

I'm heading towards the door when Ruth pops up behind me. 'Hang on a minute,' she says. 'Should you really be going out? Didn't you hear last night's news? We should avoid gatherings and crowded places. We're supposed to be limiting social contact, that's what Boris said.'

'No, I must admit, I've been avoiding the news. It's too depressing.' I love going to cafes, sampling different cakes, but glancing at Dad, broken and frail sitting there in his armchair, I experience a rush of love for him. He needs protecting. I'd never forgive myself if I unknowingly picked up the infection and passed it onto him. From what I've read you don't know you have it until it's too late.

Instead I decide to head to the attic for the morning. The rhythm of my footsteps climbing the narrow stairway to the kingdom of spiders, where cobwebs trail and secrets whisper, conjures memories of childhood when we played hide-and-seek under the eaves. The attic is also where Jay and I had an awkward moment of madness - it's where we lost our virginity. There wasn't any discussion about saving ourselves, waiting until we'd reached that year marker of going out together. We were eighteen, awaiting our A level results. It was our time for experimentation. A slow dance at the school-leaver's disco had brought us together after several months of casual flirting at the back of the school assembly. Under the glitter ball, I'd melted into his arms as we gently swayed to Lionel Richie's *Three Times a Lady*, my heart fluttering in my chest. I'd finally won the boy I'd fancied all year.

After the sex, we'd lain on the bare floorboards, straining to listen for Mum and Dad's car on the gravel returning from a party. We giggled about the word, virginity. 'Lost is a funny word for it,' I said, 'It's as if we're going to hunt for it and find it again, like you would a key, or a pound note.'

It's hard to believe he was my first. It's even harder to believe we lasted, on and off right up until we married when we were just twenty-three years old. We muddled our way through university, catching trains to come and visit each other when we could afford the fare, squeezing into a single bed but not really being able to sleep. I was at Manchester studying history, Jay was in Canterbury reading maths.

There were a couple of times when I wavered in my love for him. For a time, we drifted apart. I'd felt as if I should make an effort to move on. Jay was my prop, and while that felt comfortable it was also constraining. I needed to explore, discover myself. Looking back now, it would have been healthier if we'd parted. At the time though, neither of us was strong-willed enough; neither of us wanted to break-up. After university, any thoughts about drifting apart disappeared and we really started to align on the direction of our lives. We chose the same college to take our post-graduate certificate in education, but we never taught in the same school.

My fingers hover over the photo albums I most fear. It's time I looked at them. My heart bumps and beats like it's trying to escape, but I have to do this. It's what Helen has been telling me to do for so long. Now that I am here, back in Rivermead, I must confront the memories head on.

I pull out the album of the children. I haven't seen their faces for so long. Running away to Australia meant completely closing the door. I left their photos behind. I didn't even keep one in a wallet or a locket. I warned Mum and Dad not to send any photos of the children because it was the only way I could cope.

As soon as I open the album, the pain grabs me, but I must go on. Each photo has a strange power in reminding me the past is real. The past has crouched in the depths of my mind for so long, beating like a second heart and now it is here, spread before me.

There are tears and there are smiles as I turn each page. A picture of Sophie, not long before she died, holding a spotted umbrella in a London Disney store. If only we'd given in to her full-blown tantrum that day and bought that wretched brolly. A picture of Poppy in a hand-knitted pink cardigan. Mum knitted it and used the pattern for a doll because dolls' clothes were the only clothes that fitted her - she was so tiny, just two pounds and fourteen ounces at birth - and shockingly that was full-term. When people peered into her pram, they assumed she was premature.

There's a picture of Sophie in her highchair eating a huge bowl of broccoli. I'd forgotten how much she loved broccoli and wonder if that would have continued or would she have eventually come to hate it? As I stare at the picture, I imagine myself standing at the oven, my back to Sophie sitting in her highchair eating her dinner. I'm repeating the words 'all gone' and finally one day I heard the miracle of those words come from her mouth. There's a dull ache across my chest and my eyes warm with fresh tears. Her voice is in my head. 'All gone,' 'all gone.' I quickly turn the page leaving her to finish her broccoli. The next photo was taken on a walk to the village shop. It had been ambitious of me to attempt the walk so soon after her first steps. In the picture she has a safety harness around her and she's bending to pick up a leaf. 'What's this?' I remember her asking.

The first two years of Sophie's life was the most wonderful time and I loved every minute of it. Having her close to my breast in those early days as she nuzzled in. Brushing my cheek against her downy head. The funny way she gurgled. Watching her achieve each milestone. Her first words, 'What doing?' as I pushed the Hoover through the house and most of all her cheeky laughter. And then her second birthday came. With the candles blown out, the cake cut and divided between ten exuberant toddlers, Jay leaned in to kiss me on the neck and whisper, 'Let's have another.'

That night we began trying.

I stare down at the picture of Sophie on the settee with Poppy in her lap and shut the album.

AFTER LUNCH I take the photo album down to Dad and relieve Ruth from her duties for the afternoon. Dad is dozing in front of the sport and opens his eyes when I touch his shoulder.

'It's time for your pills, Dad.'

Dad winces in pain. Leaning forward he clutches his stomach with his toothpick thin arms. I hate watching the slow road to death that he is on. The ashen complexion he wears like an outdoor coat and the agony expressed in the lines around his eyes and mouth. And each dragging step as he walks, jarring and brutal.

I sit down next to him holding a glass of water and his tablets and watch him swallow them.

'I've been up in the attic, Dad. I thought it would be nice to look at these photos together.' I open the album and turn the pages, arriving at a picture of Sophie standing next to the oak tree where I saw the woman leave flowers. Sophie's wearing pink wellies, the ones Mum bought her from a garden centre.

Dad is staring at the page, shaking his head. 'Cut that tree down.'

'Why? What's wrong, Dad?'

'Want it gone,' he snaps, knocking the album to the floor.

He'd had a violent reaction when I showed him pictures of Jay's dad, Bob. And now this.

I leave the album on the floor, too upset to pick it up. I've been holding myself together, but I feel as if my emotions have been thrown into a pot of boiling water and are about to bubble over. I try not to cry.

'Anyone home?' Andrew breezes through the back entrance and into the kitchen where I'm helping Dad eat a sandwich for his tea. 'Didn't take me long to get here. Roads are empty.'

'I hope you didn't hammer down those lanes, Andrew, the hedgerow's very thick now, you can't easily see round bends.'

'Erm, I may have done,' Andrew says sheepishly.

'Come on Dad, you've hardly eaten a thing.' I put a sandwich to his mouth waiting for it to open.

'You give me too much,' he complains grumpily, pushing the plate away. 'I'm not hungry.'

'You've got to eat, otherwise you'll starve. You didn't have much for lunch.'

'That's what she's always saying.' He must be referring to Ruth. 'I'm not going to starve.' There's a note of aggression in his voice, which takes me back to when he used to shout at me when I got poor marks in maths. 'If you want to be a teacher,' he'd remind me, 'you'll need O Level maths.'

'Do you want a yogurt instead? You like your strawberry yogurts.'

Dad's face relaxes. 'Yes, I'd like a yogurt or some ice cream.'

'You can't live on yogurts, Dad,' Andrew tells him, pulling a chair out to join us. 'That's hardly going to fill you up.'

After tea I suggest taking Dad for a walk along the lane in his wheelchair, but Andrew points out how uneven the lane is. Dad isn't keen to go outside, he's happy sitting by the kitchen window, a blanket over his knees while he stares at more snooker on tv. I'm surprised he's not bored watching coloured balls. I am. Everytime I walk past the tv, it's on. To me, snooker is spectacularly dull, moving at its own gentle and unhurried rhythms. I think Dad likes it because it helps him get to sleep. I rarely see him actually awake and watching it.

Ruth comes back from her break. Leaving Dad in his chair, Andrew and I wander round to the back of the house, pausing to admire the daffodils, primroses and crocuses, and the chorus of blackbirds as they go about their business. I remember how much I loved this time of year. There's a kiss of coldness in the air but the sun is beaming warmth across a Wedgwood-blue sky. We are silent for a while, as if life is suspended and I sense our thoughts are synced, each enjoying the surroundings, grateful that we grew up in such a lovely place.

'In the space of a few weeks, the world has changed so much,' Andrew says. 'In January we were watching scenes from China. Doctors running around hospital wards dressed in protective gear. We didn't imagine the virus would affect the whole world. We were too busy grumbling about the torrential and relentless rain.'

Back in January I'd still been with Glen, never thinking for one moment he'd cheat on me. And here I am, back in England, Dad is dying, and I've had the shock of seeing Jay for the first time in many years. But I don't vocalise my thoughts. I'll tell him another time. I want to soak up every moment and marvel in the blooms that herald springtime.

Approaching the oak tree in the field beyond the garden, Andrew reminisces about swinging on the tree when we'd been young and the competitions we'd had, seeing who could swing the highest. I'm transfixed by its branches. The tree was our childhood friend and is now a link to our past, and like the Queen it goes on, steadfast and dependable. I've always thought of the tree watching over the house. Thankfully it was too strong and statesmanlike to come down in the 1987 storm. Touching the craggy bark, I run my fingers along the ripples feeling its roughness. Lower down the bark, I gasp. It's still there. The heart Jay etched with our initials and an arrow, in true lover's style. This was supposed to express our lifelong love for each other, but now it's only teenage graffiti.

Pointing to the wilted flowers in cellophane at the base of the tree, I ask, 'Who was the woman who put these here, Andrew, and why? Why doesn't Dad like the tree?'

'Something happened here about fifteen years ago,' he says.

'What did?'

Andrew explains that for years cows were kept in the field by a local farmer. A public footpath runs along one side of the field. Bob, Jay's dad had been walking his dog along the path, without a lead. It was springtime and there were calves in the field. The dog ran off into the field and Bob ran after him. The cows went berserk and knocked Bob to the ground. He tried to stand up, but they repeatedly attacked him, trampling him to the ground and his death. He was airlifted to a London hospital but never regained consciousness and died a week later. Dad witnessed it. Bob had blood all over his head and chest. It gave Dad nightmares for years. Jay's family blamed Mum and Dad. Jay, of course was living in New York but rushed home to be with the family. Said the cows were completely out of control. But they didn't own the cows, the farmer was renting the land. The senior coroner returned a verdict of accidental death and said the accident needed to lead to a greater awareness of the risks posed by cattle. The cattle had to be moved to private land with no public access routes. Everyone in the village was so shocked and unfortunately, a few people took their anger out on Dad. One of Jay's brothers even tried to sue Dad.

My hand flies to my mouth. I'm so stunned I can't speak for a few minutes. 'My God what an awful thing to happen. No wonder Dad had such a violent reaction when he saw the picture of Bob.' I'm so shocked, all I can do is stare at the field. Poor Jay, what the family must have gone through. Several minutes pass as I digest what happened. It's just so hard to comprehend. Trampled on by cows. What that must have been like. Truly horrific. Whoever would have thought that about cows? They always seem such docile, placid creatures. And Bob - such a nice gentle man who was kind to everybody. He'd probably walked these tranquil fields for years, never imagining he was in any danger. Well you don't, do you? The English countryside feels so safe.

'You should have told me, Andrew,' I say, turning and staring at him in astonishment. 'I can't believe you didn't tell me about this. He was my bloody father-in-law for God's sake.'

Andrew lets out a sigh and rubs his head. 'All I was trying to do was protect you, after everything you'd been through, you really didn't need to hear about it.'

I find his worry for me both touching and surprising. He's caught between a rock and a hard place. He's tried to protect and shield me all these years from anything that might upset me, but at the same time he's felt bad for lying or staying quiet.

'But I was bound to find out at some point, especially coming back here. I don't want to be wrapped in cotton wool, Andrew. Now that I'm back I'm trying to confront all the bad things that happened here.'

'I'm sorry. Mum and Dad told me not to say anything.'

'What is it about this bloody family? I'm sorry, Andrew, I know you thought you were doing the right thing in not telling me, but I'm not a kid, I'm an adult and I had a right to know. Our bloody parents. They never were very good at confronting things and discussing stuff. And talking of Mum and Dad, there are some strange clothes in Dad's wardrobe. Was he involved in amateur dramatics? Or fancy dress? I can't imagine it somehow. They can't be Mum's clothes, they're much too flamboyant.'

Andrew hesitates and is about to answer me, but the next sound is his phone ringing, breaking the spell with its convenient timing.

'No way, poor Emily, what the hell will happen now? Her GCSES. And Izzy, you'll have to teach her at home.' There's a pause as he listens. 'I'll leave now, yes, of course.'

'Look I've got to go. Boris has announced that all schools will close on Friday, to stop the spread of the virus. Emily's distraught, poor kid. She said several of the teachers were crying. She's got tonight and tomorrow to revise for her exams. They're going to sit four exams on Friday and the results, together with the teacher's assessments, will form her GCSE results.' He's in a fluster and although I haven't forgotten the conversation we were going to have, he clearly has. None of it is important compared to the crisis that awaits him when he gets back to his family. Emily is nearly sixteen and Izzy is eleven. As we walk back to the house, I consider how things would have been if I'd still been teaching. I hated teaching. I would have relished the break from those unruly classes.

'I'll come back tomorrow, sis, we can chat then.' I get the sense that he is relieved not to have to discuss the things that are troubling me, but I need to get to the bottom of this.

I wave Andrew goodbye as he drives down the lane. Right that's it. I need to get to the bottom of all this. If Andrew won't answer my questions, I'm just going to have to confront Dad. Dad, are you into cross-dressing? Shit. Am I really going to just blurt it out like that? I was never known for my tact, but how on earth do I broach the subject? It's a complete minefield. The whole thing feels insane, preposterous. But of course, Dad wasn't a cross-dresser. It's just my wild imagination getting the better of me. There will be a simple explanation for why he has women's clothing in his wardrobe.

I linger in the hallway outside the kitchen. The door is ajar and, peering in, I can see one edge of the television screen and Dad's slippered foot. Ruth is singing while she washes up. Now's not the time. I need to wait till Ruth is on her break tomorrow. And then an idea comes to me. I might find some clues in the attic.

I splice through packing tape and inside a box that Dad has marked, 'Pam's stuff,' I find Mum's diaries and letters. I untie the frayed ribbon holding them together and slip the folded paper from one of the envelopes. I scan-read Dad's letters to Mum written from East Africa during his National Service in the 1950s. African landscapes. Not what I'm looking for and not exactly a hot romance.

I'm drowning in paper, diaries, sifting through, not knowing what I'll find. Just when I'm about to give up, I spot Mum's diary. It's marked 1965, the year I was born.

My fingers are careful, my touch delicate. The pages are nicotine-yellow. I scan through the pregnancy, intrigued to learn about my birth.

April 16th 1965

Met this ghastly woman on the ward of the maternity home after I gave birth to Dee. Horrible Essex accent. She's in the bed next to mine. Common as muck. Lives at the bottom of Summer Lane in one of those poky council houses. Eileen Goldring. This is her sixth child. Obviously doesn't know how to keep her legs closed. 'Got a name for littlun?' she asked me, attaching her screaming baby boy to her fat boob. As it happens, I tell her, Ron and I haven't the foggiest. We're narrowing it down to a list of names beginning with the letter D. Denise, Debbie, Deirdre, Dawn, Diana. We like them all. But we've come up with an idea to give her the first letter, D, then when she's older she can decide what it stands for.

'What a good idea,' this Eileen woman with the horrible accent

says. Copy-cat. She's going to do the same thing and call her baby, J. 'In years to come he can decide whether the J will be Julian, James or Jeff, but Jay is a very nice name too.'

When Essex woman laughs, she's a snorting pig, and you can see right inside her mouth and her teeth are crumbling. Honestly, the state of the woman, and you should see her raggy nightdress. You'd think she'd have bought a new one for her hospital stay. 'We were desperate for a girl,' she squawks. 'We wouldn't have kept trying if we'd had a girl sooner. I want me 'usband to be sterilised. Thanks for the tip about the name,' she said, wiping her runny nose on her arm, filthy cow. Sooner I get home the better. She's human trash. Then she added, 'As long as your daughter and my son don't get together. They'd be DJ. Disc jockey.' Lord give me strength.

∽

MUM, how could you? Poor Eileen, she can't help her accent or living in a council house. What a stuck-up snob. You never were keen on Jay and me marrying. I should have left the diary well alone. You always thought his family were beneath you, that he wasn't good enough. And no wonder you didn't bust a gut to find out where Jay disappeared to after the children's death.

Despite my fury, I flick the pages scanning for anything about Dad and cross-dressing, until I arrive at 1985. Jay and I were at university. I might learn more about Mum and Dad's relationship here.

There are sketches of sheep and flowers with captions. A beautiful record, a country diary. Of course, there weren't any cracks in their marriage, this diary reflects the harmony that existed here. Mum writes about the sheep shearing, Dad supervising the operation. There's a whole passage on Mum's patchwork quilt-making and the village competition she entered it in. Blissful country life…until…

. . .

October 20th, 1985

Ronnie's off on one of his weekends away. He makes me sick. I'm glad they only happen twice a year. It's not right. He's a married man. This shouldn't be happening. Why is he like this? I can't bear it. When he's away I get my patchworking out and try to blank it from my mind otherwise the images come, and they won't go away. He should never have married me. I love him, I can't leave him. But he's putting me through pure torture. I don't like this obsession with dressing up as a woman.

October 21st, 1985

Andrew has chosen the same weekend to go away and would you believe it, he's going to Brighton too. His new girlfriend lives in Brighton. Oh God, I just hope they don't bump into each other. I don't want Andrew or Dee to find out what Ron does. But Ron would cover it up. He's good at pretending.

~

I'M SO shocked that the ground seems to fall from under my feet. I never would have suspected this. Not in a million years. My mind goes blank as I stare at the words, a chill sweeping through me, taking with it the security of my youth. Tomorrow morning I'm going to send Ruth out on an errand. I need to ask Dad some questions. But just when I think I couldn't be more shocked; as I put the diary back in the box, I notice a photo. Taking it out I look at it, my heart banging in my chest. It's a picture of Dad and three other men arm-in-arm. They are wearing glamorous ladies' shoes, flamboyant dresses, long necklaces, make-up and wigs. Oh hell. I'm staring straight into my dad's eyes, connecting with his thoughts. He's happy. Happier than I've ever seen him. He's positively glowing, radiant, shining. Even though none of this feels real, I know that it is real, simply because I've never seen Dad look so full of life. It's as if he was going through the motions with us. The dutiful husband and father. But this hidden life was who he was supposed to be, even born to be.

As I process my thoughts, I'm trying so hard to convince myself he was just performing in a pantomime or posing for a photo at a fancy-dress party. A small voice in my head asks, how can this be true? This can't be happening. You've got it all wrong. I don't want to believe it.

I stare at the photo for ages in complete disbelief. Who is this woman with brown hair and a floral dress? The smile looks the same, the eyes, the chin, but it isn't my dad. My dad wore brogues and a tweed jacket, drove a Jag with his arm casually slung out of the window, a fag between his hairy fingers. My dad was stereotypically masculine; he loved cars and speed and he was the male breadwinner with a cut-throat desire to make money to support his family and always discouraging Mum from working, 'Because you don't need to, dear,' he'd say.

13

I'm aware of Dad's life slipping away. I need to know who he really is - or was. Soon it will be too late. Dad, a cross-dresser. Even though it goes against my liberal views, I can't help feeling disgusted. And the more disgusted I feel, the more annoyed I am with myself for being like this. I'm not supposed to feel this way. In this day and age, we're encouraged not to be judgemental, that people can be who they want to be. What does it matter? People should be able to explore their sexuality, because sexuality doesn't fit into neat boxes and in any case, what right do we have to judge? Life is short. But no matter how hard I try, I just can't get my head around the whole thing. He's my dad and I am judging because this affects me and who I am and how my family life has been for the past fifty-five years. It feels so outlandish.

But what I'm most cross about is the fact that Andrew and Mum didn't tell me. Yet again, something they decided to keep to themselves. It's as if the dad I knew doesn't exist. My life has turned upside-down, it's all topsy-turvy. All the things I took for granted have been pulled from under my feet. Who even am I? My mind is racing, so many questions filling my head. What does it all mean? Did he want to be a woman? Was he actually gay but married a woman just to fit into society? Did he still love Mum despite what he did? It doesn't make sense.

After lunch I take Dad's hand and we walk into the garden. I guide him to the bench Dad made years ago, fashioned from a wind-felled tree, Dad had varnished it meticulously each year. It had become a place of contemplation and reflection over the years. Moments of stillness sitting on the bench, taking stock. It's also a good vantage point to survey the whole garden and relax. When we're seated, I give his hand a squeeze. I wish he'd use my name. I'm not a stranger, I'm just a different version of Dee. If he doesn't recognise me, what hope have I got of him talking about the past? I breathe in the perfume of spring and glance around me. Everything is blooming recklessly. Andrew's said we need to get a new gardener in, but I haven't got around to making enquiries yet.

I take a moment to study Dad from the corner of my eye, as he stares ahead to the row of daffodils dancing in the breeze. Rivers of thread veins weave around his face. His bulbous nose is an angry mauve and his hands are covered in bruises which look like blackberry stains. I wish I could erase the image of him wearing a dress out of my mind, but now it's lodged there it's never going away.

I want to get Dad's memory working. 'Do you remember the parties, Dad, here, in the garden?' My mind is whirling back to the eighties. I'm back there; Dad has mown the lawn using a petrol mower, making perfect emerald stripes, the tips of his shoes turning green. Mum and Dad's friends, mainly from the village cricket club, holding glasses, plates of food, mingling, chatting. Us kids running round playing chase.

Dad stays silent. His eyes are vacant. Maybe I need to go further back, transport him to his childhood where his mind might be clearer. That's what they say about dementia, that sufferers remember the distant past, but can't recall what happened the day before. Sometimes I wish somebody would rob my memories, in the way that dementia does, because then I wouldn't have to wake at night remembering the death of my children.

'What did you like doing when you were little, Dad?'

A spark ignites in his eyes, his thick eyebrows lift as his brain ticks over, an engine cranking to life. 'Well you know…' He digs his hands in his pockets, his face has more expression now that he's engaging. He splutters for a few seconds as if organising the words in his head. 'My brothers were always using their fists.' This is a start. I follow his eyes, trying to enter Dad's world. 'I loved my mum's company. I was the odd one out.'

I silently will him to carry on before asking, 'Why?'

He looks around him. 'The bloody lawn needs mowing. Why's nobody mown the lawn?' I sigh. This is hopeless.

From my pocket I pull out the photo that I found in the attic.

'Dad, look at this photo.'

He smiles. 'Good times. You mustn't tell my daughter, Dee, she doesn't know. I don't want her to know. You won't tell her, will you?' He reaches out for my arm and grabs it. 'It's a secret.'

'Where was this photo taken?'

'In Brighton, of course.'

'Why were you in a woman's dress? For a play, a fancy-dress party, what was the occasion?'

'They were my special weekends. They were good friends, came from all over the country, they did.' He says it in a way that makes me feel stupid, as if I should already know all this. As if it's common knowledge. 'I miss those weekends. What were the names of the other fellas? They all had different names.' He shakes his head. 'Oh,' he says spluttering again, 'I can't remember.'

'Why, Dad? Why did you dress up as a woman? Didn't you

like being a man? Did you have an affair with a man?' I'm on full-grill mode now, my heart's racing, it's intrusive I know, but I'm not stopping. I need to know. In fact, it's my bloody right to know. But shit, I've gone too far, I need to back off, but I'm waving the photo at him, my voice is raised, and although I know I'm being cruel with my persistence I can't help myself. What he did was wrong. 'Why did you marry Mum, I mean, Pam?' My heart is thumping in my chest but I'm on a roll and will not stop till I've got it out of him. 'Why did you have Andrew and Dee? If you wanted to be a woman, why have a family?' But Dad doesn't answer. He stares at two blackbirds fighting over a worm, one tugging it from the ground, the other hopping and pecking at it. I need my brother. I can't do this on my own.

Just as I'm glancing at the time on my phone, wondering where the hell Andrew is, I hear his car crunch over the gravelled driveway. I guide Dad back to the kitchen as Andrew bustles in, his arms laden with toilet rolls and rejoicing in the fact that finally he's found a supermarket well-stocked with essentials - apart from eggs. The only eggs he could find were two broken quail's eggs.

'How are the girls?' I ask Andrew, remembering why he'd rushed off yesterday.

'Emily was distraught when I got home. She said even the teachers were upset that the schools are closing tomorrow.'

'So, what happens now?' I ask.

'Emily is revising today, and they'll sit four exams tomorrow, Friday, their last day at school. The results from those exams and their mocks will form the grades they get in August. She's devastated that the prom is cancelled.'

Ruth is back from her break.

'Let's go in the garden, Andrew, we need to talk.' I can see he's reluctant, I sense he knows I'm going to press him about Dad again, but he follows me all the same.

I take a deep breath. 'I found Mum's diary in the attic.'
'Chuck it away, it'll only upset you.'
'Will you just listen a minute.' My words feel like arrows, but I'm going to have it out with him once and for all. 'The diary says something about Dad going off on weekends. Seems these weekends away caused arguments between them. I was at university. You were still living here. You were about twenty-two. You must know. Where did Dad go?'
'Just leave it. Dump the lot.'
'I know when you're hiding something, I can hear it in your voice. I'm not going to be fobbed off, Andrew. Whatever went on, it can't possibly upset me any more than losing two children.'
'It was just a bit of this, that and the other.'
'Oh, for pity's sake. Stop being so bloody vague.' This, that and the other are three particular words Andrew uses to avoid tricky subjects and they send me over the edge.
'You really want to know the truth? Well I think you've already put two and two together. You found the clothes in his wardrobe. Yes, Dad was into dressing up as a woman.'
Even though I've already worked this out, from Mum's diary and talking with Dad, Andrew's words stun me into silence. I glance at him and before turning away I catch an expression of shame on his face. Shame, because he's probably feeling guilty for not telling me. His eyes look to the ground.
When he looks up, the shame is gone, replaced by a defensive look. 'Now can you see why my relationship with him has been so difficult over the years? Christ, Dee, you've no bloody idea what it did to me.' He's shouting now. 'I moved out. I couldn't be around him. He disgusted me. I was on anti-depressants for years.'
'Was? I saw Valium in your car, the day you picked me up from Heathrow.' I walk towards the French lattice bench by the pond and sit down.

'Yeah, I knew you'd clocked the packet, what was I supposed to say? That deep down I'm a complete wreck because my father messed with my mind? He wasn't our dad, he was a stand-in, he covered it up for years. He's not the person you thought he was. My whole childhood is one big lie. Our childhood is a lie.'

'Oh, come on, Andrew, stop being so melodramatic. He probably went to fancy dress parties, maybe he was in a pantomime, that kind of thing.' Deep down I'm still in denial, part of me refusing to believe, hoping this is all very innocent and that maybe I misunderstood Mum's diary entries.

'You really want to know all the sordid details? Well I'll bloody well tell you. But you won't like it.' His face has turned a deep shade of red. 'I went down to Brighton one weekend to stay at a hotel with Tracy. We were going to a concert. I can remember it all as if it were yesterday. Going up the steps into the hotel, glancing round the foyer thinking - this is a nice lively hotel, lots of people drinking and enjoying themselves. But then...something didn't feel right. The lobby was full of fellas in colourful dresses. I glanced at Tracy, her face was a picture, thinking the same as me, blimey, what have we come to, a bleeding tranny's festival?'

'Go on.' As I listen to Andrew's story, predicting what he's about to tell me, I feel as if I'm looking at the past through fresh eyes, as if I'm staring into a kaleidoscope and somebody is slowly turning it to form a new and unfamiliar picture. The patterns are wrong, they don't fit, everything's in flux. If only I could wake up and peer through the correct kaleidoscope. This is all so amiss.

'We checked in, bought drinks from the bar and somehow got chatting to a few of the trannies. I think back then we called them cross-dressers. They were really nice guys, so open about what they did, going away for weekends, leaving their wives at home and dressing and acting like women. They said they go down to Brighton every year, a big group of them to that hotel because the hotel was welcoming and didn't judge. Tracy had the guts to ask them about why they dressed up. They said it felt as if they were leading double lives, coming away from their wives, being who they truly wanted to be - women. I didn't care what they did, it didn't bother me, I found it amusing, until I went to the loo and bumped into Dad dressed in a red dress and high heels, full make-up on, standing at the urinal. I had to do a double-take. It couldn't be him. But it was, Dee, it was our dad.'

I'm not sure whether to laugh or cry. There's a disconnect. He's not talking about Dad. He's got the wrong man. This is so totally absurd. Or have I been blinkered all these years? Did I miss the vital clues? I scroll through my mind. Dad wears cords and Fred Perry shirts, v-neck cashmere jumpers from M&S. There's nothing in the slightest bit feminine about Dad. Curiosity as well as revulsion crouches in my head, daring me to ask questions, wanting to know more. Did he dress-up because he felt like a woman inside or because he preferred women's clothes? Was he bi-sexual? Did he have affairs with men? A sick feeling curdles in my stomach. 'I can't believe it, Andrew. Maybe I'll wake up to find this is all a bad dream.'

'Standing next to my own dad dressed as a woman at the urinals, was without a shadow of a doubt the worst moment of my life.'

'Hang on a minute...' My mind is whirring. 'You found this out long before my children died. I was at university. Why didn't you tell me? You had no excuse.'

'I think you were in the middle of studying for your finals. There was no way I was going to ruin your studies. You were at a vulnerable age.'

'Protecting me again? All very sweet, Andrew, but you really should have told me. I had a right to know.'

'I'm sorry, I've been very good at doing that, haven't I?' Andrew kicks the ground with one foot.

I glare at him. 'If there are any more secrets about this family, you need to tell me, okay?'

He shrugs. 'There's nothing.'

'You quite sure about that?' I say, grabbing his shoulder, forcing him to look at me.

'Yeah, that's pretty much it.'

I'm still getting my head round the idea of Dad as a cross-dresser. I'm revolted. But tucked behind my revulsion there's also compassion, and I'm pleased with myself for feeling this. Poor Dad, has he spent a lifetime bottling it up, quelling it, never really showing his true self? But there again, what if he hadn't kept it a secret? I would have ended up a pretty messed-up teenager. Perhaps that's why Dad took his urges outside, getting it all out of his system on those sordid little weekends away. But in doing that he was sacrificing who he really was. How awful that must have been.

'After you went away to Australia, Mum became very bitter towards him. I pleaded with them to have counselling. Mum was already traumatised by the loss of Sophie and Poppy. Their deaths changed her, Dee, I don't think you realise just how much.' Sucking in air, he adds, 'And she always felt she'd lost you too.'

My eyes fill with tears. 'I'm sorry, I never knew.'

'Dad and I had a few run-ins. I couldn't stay living here. That's why I asked Tracy to marry me, which was a bit premature given we hadn't been going out for very long.'

'Run-ins? What happened?'

His jaw tightens at the question and as he goes to speak, I catch a hint of contempt for Dad in the curl of his mouth. 'I screamed at him one evening, pinned him by the neck against the wall and told him to leave Mum. I could see what it was doing to her.'

I think of Mum, her voice, her sweet smile. Despite her bitchy side, she was caring and obviously endured a lot. I think of the way she tried to help me through my pain, but kept her own pain locked inside, staying strong for me, while all the time she had her own demons she was battling with. No wonder she said, 'Confront your demons, don't run away.' She stuck with Dad. She didn't run, or hide, she didn't take the coward's way out and whatever arguments and silent periods Mum and Dad had - they stayed together. Till death do us part meant everything. The tears now flowing down my hot cheeks are a reaction to her suffering. I can totally empathise with what she must have gone through. My mum, for all her faults was a proud woman. I'm gripped with compassion. I didn't treasure her enough. I wish I'd been there for her.

'What did Mum do?'

'She cowered in the kitchen, begged me to let him go, kept shouting for me to leave.'

'She must have really suffered.'

'I could have killed him that night. I was livid, it was as if a fog had descended and all I wanted was him gone. Please say you understand, sis?'

'I don't know what I would have done, I honestly don't. I can't judge your actions.'

'My head was all over the place.'

'Yeah, my head feels messed up too.' I turn and look him in the eyes. 'Andrew, he was a good man.'

'It's all just plain weird. Because he's my dad, our dad. I'll never come to terms with it. The moment I saw him in that hotel, he was no longer my dad. It blew everything away. I'd lost all respect for him. I can only deal with him in small doses. I don't actually like being in his company. That's why I called you back. I'm just going through the motions because I know he won't be around forever.'

'You're willing his death.'

'I didn't say that. I'm just doing what I have to do.'

'He still doesn't know who I am. I showed him a photo of him in a dress. He said he doesn't want his daughter, Dee, to know about his secret.'

'You were the precious one. He wanted it kept a secret from you. He'd have been horrified at you knowing. You were daddy's little girl.'

It hurts that this was kept from me. 'He's never volunteered to tell me, I suppose I didn't have the right to ask him about it this morning. And Andrew, he loved you very much.'

'It means nothing. I think he didn't like the fact that I was a real man, and he wasn't.'

'Don't be stupid, Andrew. That's all in your mind.'

'He hurt me. He hurt Mum. Not directly, but he wasn't the man she married. Think of how it was for her. Poor soul.'

'At least he wasn't an alcoholic. Plenty of alcoholics end up beating their wives. He didn't have a nasty bone in his body.' Tears fill my eyes. 'So, what if he liked to throw on a dress every once in a while? He's still the same man, just liked to wear dresses and paint his nails. In the end it's just lipstick and fabric.' I'm trying to get myself to look at it from a different and more rational perspective and to control my own emotions. But I'm having a hard time, it isn't easy. I'm also aware that I'm partly playing devil's advocate because Andrew is annoying me. He's had over thirty years to come to terms with all this and get used to Dad's lifestyle. He shouldn't be still finding it weird. He should have moved on in his thinking.

'Dee, for pity's sake stop down-playing the whole thing.'

'What do you want me to do? Wallow in self-pity and chuck pills down my neck, like you obviously have all these years?' I never realised my brother was such a weak person. After everything I've been through, it would seem that this is the worst thing he's ever been through. It's pathetic. After all this time he needs to get a grip.

'The government's telling us to reduce our social contact. And quite honestly, I'm glad. It means I don't have to come over here for a while and see that old Nancy. That excuse for a father.' Andrew, red with rage stands to go, but as he storms from the garden, he lobs me a passing shot like a hand grenade. 'I've done what I can for the old bugger, it's your turn now.'

He pulls a childish grimace at my shocked face and strides round the side of the house towards his car. I'm dumbfounded. All this helping Dad in his hour of need was just a show, something he had to do out of duty. He's been acting on auto-pilot for weeks dealing with Dad, and has clearly held it all in for years. I don't know the half of what went on in this family. The atmosphere between the three of them must have been dreadful. And the façade they all put on, just for me. There's so much I don't know. I've been so blinkered. I wish I could have picked up on the tension between them. Any tension between Andrew and Dad that I did observe, well it was all pretty normal father-son angst. Andrew and Dad never did see eye-to-eye on very much.

14

It's Sunday and Andrew hasn't phoned since our awkward conversation in the garden on Thursday. Still sulking no doubt. Ruth has gone home for a forty-eight hour break, and so tonight is my first night alone with Dad. Ruth has shown me what to do, but I'm nervous about undressing him. My own dad. Who would have thought it would come to this? I'm squeamish and have no idea how I'll cope, but I'll just have to get on with it.

Ruth spends all morning cleaning Dad's room which is on the ground floor of the house next to a small room where she has been sleeping. She changes the sheets of her bed so that I can sleep there while she's away. She leaves in the early afternoon after cooking Dad's lunch and helping him to eat.

I'm suddenly frightened to be left alone with him. The man sitting here is a crumpled version of Dad. He looks like a human lizard, all wizened and a shell of his former self. I don't know how to behave in front of him. I haven't a clue what to say, especially after yesterday, in the garden when I showed him the photo of himself in a dress. I shouldn't have put him on the spot. It was a well-kept secret and the best thing I can do now is to help protect that secret for him.

I kill some time by Hoovering round, but Dad is alarmed by the noise. 'What's that roaring noise?' he asks. So instead of being useful I sit with him, the television blaring as he drifts in and out of sleep. When it's bedtime, I wake him, nervous about what lies in store. 'Shall I help you to bed now, Dad? It's getting late.' I take his arm to help him stand. It feels like a vicious act, but at this rate we're never going to get to bed.

'Go home,' he snaps.

'Dad, this is home. I'm tired. Let's go to bed.' I yawn dramatically.

'This isn't my home. Where am I?' He looks round, confused.

How is it possible to lose my dad while he is still here, living, breathing? This is not the man who rushed up to Great Ormond Street in the middle of the night to be with me just after Poppy died. Or stood with me at the funeral of my children willing me to be strong.

'Well what are we waiting for?' He says a few minutes later, just as I'm drifting off beside him. He clutches the edge of the settee and slowly gets himself up. Tottering as he stands, I'm terrified he will fall. I reach to grab his arm.

'You've not drawn the curtains. You've missed a gap.' He shuffles towards the window, fiddling with the pleats. I can see this is going to take an age. I guide him away from the curtains and he stops, a confused expression on his face. 'Where is she?'

'Who?'

'That woman.' He's frowning.

'Ruth has gone home for a couple of days. She did tell you.'

His nose is purple, his eyes are red-rimmed and he's out of breath. Is he desperately ill or this how he's been for a while? I can't work it out, because I've not been here. I'm out of my depth. I keep reminding myself that the agency had said they could provide a stand-in carer, or bank worker as they are called, but I was determined to look after Dad myself. It's almost as if I've set myself a test. It's something I have to do.

Dad frowns at me, shakes his head and mumbles something I don't understand. 'I don't know,' he mutters. 'What's to do, what's to do?' I hold his arm as we walk towards the lounge door where he stops and glances round. 'Turn these lights off,' he says, waving to the lamps. I go to the first lamp and switch it off. 'No, you fool,' he shrieks, taking me by surprise. In an instant I'm back at the kitchen table, the seven-year-old struggling with her homework, Dad standing over me with his disparaging remarks, pointing to each mathematical puzzle with his pencil. 'You'll bugger the system. The switch is here.' It's confusing, this dementia. Sometimes he's so sharp, but at other times he hasn't a clue.

In his bedroom I help him sit on the bed, while I fumble under the pillows for his pyjamas. Just as I'm removing his jumper, revealing the scar where his pacemaker was fitted, he looks at me and says, 'Is there a proper person working this evening?'

'Dad, I'm not working, I'm your daughter, remember?' My voice begins to crack. 'I've come all the way from Australia to look after you.' There are tears in my eyes, but I try not to cry. He was there for *me*, he stayed strong when my children died and after Jay left me. He was my steadfast rock. He took me into his arms, and we clung to each other. There was no holding back. I wish I could get my old dad back. There's so much I want to tell him, so much I want to thank him for. I want to thank him for being so capable when I was a wreck. I want to tell him how sorry I am for leaving England and letting him and Mum worry about me from a distance.

'One minute, Dad.' Emotional, I rush to the bathroom and as I grab some loo roll to blow my nose, I catch my reflection in the mirror. I look a wreck.

'Where is she? The usual woman? She knows the drill,' Dad calls through to me.

I suddenly feel sorry for myself. I'm exhausted. I just want to crash. I want to hug the pillow and wallow in self-pity, lie in bed all morning and pretend this is a horrible nightmare.

'Are you listening?' Dad says.

Ignoring him because that is all I can do, I guide him through to the bathroom and help him take out his dentures to rinse in Steradent and then get him ready for bed. I'm suddenly unnerved by the thought of doing all this. I must take his trousers down. And his nappy pants. My dad naked. I can't do it. I want to run. But a voice inside my head takes over, driving me on. I have to do this. Ruth needed a break.

DAD SLEPT THROUGH, which was a big relief, but I didn't. I was half awake, listening for movement in his room, worried he might get up.

Tonight follows the same pattern as last night. Dad watches more sport. Groan. I wish I could get him to watch something else. I'm sure he used to enjoy *Morse* and *Last of the Summer Wine* and maybe even a soap opera or two, but if I dare to switch channels he'll have a hissy fit.

'Shall we see what else is on? I suggest, picking the remote up, finger poised to click the guide button.

'Leave it.' His gnarled hand comes out, grabbing the remote from me but he doesn't know what to do with it. For a doddery old man, he still has a feisty spirit. I give up, go to close the curtains on the pale moonlight skimming the walls. I'm tired, my brain is running on five percent battery, I need sleep.

'Come on, Dad,' I coax, touching his arm. 'We really need to go to bed now.'

I don't like being bossy with Dad, I find it hard. I've been away for years and he doesn't know who I am. It makes me cringe, but what choice do I have? I need some strength left in me, to get him to bed. His eyelids flutter, he's about to nod off again then his head jerks and he says, 'I've not watched the news.'

I sigh. I think I can manage five minutes of news. I pick up the remote and press 1. Prime Minister Boris Johnson's face fills the screen and there is a Union Jack propped against a wall. Boris reminds me of an alpaca, or a grown-up version of the Milky bar kid - the boy dressed as a cowboy who appeared in adverts for Nestlé in the sixties and seventies. I want to turn the tv off, but something makes me continue watching. It's Boris's tone, it's more sombre than usual. There's a deeper edge to his voice. But I know what's coming before the dreaded words leave his mouth. We've been expecting it. Lockdown. There's something about the word that makes me shiver. The word conjures all sorts of images: of Northern Ireland during the Troubles or a giant chain and padlock wrapped around the house, the army on the street stopping people leaving their homes. 'We've been asking people to stay at home... I must give the British people a simple message... people will only be allowed to leave their home for the following four reasons...'

A cold chill sweeps through me. How has it come to this? Even though we've been half expecting this to happen, I didn't really believe Boris would do it. He's been dithering for weeks. Things must be pretty bad. The virus is out of control, otherwise why would he resort to this drastic action? Looks like I'm definitely staying in England for a while. But I'd already made that decision. It's just that it's now been taken out of my control. I'm not sure how I feel about that.

'We're in lockdown,' I mumble to Dad, but I don't think he understands what's happening.

I help Dad out of his chair, and as we pass the curtains he tuts. They don't meet in the middle. There's an inch gap. Silly me. 'You haven't pulled them across properly, what do I pay you for?' I want to scream at him, Dad, it's me, Dee. Your daughter. His tone is stern and he sends a spray of spittle which lands on my shoulder. He fiddles with the edges of the curtain until they meet, then stepping around he notices his used tissues on the coffee table and heads towards them. 'You've forgotten these,' he tuts and his shaking hand picks them up and stuffs them up his sleeve.

With Dad in bed I settle into my own, flicking through messages on my phone, in two minds whether to call Andrew, but deciding that it's too late.

I'm just drifting off under the warmth of the duvet, in the room next to Dad's, snuggled against a hot water bottle, when I hear Dad shuffling around in his room. I fling the covers off, switch the table lamp on and head to his room. He's staggering towards the bathroom, clutching his stomach and groaning. Something is hurting him. Poor Dad, I hate seeing him in this much pain. I wince at the thought of the cancer, causing havoc throughout his body. Pulling his pyjama bottoms down he inches towards the loo, glancing back at me with a grimace. Hell, what am I supposed to do? Just watch. He's my dad, he deserves privacy, yet I know something is wrong.

'I'll just be out here if you need me.' I face away from him, staring at the pictures on the wall above his bed. He's still groaning. As I turn to check on him, I gasp. There's blood pouring in torrents from his bottom. What the hell do I do? Why is he bleeding? I make a dash for the kitchen, grabbing handfuls of kitchen roll, my heart racing. 'It's okay, Dad, stay there, don't move,' I shout coming back into the bedroom. He's still bleeding. It's not stopping. Oh my God, what the hell do I do? My nose wrinkles, the smell of iron is overwhelming and makes me think of an abattoir. I stem the flow of blood with more kitchen towels but it's still coming. Jesus, he'll need a blood transfusion if this doesn't stop soon. My mind is all over the place. Leaving him standing in front of the toilet, I dash to my room and return with my phone. I hurriedly dial 111 and wait. 'Turn round Dad, sit on the loo,' I order and while waiting for someone to answer the phone I use my other hand to hold his arm and twist him round, easing him onto the toilet.

A woman on the end of the line asks how much blood is coming out. 'A teaspoon?'

'No, more,' I tell her.

'A small cup?'

'More.'

'A pint?'

'More.'

There's a slight pause. 'Okay.' She takes a sharp intake of breath. 'An ambulance is on its way.' Another pause. 'Stay with me on the phone, I need to ask some more questions. After she's asked a string of questions about Dad and his illness, she says, 'I have a few questions related to Coronavirus. Does anybody in the household, including your father have any of the symptoms of the virus? Are you aware of what the symptoms are?' As she asks these questions a new panic rises inside me. What if Dad gets the virus in hospital? From what I've heard, it's so contagious, it'll be rife in that place. But what choice is there? He's ill. I'm going through the motions of answering her questions, but my head is spinning with worry. 'I can hear a dog,' she says. Pippin is making whining noises. I wonder if Pippin senses that Dad is ill. 'Please make sure the dog is shut away in a room before the paramedics arrive.'

Coming off the phone I urge Dad to stay sitting on the loo, while I grab Pippin's collar and tug her towards the kitchen. She chokes and tries to resist, looks back at Dad through pitiful eyes. I coax her towards her basket, she stops, looks up at me sadly, as if she understands what is going on. Then she pads, head down towards her bed with an air of resignation about her.

Expecting to wait ages for the ambulance, I'm relieved

when I hear tyres crunching over gravel, blue light streaming through the hallway. I open the door to two paramedics gowned up and wearing visors, masks and plastic gloves, looking young enough to be still at school. I stand back, respecting the new social-distancing rules, waving them through to the bedroom. 'Who is his doctor?' 'What medication is he on?' 'Does he have any medical conditions?' My mind goes blank then I remember where his notes are kept. Tearing back into the kitchen, I've forgotten about the dog being there. She rushes out, barking frantically, lurching towards one of the paramedics who is crouching over Dad. I tear her away, clutching her tightly, returning her to the kitchen, then open the drawer for the medication dosset box and Dad's medical notes.

The paramedics have helped Dad to his bed and sitting up he is relaxed, even jovial, taking everything in his stride, holding his arm out for his blood pressure to be checked. I think the blood coming from his bottom has stopped. I hover like a spare part in the room, not knowing what to do and feeling useless so I go into the kitchen, pick up Pippin and comfort her, buying my face in her warm fur before returning to the bedroom to see how the paramedics are getting on.

'You were very quick getting here,' I say to them.

'A&E is empty. He'll be seen immediately. We've never known it to be so quiet. Everyone's staying away from hospitals, scared of getting the virus.'

'But people must still need emergency treatment. Accidents still happen.'

'You would think so,' one of them says shrugging.

'Can I come in the ambulance, or shall I follow in the car?' I ask as they carry Dad on a stretcher towards the door. I can keep him company in A&E, bring him tea from the machine and make sure he gets seen quickly. At least Dad has me here with him. I'm so glad I flew home. At last, I can make myself useful. The thought of him going to hospital alone fills me with horror. But the dog. I'd almost forgotten her. Poor little creature. She loves Dad. Follows him everywhere. She's scratching the door, barking frantically, probably anxious about what's happening to Dad, but she'll just have to stay here. She'll be fine for a few hours.

'I'm very sorry, but the hospital has just this morning announced tight restrictions on visitors to protect patients and staff in preventing the spread of Covid-19.'

Eek. My hands fly to my mouth. They can't do this. I want to be with him. 'But I can't let him go on his own.' All sorts of things happen in hospitals. You read about it all the time. Patients left to die in corridors through neglect and what about that illness, MRSA? I remember it being in the papers, quite a national scandal.

'We'll look after him.' There's an officious tone to the paramedic's voice, as if she's talking to a child. 'Someone will ring you as soon as we know more.'

I watch helplessly as they wheel the stretcher up a ramp and into the ambulance. In the background, Pippin is going crazy, locked in the kitchen, parted from Dad.

I am lost in a torrid vortex. The doors slam shut. Dad gone. And I didn't even say goodbye. What if this is it? I've failed him. I let out a sob. Please, no. Through tears I watch the rear lights of the ambulance fade from view until darkness closes in on me. I turn towards the house, some of the lights are on, but there's no welcoming feel. It's almost creepy. All the people who lived here, our family, Mum, Dad, Andrew, they're all gone. It's just me. I'm alone in this ghost house where only memories live on.

Andrew, I must phone him, let him know, even though it's very late.

'Oh no,' he says, but am I imagining it, is there relief in his voice? 'I didn't say goodbye to him the other day. Maybe this is some cruel fate. But I was so wound up, sis. Talking to you about the past and what went on, well it stoked it all up again. I wish to God I'd said goodbye. This could be it.'

'Andrew, we've both known that Dad was going to go downhill at some point.'

'I'm not sure I'm ready though… to be an orphan.'

His words spark fresh tears. 'Me neither,' I say through misty eyes. An orphan. What a strange and sobering label, but that's exactly how I feel right now. I don't have a family of my own. Who's going to be there for me when I grow old? And then a thought jars me. Other than my brother and nieces, there's only one person I'm linked to. Jay, the man I'm still married to, but shouldn't still be married to and we're both here, living back in this small village after all this time.

15

I'm still in bed the following morning after Dad was rushed to hospital when I hear the landline ringing. Where the hell is it? I remember seeing it somewhere in the house. Stumbling out of bed, I barrel down the stairs, towards the sound. I pass Pippin, in a cinnamon bun position under the kitchen table as I head for the utility room, the nimble tap of Pippin's nails on the flagstones as she follows me.

I'm aware of a debilitating tiredness, the kind I felt when Poppy was in hospital. It feels as if I'm running after life, as though it's ten minutes ahead of me. I reach for the phone. Please let it be the hospital and please let Dad be okay. But what if he dies there, without us at his bedside? My head buzzes with questions, there are so many uncertainties. A new thought slams into me. I'm on my own. With the lockdown now in place I can't see anybody. Andrew won't be able to come over. The police will be out, checking where people are going. We can only go out for essential items or for daily exercise. They've shut down society with a flick of a button. This is hard to deal with alone.

Picking up the phone fires up a long-held dread of uniforms

and bad news and I tense as I listen to the doctor's voice on the other end. My head feels suddenly light, a familiar feeling from years ago. I don't want to be here again, waiting. Hope dashed, hope raised. I hate this process. 'I'm very sorry but...' the voice at the end of the line says. I know what it means to go weak at the knees. It's not just an old cliché. I grab the utility room stool, sit down and wait to hear those dreaded words: death, dead, passed away.

'Your father unfortunately had a fall in the night. We've given him strong painkillers and he's sleeping now.'

'A fall? How on earth did that happen? Was nobody watching him?'

'We're not sure how he fell or why.'

This isn't good enough. If I'd been there with him this wouldn't have happened. 'He must be in agony and you won't let me visit. He needs me there. And what about the bleeding?' I feel so damn helpless.

'He needs a hip replacement before we can assess the reason why he was admitted. He's in a great deal of pain.' Poor Dad, I can't believe this. Going into hospital and having an accident.

Coming off the phone I ring Andrew to update him. He's as cross as I am. 'Broken his hip? It's a disgrace. We need to put in a formal complaint.'

We talk about Dad's illness, sharing our concerns and then I ask how he is.

'Stressed. Worried about Dad and I've got Tracy moaning about the lockdown. Says she needs a haircut and Emily's moping about the house. The bands on her braces have split and the orthodontist said he'll fix them when the lockdown ends. Not that we know how long this is going on for.'

'I've got to go, Andrew. Pippin needs to be let out for a wee.'

After letting Pippin out, I call Ruth to let her know what's happened.

'The poor sausage and poor you having to deal with it all alone. I wish I'd been there.'

'Not your fault Ruth, you weren't to know.'

THERE'S NOT MUCH I can do over the next few days, so I spend the time taking Pippin for long walks, trying to come to terms with the dad I didn't really know. Pippin is such a gentle dog and is adjusting well to Dad not being here, but occasionally I catch glimpses of sadness in her eyes. There's a dog bowl by the bench and I pour some tea for Pippin who laps it up with a greedy tongue.

In the garden, neglect has set in. Ivy cascades over the fence, growing tendrils in each direction and the disheveled lawn is more moss than grass. Clusters of daffodils rear their golden heads amidst the tall grass and there are smatters of saffron-hued primroses. I don't like gardening, the only thing I can take care of is a pot plant and most of them die on me. I either overwater them or forget to water them. This garden is far too large to tackle. And it is hard graft pushing a mower through long grass. I stroll past the herb garden. The beautiful aromas of rosemary, chives and sage whisk me off to pleasant evocations of Italian restaurants. The smells make me hungry and I think of fresh omelette and spaghetti bolognese. I pull a chive leaf and chew it as I walk back to the house.

After my walks I retreat to the attic, despite the attic feeling like a cage of pain where secrets are stored, the past unearthed. Never mind Mum and Dad's dramas, I have my own past to come to terms with. It's all in my journal and now I have time to read it.

I pick up from where I left off, March 11th, the day I found out I was pregnant with Sophie, my eldest.

. . .

March 11th, 1991

When Jay found out I was pregnant his reaction was, 'Fudging Nora. I'm going to be a dad. But I don't know the first thing about raising a kid!'

'It's on-the-job training I'm afraid. A steep learning curve, my love,' I told him.

I can't believe a tiny bud is developing inside me. Something pink will be wriggling and kicking inside me soon. Like an alien trying to burst forth. Heck, what will that feel like? This is a super-new experience. I don't know what to expect.

'If you get unwell,' Jay said, 'you'll just have to start your maternity leave early. We'll manage.'

30th May 1991

I'm so tired of traipsing up and down the stairs to my classroom, and teaching a rowdy bunch of unresponsive, disruptive pupils isn't helping. This afternoon a quiet well-behaved child said to me, 'You can't control us, can you? You shouldn't be a teacher.' Her words were like a punch in my gut but also a thunderbolt. When the bell rang at the end of the day, I opened the drawers of my desk and tipped everything into a carrier bag. Damn it, I'm not going back. I've had enough.

∼

I FLICK through the pages of notes about Sophie's pregnancy and early life, until I come to my second pregnancy and the birth of Poppy. The second time around I felt like a waddling encyclopedia on the a-to-z of pregnancy: morning sickness, food cravings, heartburn, back ache, Braxton's Hicks, the whole shebang. I considered myself an old hat at this having-a-baby lark. How wrong I was. I was soon to find out that pregnancy can spring some very nasty surprises. It doesn't always go to plan or follow a fixed agenda.

Poppy was due in December 1994. At least that's the date I told the doctors I was due, going by the first day of my last period. It's all very simple to work out, using a pregnancy wheel/gestation calculator. But the doctors didn't agree with me. That's when my nightmare began.

16TH NOVEMBER 1994

It's just three weeks to go until my due date, 7th December, the date I thought I was due. Lyn made an off-the-cuff remark today and that got me worried. 'You're carrying it well, Dee. If I didn't know you were pregnant, I'd have a hard time believing you were.'

'Oh, come on, surely not? I feel like a whale.' Of course, I look pregnant. What was she talking about? Sophie was a football-shaped bump. This one was spread out and was more like a vat of jelly. The main thing was though, my midwife wasn't worried. She checked my blood pressure, weight gain, height of fundus. At the main scan they said the baby was small for the due-date, and they did keep questioning my dates, saying they thought the baby was due nearer the end of December, rather than the first week of December, but overall they weren't worried.

Lyn's words troubled me, so I booked a doctor's appointment.

20TH NOVEMBER 1994

The doctor measured the height of the fundus and to be on the safe side he sent me to the hospital for another ultrasound scan. The sonographer put cold gel on my belly and moved a probe around. She called a doctor in and they stared at the screen while the sonographer continued to poke and prod me. I craned my neck to see the screen. It didn't mean anything to me and was like watching a near- extinct prehistoric creature swimming in the eerie underwater in an old Jacques Cousteau documentary. The sonographer asked me to sit up and for the next twenty minutes they studied figures on a growth chart. I felt like a tomato plant waiting to bloom.

The doctor had the posture of a soldier. His actions were precise and purposeful. 'These due dates have been changed several times,' he said. 'According to the date of your last period the due date is December 7th, but we then thought it was due on December 21st, then that was changed to December 28th, but now - judging by the baby's size - I would say January 2nd. There's been quite a fall-off in growth which is concerning.'

'What do mean? A fall-off?' I asked.

'The baby is much smaller than the lower line of expected growth. There are three growth curves - higher, medium and lower. Five percent of babies are exceptionally small and maybe yours is one of those. It will be a small baby.'

'How small?'

'The size of a bag of sugar, about two pounds.'

'Why? Why's it not growing?' A voice in my head immediately zoomed in on all the things I hadn't done. I hadn't been taking folic acid tablets. I hadn't rested enough, and I should have drunk more milk. Was there something wrong with me? Maybe my womb wasn't big enough for the baby to grow. The doctor had a brusque manner, as if he needed to finish the appointment to get onto his next tomato plant.

'I'd like to admit you to hospital for bed rest, while we await an appointment to see a top gynaecologist at a London hospital. He's a professor and the best consultant in the country.' As I left the room, I tried hard to visualise a bag of Tate and Lyles sugar.

21TH NOVEMBER 1994

Rest? They've got to be joking. I don't know how to! And not sure why I have to. What difference is resting going to make? Nobody's explained that one, but I got the impression that one wrong move might set off a Cuban missile crisis in my uterus.

Jay and Sophie came in to visit me during the evening, bringing chocolates, and after they left, I was so hungry having not eating the yukky hospital dinner, that I scoffed the lot.

22ND NOVEMBER 1994

Jay arrived in the morning to drive me to the appointment in London. Last night we shared our worries about the baby but in the car a distance opened up between us. Jay chattered on about work. None of this mattered when our baby had something wrong with it! He really does stress about work. Jay puts his heart and soul into teaching, it's in his bones. I've never seen him teach but I just know that he's an incredible teacher. Unlike me, he's got what it takes. I couldn't wait to escape the chalk-face. Jay's patient, kind and has the most amazing strength and resilience. He's one of the staffroom's shining stars and in the classroom he's a celebrity. It was hard when we were both teachers. I felt as if I was somehow in competition with him. Even though we taught in different schools, in different catchment areas his classes always achieved better grades than mine. Sometimes it felt as if he enjoyed bragging. But now that I'm well-shot of the job - with no idea yet what I'll do when I return to work - it's tough being married to a teacher, especially a teacher like Jay, because, let's face it, Jay is married to the job. He's up till stupid-o-clock most nights slaving over homework and exams papers.

'Stop staring out of the window and look at the map, Dee, will you? I'm struggling. It's the first time I've driven this far into London.'

When we reached the hospital, Jay manoeuvred the car into a tight spot in a side road. Killing the engine, he flumped onto the steering wheel letting out a howl. I gasped. He seemed so in control - but was clearly cracking. Jay is the type of person who is outwardly strong, but it's only a polished veneer. I reached over and gathered him into my arms. We sank into each other losing ourselves in our warmth and vulnerability. I breathed in the smell of everything I love about him. He pulled away from me and although I saw the pain in his wet eyes, he switched to practical mode. 'We better get a ticket. It's London, the traffic wardens are everywhere.'

'It's going to be all right, Jay,' I said, trying to sound strong even though inside I was wobbly. 'We've been sent here because it's the best place.' My words were just as much to reassure myself as they were to reassure him. 'Let's be positive, the baby's still alive,' I told him. Shit, I hope I'm right. I hope this place has some answers. It is a teaching hospital so it should do. I hope our baby's going to be okay.

16

The queue outside the professor's room was long. There were chairs either side of the noisy corridor. Women of all nationalities, partners too and small children. I muted their voices. There were only two places I'd seen such long queues: the airport and Disneyland. A notice flashed above in orange, 'We apologise for the delay...waiting time is currently running one-hour behind..' The wait was nearer two hours. Jay read his *Terry Pratchett* novel and I flicked through a dog-eared copy of *Home and Garden* magazine.

When my name was called, we headed into the professor's room where I was asked to lie on a couch and pull up my shirt in preparation for the scan. The professor had a Greek name that was hard to pronounce and looked like a human version of a statue of Cicero. Just then the door swung open and in trooped seven young doctors in white coats. The seven dwarfs had more manners than this bunch of gormless, insensitive creatures. At least those dwarfs would have smiled and introduced themselves. The white-coated doctors gathered around the couch and stared at me, as if I was an alien just landed from space. My cheeks flushed. While the probe moved over my belly, my eyes fixed on the white ceiling, trying to ignore the fact that there were so many people in the room, all holding clip boards and pens poised ready to write notes. God, they were officious and intimidating. I wanted to tell them to step away, give me some space. They were like the flipping paparazzi swarming round. There was another doctor sitting at a computer and I wondered if he was calculating measurements and entering my details. 'Dee,' Jay said, with a sparkle in his eyes. 'Look at the screen, that's our baby.' I turned my head and watched the screen in amazement through a small gap between the white coats. The picture of our unborn baby was much clearer than on the screen at our local hospital. It took a while for the professor to examine the screen as he pressed and prodded my belly.

'How old are you, Mrs Goldring?'

'Twenty-nine.' *Can't he read the notes?*

He frowned. 'Twenty-nine?'

'Yes.'

Silence. I glanced at each of the doctors in the room while the professor pondered my answer. Everybody seemed to be waiting for this great professor to give his verdict.

'When was your last period?'

'Second of March.' He stared at his notes, frowning. 'But I have long cycles. Sometimes fifty days.' My voice splintered as I tried to stay calm. I closed my eyes. *Go away all of you,* I willed. But when I opened my eyes, they were staring at me. I felt like a corpse on a gurney.

The room was silent as everybody waited for the professor to say something, but he was deep in thought. Jay squeezed my hand as we waited.

When the professor spoke, tendrils of fear crept through me and the team of doctors were poised, hanging on his every word. He addressed them, without looking at us. And for the next few minutes, it was as if we weren't even in the room. I might as well have been meat on a butcher's counter. 'It is wrong to keep altering a woman's due dates. To change them once, fair enough. Twice raises a concern.' Beyond this sentence I didn't understand what he was saying. It was all medical jargon. Latin words. When was he going to look at me, speak directly to us, the parents, or didn't we matter? This, it was dehumanising. I was a lab rat for him to poke and prod and discuss with his medical students. They won't remember me, but I might make case history. They just needed to learn a list of jargon to pass an exam to determine their future. I squeezed Jay's hand. It felt as if he was the only human in the room.

The professor turned to us, as if we were an after-thought and reeled off a 'shopping list' of problems. I caught the term, birth defects and my mind glazed over. '...cleft palette, hair lip, overlapping fingers, hole in the heart, twisted heart valves, gross retardation...' The words swam before me. This was every parent's worst nightmare.

The professor had just slammed us with the ghastly news and yet my body was screaming for a cup of tea. 'Can I please have a cup of tea?'

The professor ignored me and called for a nurse. The medical students left the room, clutching their clipboards. They didn't smile at me or offer good wishes, I was invisible, just the patient. I fought tears, refusing to cry because professionals don't like tears. They are indifferent and tears take up time. There was a long queue outside waiting to be seen. I saved my tears for when Jay and I were alone, curled up in bed like a question mark. 'Why was this happening to us?'

A nurse came in with a dish containing needles and tubes. 'Now,' the professor said in his brusque tone, 'what this amounts to, I am more or less certain is Down's Syndrome. If this is the case, the baby won't survive the birth. We have to do a cordocentesis to confirm this chromosomal abnormality and to detect any blood abnormalities. This is similar to an amniocentesis except that we are going to take blood from the baby rather than amniotic fluid. I'm going to insert a needle through your abdomen and into the umbilical cord. His words sound rehearsed. 'But there is a small risk of miscarriage.'

'Can we have five minutes to think about it?' I looked at Jay. He wasn't saying anything - but continued to grip my hand.

'There's nothing to think about,' the professor said firmly. 'It needs to be done.' A long needle came towards me. Shit. It was heading for my stomach. I looked away, tensing, willing myself to stay calm. 'Can you watch the screen,' the professor asked. 'I need you to watch the screen.' Watch? How much more did he want me to suffer? It wasn't a quick procedure, he wiggled the needle, pushed in further, further. I wanted to be sick, bile was rising. Tears flowing. Please let this be over.

Then it was over, and he told us that they would ring with the result in a few days time. Out of the room, I begged the first nurse I saw for a cup of tea. 'Oh, I don't know, the coffee machine isn't working, the café on the ground floor might be still open, go downstairs, first left, along the corridor, left again, past the florists and it's on your right.' I felt so sick, all I wanted was a cup of tea to make me feel better. But it wasn't going to happen.

26TH NOVEMBER 1994

The past few days have dragged by at home while we waited for the hospital to ring with the results. Mum has been looking after Sophie. I'd been in such a state over all this, there was no way I could look after my little girl. Friends popped by to see us. Nobody could believe what was happening. They brought gifts, took us out for lunch. It helped to take our minds off the agony of waiting. But after they left, Jay and I melted into each other, salty tears keeping our souls alive in this furnace of pain.

Last night in bed I watched the muscles of Jay's chin tremble like a small child, there was static in my head, the side-effect of living with the not knowing. Something had been snatched from us, yeah, that's how it felt. Robbed. A baby swap. This one was deformed, I'm carrying a monster. Babies are supposed to be perfect, angelic, tiny new creatures.

. . .

27ᵀᴴ November 1994

The house felt unusually quiet without Sophie. I missed her bounding in, climbing into bed with us, her blissful and familiar scent, her dog-eared toy rabbit tucked under her arm.

Jay had a pensive expression on his face this morning. He was awake for hours, I just knew it, fretting, worrying, mulling things over. Should I have done the same? Am I a lesser human being because I'd slept right through?

'Dee, they said it could be Down's Syndrome. We need to find out all we can about the condition.' Jay threw his legs over the side of the bed, reached for his underpants with a determination that said, I'm onto the case, I'm not wasting time languishing here, I'm going to confront this problem. I sighed. Good old Jay, in practical gear, turning to books and helplines for answers. I turned away from him and stared at the wall. I didn't want to read all about it, I knew enough to know that...oh God, my thoughts are too ugly to confront.

I just want this to go away. Jay has what it takes. Look at the success he's made of teaching. He comes from a large family. He's strong, he can take on any challenge. But me. I pulled the duvet over my head, silent tears wetting my face. And that's where I stayed, all morning, listening to Jay asking questions on the phone. And then he called out to me, 'Just nipping down to the library.' Don't know why he doesn't research using his computer. I think it may have crashed. It's always crashing. He spends hours holed up in front of that damn machine, sitting there in his ridiculous Star Trek slippers and matching towelling robe like an overgrown boy, trying to get it up and running, talking to other computer geeks on the phone, about DOS, whatever that is. And the black computer screen with white writing I've come to dread. Stupid machine is broken more times that it actually is working. Don't see the point of it. The hours he spends trying to fix it on a Saturday morning when we could be enjoying a family day out. The wires trailing round the lounge, the screeching noise as it connects to the internet, or world wide web, I don't know the difference. Do I care?

A couple of hours later I heard the front door bang, feet on the stairs, Jay breathless in the room, flinging his leather jacket off, dumping it on the bed. I hadn't bothered to get up. The bed dipped as he sat.

'I've got some leaflets. The library assistant was really helpful.' Jay blabbered on. 'They have sunny personalities,' he said reading from a leaflet. What the actual heck? What was that supposed to mean? He irritated me, the way he flapped the damn leaflet in front of me, then when I wouldn't take it, he read it for me, but in a slow and deliberate voice as if it was the Holy Grail. I think Jay thinks that by being well-informed everything will be okay. No, it won't be. This isn't what I signed up for when I got pregnant.

'There's plenty of support and help out there, Dee.' Yeah, I bet there is, but they can't 'fix' our baby. He may be coming to terms with this, but I'm not. I'll end up in a psychiatric hospital with a nervous breakdown. I can't do it. I wanted to throw the bloody leaflets at him but instead I smiled sweetly. Underneath the duvet, my fingers sunk into my thighs in frustration. I wanted to tell him what a shame it was that the pregnancy had come this far, that if we'd known about all of these birth defects early on, we could have aborted it, erased the problem and started again. I felt cruel for thinking all this and knew I shouldn't. But this was going to change our lives forever. I was desperate to fling my arms around him and tell him how I felt, but he would have been shocked. I can't speak the unthinkable. Jay was nearly an abortion. His mother had been warned not to go through with the pregnancy, though I've no idea why. He's the youngest of six. I think she had problems with number five and was told by doctors not to have any more.

30ᵗʰ November 1994

We weren't prepared for the call when it came, two days earlier than expected, the phone ringing like an annoyed rattlesnake from the hallway. I was in the kitchen clearing debris from a takeaway we'd had the previous evening. My hands were dripping so Jay answered it.

Tears were streaming down Jay's face when he came off the phone, his arms ready to embrace me.

'It was them?' I dried my hands, bracing myself.

'We're going to have a healthy girl. Everything's going to be all right,' he blurted.

I was speechless. There had to be a catch because something didn't add up. 'How can it be all right? Birth defects don't magically disappear.'

'She...' Why have they announced the sex? Although this isn't important, I feel miffed they've spoilt our surprise and worst, annoyed with myself for thinking this. 'She doesn't have Downs Syndrome, it's good news.'

'So, what now?'

'We need to get back up to London to the same hospital tomorrow with a packed bag. Sounds as if they'll deliver the baby tomorrow. They said something about an emergency caesarean.' There's relief in his voice, and excitement even, but I'm holding back. I can't let my guard down. There are too many questions bobbing around my head.

1ST DECEMBER 1994

I was right. While the baby doesn't have Down's Syndrome, she has some sort of syndrome, but they don't know what it is. I stared at the professor, as he delivered this news in his consulting room. This was worse, not knowing the name of whatever it was she has. It's just a collection of problems. But why? I want to scream at him. Why don't you know? Why has this happened and what is the long-term prognosis? A few hours ago, it felt as if we were climbing a ladder, and soon we'd peep through a cloud and the landscape would be clear and hopeful and every professional would rally round and take care of us. But now it felt as if we were standing on the edge of a dark and forbidding forest. We'd arrived in the middle of that forest, looking up, tall trees around us, overwhelmed, scared, not knowing what direction the next few days would take.

The professor asked me to lie down and pull my top up. More probing, another scan. My belly was beginning to feel like a lump of bread dough to be kneaded. The professor stared at the screen. He was the top guy in the country and yet I felt as if my baby had flummoxed him. He was at a loss for answers. Today was a wasted day. We were no further on, slinking deeper into that forest. At least with Down's Syndrome we could read the leaflets, study the outlook. But a syndrome with no name?

'I'm going to refer you for more scans.' Surely not? 'To one of the heart hospitals in London. We need a full cardiac assessment of the baby's heart. The nurse will take you to a room while you wait for the paperwork to take with you. A team of the hospital's specialists will see you tomorrow.

The nurse guided us into a room to wait for the paperwork, but before she left, she turned and said something completely out of the blue and without context and it shocked and totally overwhelmed both of us. 'How would you feel if your child is mentally handicapped?'

What were we to say to this cold, heartless question put to us in such an unprofessional way? All she did was scare us. There was no basis to her question. And yet, she planted a seed in my mind.

∼

2ⁿᵈ December 1994

The grey world outside our metal box as we drove back up to London the following morning for the cardiac assessment mirrored my own sadness. It was one of those days when you think, come on weather, frosty mornings please, help us build a Christmas mood. Except that we weren't in a festive mood and all this driving back and forth between home and central London was stressful. Mum, in her pastel blue raincoat was crammed into the back of our little Fiat, her puffy legs digging into my seat. She insisted on coming. 'I'm worried love, you need me there.' Jay's mum was looking after Sophie. My hand cradled the bump, which still felt no bigger than a cake-and-pudding tummy. I sang lullabies in my head to the little princess asleep inside me who was oblivious to the worry she was causing. It passed the time as we sat in traffic queues in bland suburbia. 'I'll love you forever, not matter what, as long as I'm living, my baby you'll be.' The lullabies helped me to bond. I was frightened I wouldn't love her, that when she was born, I'd reject her, run away from the problems. The path was unknown, but it would be a cruel one.

St John's Hospital was a sprawling red-brick building with a tiny carpark that was already full and way too small for the numbers of patients and visitors this place must see. It niggled me as we crossed the road - staring up at it I couldn't help wondering if institutions like this needed to be rebuilt out of town where there was plenty of land. If Tesco can take over greenfield land, why can't hospitals?

Inside was a maze of corridors, and old-fashioned noisy lifts - the type with metal chains and pulleys that clang and clunk as you ascend, inch by painful inch. A notice above informed us that we'd arrived in the cardiac department. We were told to wait along another corridor and Mum was the first to collapse into a plastic chair. 'Oww, my pins are aching, so much walking, funny place this isn't it, dear?' she said rubbing her legs, looking around her. 'Least you're not as big as that lassie coming towards us. Her belly looks as if it's been pumped up like a beach ball,' Mum whispered. I looked at the woman as she waddled along nursing her beach ball. It was a normal bump I wanted to tell Mum. That was how I was with Sophie. My belly was stretched like a drum and I had the classic waddle. But this time around, accommodating my neat bag of sugar doesn't leave me waddling like a bloated guineafowl. I wished it did. Because that would mean being normal. I so want to be normal, I want my baby to be normal too. What is normal? We're always told not to use that word, not to compare ourselves with others. Why is life so futile?

We left Mum reading a tatty copy of Woman's Own while a nurse ushered us into the consultant's room. A cardiologist sat at a screen reading notes; barely turning to greet us, he waved an arm for me to lie on the couch. Like the last scan, I was just a piece of meat on a slab for him to dig his implements into and he didn't waste time in doing just that. The room was warm, and I drifted into a light sleep, sensing Jay close by, but he didn't hold my hand this time, as if he had temporarily removed himself from the situation. Why was he staring at the floor? I needed him to be with me, now more than ever.

The cardiologist put the probe down and told me to sit up. 'Let me explain...' he said. Getting paper and a pen he drew a diagram of the heart explaining to us how a normal heart works and what was different about our baby's heart. Our baby had several holes that would probably close in the first months of life. He wanted her to be delivered at St. Julian's, the top cardiac hospital in London, just in case there were problems during birth. On the piece of paper, he wrote large secundum ASD. I knew that Jay would look the word up later in his medical encyclopaedia. He had a library full of books at home. You can take the teacher out of the school but not the school out of the teacher.

It was a long day, but as we left the treatment room with instructions to head to St Julian's in the morning there was only one thing dominating my mind. I grabbed the doorframe for support and breathed slowly as pain seared through me like a branding iron. I'd struggled all day, ignoring the waves. Jay asked, 'What's wrong?'

17

I had thrush. It was agony and the hospital's pharmacy was closed. Why had I been ignoring it hoping it would just go away? Without Canesten I knew that the pain would keep me awake all night. I kept my eyes peeled through the streets of London, leaning forward to peer through the rain splattered screen, but nowhere was open. At last a Tesco, on the Purley Way. I left Mum and Jay in the car while I dashed in, hurrying down aisles until I found the pharmacy counter. 'I'm sorry, we're out of Canesten. There should be a delivery in the morning,' said the assistant. I couldn't wait till the morning, but even if I could get it, it wouldn't be enough. I needed something stronger, but nothing seemed to work. It's gone on for weeks, but never been as bad as this. Natural yogurt, that's what I'll get. It's better than nothing, will soothe the burning pain. I needed to feel relief now. Taking the large pot, I dashed to the toilets, taking down my knickers and ripping open the lid to scoop a generous amount onto my fingers, lathering it over my personal area, inserting it as deep as I could, enjoying the cool relief it gave. I sat on the toilet for several minutes, thinking over the events of the days, while the yogurt soothed me.

When we got home, I was ready to hit the sack. The pain was

intense as my head hit the pillow, but it was a long day and tomorrow would be longer. I just wanted my mind to switch off, sleep to take me. Our limbs were entwined, Jay pressed against my back, whispering something in my ear. But I was drifting. Tiredness beating against my eyelids, sleep towing me under.

WAKING the following morning there was a moment when I was whole again, but it evaporated as fast as summer rain on scorched mud. By the time my eyes were open my brain was overwhelmed all over again as if it was all new, fresh and raw. I wished I could linger in that blissful ignorance of waking or never wake at all. Down below the pain was worse. The itching, the throbbing, the stabbing sensations. I wasn't up to having my baby today. Not with this going on. They'd poke and prod. I curled into a fetal position, my hand between my legs pressing away the pain. I didn't want those doctors and midwives anywhere near me, with their nasty metal implements and their gloved hands. This baby was staying where it was until the thrush had gone. But as Jay brought fresh coffee to my bedside with a kiss on my forehead, I knew that today was the day, regardless of the pain I was in.

HOURS later when Jay had gone home leaving me lying in a dark hellish room in a hospital gown, mild period pains came in waves several hours on from the insertion of a pessary to bring on labour. Fear and adrenaline flooded my body. The thrush was worse. I pressed the red button above the bed, lying back clenching my fists, willing the pain to go.

A flustered nurse appeared in the doorway.

'Please, I need something for the thrush.'

'I'm sorry, I called the doctor to see you, but really it will disappear as soon as the baby is delivered. It's a symptom of pregnancy. Have a bath, the warm water might help.' She hurried off and I staggered to the bathroom, gripping my stomach as the labour pains squeezed my stomach then eased. I stood in the bathroom, my legs wide apart to ease the burning below, as if I was John Wayne getting off his horse after a long journey through the Wild West. In the bath, I sloshed warm water over the bump and afterwards patted the sore area gently with the abrasive hospital towel they provided me with.

In bed again, the warming effects of the bath soon wore off. I lay there staring at the ceiling wishing I could be put under, wake and find it was all over. But that wasn't going to happen. Instead I imagined myself running in my gown to the top of the building and jumping off. The roar of the air in my ears as I plunged forward, arms outstretched, weightless at first, then growing heavy as gravity sucked me down. Hitting the ground, the force would break every bone in my body, but the pain would be gone, I would be gone. A crowd would gather and gawp and wonder what could have been so bad? So awful, so tragic.

I drifted in and out of sleep and when sunlight pushed through the blinds, I wondered why labour hadn't started. I thought that was the whole idea of the pessary, to get things moving.

At midday Jay arrived, his face full of concern as he held my hand while we waited for the doctors to do their rounds. Several doctors came in, holding their clipboards and one of them asked us, 'Given the high chance that this baby could be mentally handicapped, how much do you want us to resuscitate her?' There they were again, flippantly alluding to the idea that she might be mentally handicapped. When the professor gave us his shopping list of defects, he hadn't mentioned mental handicap.

Jay and I looked at each other. It felt as if I was stuck underwater, everything was slow and warbled. I didn't know what to say. Jay shrugged, he didn't either. My mind went blank, Jay's eyes desperately searched mine...waiting for me to say something. My heart answered for me. 'Do what you can.' Jay nodded. They would do anyway, surely?

The fetal heartbeat was being closely monitored but in the early hours of the afternoon the nurse called for the doctor who stared at the machine and said, 'The baby's heart is in distress. It won't be able to cope with a normal birth. We need to deliver her by caesarian, otherwise she will die. Do you want to be awake or would you prefer to be completely under?' they asked me. 'There are risks though with a general anaesthetic.'

Despite the risks, I didn't hesitate, I agreed to a general anesthetic. I wanted to be out of it, to wake up and it be all over. I was scared of seeing the baby. And also, other women had told me how horrible being awake was. Apparently, it felt like having the washing up done in your stomach, lots of pushing and tugging, and removing the baby through a small slit in your stomach, rather like a cat flap. Asleep, I wouldn't be aware of what was going on. I wouldn't feel the pain of the thrush, I wouldn't see the baby. I was frightened, terrified, what would she be like? Would I love her?

They wheeled me into the operating theatre. Bright lights and chrome. I was dazed, scared. 'First, we need to fit a catheter,' a nurse said. That's good I thought, when I go to the loo next it won't sting. Everything was being taken care of. Soon I would be asleep. But as she began to fit the catheter, a sharp pain seared through me, a pain I will never forget. A scream forced its way from my mouth as if my soul had unleashed a demon, but it was muffled by a mask the nurse placed over my face. I could taste something odd. I was drowsy. Then under.

SOMETIME AFTER THE OPERATION, minutes, hours, I was aware of Jay standing beside me. Then a burning sensation across my stomach, like a red-hot iron. I was too frightened to move. I needed painkillers.

24TH DECEMBER 1994

. . .

I SLEPT for hours after giving birth to Poppy and when I woke, I felt groggy and disorientated. I was too frightened to move. A catheter was still attached and thank God. I really didn't want to go to the loo and experience once again the searing pain of urination.

My eyes shot around the room. Where was my baby? Was she okay? But sleep was dragging me under, I had no energy to lift my arm to press the call button to ask about her. Dealing with the pain was energy expenditure and stole a part of me, robbing me of my ability to be a mother. I felt helpless. Wherever she was, I was of no use to her. I didn't want to be conscious. I wanted to sink into oblivion, into my own protective bubble.

Minutes, hours later - I had no concept of time - I woke again. Jay and Sophie were standing at the foot of the bed calling my name. The pain was taking over a portion of my brain, increasing in waves. Where was the nurse? I needed painkillers.

'Painkillers, Jay, get the nurse, please.' In that moment I leaned over and grabbing a cardboard bowl next to my bed, I vomited into it. Sophie took a few steps back, pulled a face and clutched her brown teddy.

'Sophie, I've missed you, darling.' I held out my limp hand for her and squeezed hers tightly.

'Why are you sick, Mummy?'

'I've just had a baby, darling. Your sister.'

Jay came back bringing the nurse who administered strong painkillers. I noticed dark circles under Jay's eyes and his skin was pale. He looked stressed.

'Dee, the baby's doing well, she's in the special care baby unit on the tenth floor. We can put you in a wheelchair and take you up there to see her.'

'I can't move, Jay, I want to, but I'm in too much pain and I feel really rough. Tomorrow, yeah?'

After Jay and Sophie left, I slept again for hours only waking when a nurse appeared at my bedside with a wheelchair.

'I've come to take you to see your baby daughter.'

Panic set in like a cluster of sparks in my abdomen. Terror. I had no idea what to expect. Overlapping fingers, a cleft lip. That's what the professor had said. 'It's okay, there's no rush, I'll go tomorrow.' I'd put it off as long as I could.

'Okay, well I need to remove your catheter today. You'll have to start moving, you've been in bed too long.'

Adrenaline flooded my body, pumping and beating as if it was trying to escape. There was only one thing to do - stay calm and still and hope that it didn't take long. I held my breath, tensed my muscles and willed myself to relax. Thankfully it didn't hurt and was over quickly. But then I was terrified to go to the loo fearing the burning pain.

'I'll help you to the loo, but the next time, you need to try and walk there yourself. It isn't far. The quicker you mobilise, the better.'

As soon as I stood, waves of nausea crashed over me. I swayed for a moment before the nurse took my arm. It was as if the blood in my body had rushed down to my feet. I was glad when I was safely sitting in the wheelchair. I tried not to cough, or sneeze. Reaching the toilet, the nurse helped me onto the loo and waited outside. I leaned forward clutching my stomach. When the trickle came it stung. It felt like I had an invisible flame inside me, and I tensed my leg muscles willing it to go away. Beside me was a bidet. I couldn't believe it, why hadn't I see that before? I got up from the loo and lowered myself onto the bidet, turned on the tap and let out a sigh of relief when I felt the fountain of warm water splash across my private area. I wanted to sit there all day and wondered about bolting the door and holding the little ceramic beauty hostage.

In and out of the toilet for most of the day, I tried to wash away the vaginal infection. The following day, Jay and Sophie returned, and Jay was determined I should see baby Poppy. Sophie jumped up and down. 'Mummy, I want to see my sister.' She grabbed my hand and started to tug me along the corridor.

'Mummy needs a wheelchair,' Jay told her.

'I want to sit in there too, on Mummy's lap.'

Jay lowered her gently onto my lap in the wheelchair, warning her not to press against my tender tummy. I kissed her head, smoothing the soft blonde curls from her face, breathing in the dreamy smell of peach and spun sugar. I'd missed her so much. I wanted to snuggle up with her in bed, read her stories, touch her delicate face. Do all the things we used to do. They were fleeting memories. As if they'd happened in another lifetime. I felt as though I'd been in hospital for months, not days. Where had time gone?

Out of the lift on the tenth floor we followed the signs to the special baby care unit. Through the doors of the unit, the heat slapped me in the face. It was like stepping into a tropical greenhouse. It was also like entering a children's nursery school. There were rhymes on the walls and colourful decorations hanging from the ceilings and the walls were covered with success stories - pictures of babies, toddlers, small children. Children who had survived illness and premature birth.

But Poppy, although tiny, wasn't a prem baby. Her illness didn't have a name. There were no precedents to follow, no indicators to work towards, no examples to compare. We were alone in our experience. There were no other parents to compare notes with. I wished we'd fitted into a pigeonhole. I wanted the doctors to be able to say, 'Well this normally happens,' or, 'This could happen.' But they couldn't, they were groping in the dark. Poppy had a syndrome without a name.

So much was happening around us: different noises, machines ticking, bleeping, clicking. The bleeping was like a busy lunchtime in McDonalds with timers going off and the clicking reminded me of the gentle sound of halyards on masts in a marina. So much machinery, breathing monitors, ventilators and staff rushing around flicking switches, checking tubes. It was a hive of activity I'd never seen before in a hospital.

Poppy's incubator reminded me of a giant Tupperware pot. I looked down at her and gasped. She was tinier than I'd imagined, her face was red and wrinkled and her legs and arms were the size of a man's fingers. What had the professor been talking about? Her fingers weren't overlapping? They were perfect, but small. A pink bonnet which looked like a tea cosy, covered her head. Although she was mine, my baby, my creation, my flesh and blood, there was a disconnect. I stared at her and couldn't feel anything. I wanted to feel the same rush of love I felt when Sophie was born, but it just wasn't there. This little baby was so fragile, I was frightened for her. I didn't want to get attached in case she didn't make it.

The nurse put Poppy in my arms. Afraid of breaking her, I held her at arm's length, marvelling at the fact that her head fitted neatly into my palm. I was scared I would harm her because she was so scrawny, as delicate as fine bone china. Taking her tiny hand, I watched her fingers wrap around my smallest finger and grip it. It was the beginning of a journey. How was I going to protect someone so small?

Over the next ten days I stayed in hospital recovering from the caesarean, popping up to the special baby unit to be with Poppy, between sleeping and reading. Even though I had a role to play in producing milk for her, I felt redundant, just watching my baby sleep for hours on end. It was as uneventful as watching a geranium grow, but I felt excited when she occasionally stretched her arms or legs.

Two days after giving birth my milk came in. I peered down at my wet nighty and gasped at the size of my boobs! I looked like Bridget Bardot. Every few hours I attached my nipples to the machine they called Daisy. I felt bruised and sore all the way up my arms and across my chest. I'd never seen such huge knockers and don't remember being this big with Sophie. It felt as if this was nature's way; they are bigger this time around because I had a tiny baby who needed a lot of milk to get big and strong. Except that a tiny baby could only drink bird-sized portions and how was I going to store the excess milk that I produced? With the milk coming in, my mood changed. I was tearful and surprised myself by feeling a tremendous rush of love towards Poppy that wasn't there before the *milk came through. It was as if hormones rather than brain cells were now controlling my body.*

One day a nurse said to me, 'We'd like you to be as much involved with Poppy's care as possible. Her next feed is at midday. She has ten mls through her nasal tube. And how about changing her nappy?' I was horrified. I couldn't change her nappy. She was too tiny. What if I broke her? The nurse watched over me and guided me, but I was very scared that I was going to hurt her because she was so delicate. 'Take a firm grip of her legs. She won't break,' the nurse said. 'They're tough little things.'

18

From London where she was born, Poppy was transferred in early January to the special baby care unit of our local hospital and came home a few weeks later. When Poppy was twelve weeks old we were invited to lunch with the women I met when I stayed the night in hospital, after the doctor told me I was carrying a bag of sugar. We lined the babies on the carpet and took photos. Poppy was scrawny and half the size of the other babies. They smiled up at their mothers, but Poppy hasn't smiled yet, not even through her eyes. Her eyes were distant, she didn't look at me. But she did have a cute sound when she broke off from feeding. 'Oia oia' she says. It annoyed me when the mothers started comparing every aspect of what we were going through, because Poppy's milestones were different. Poppy won't be eating mashed butternut squash or Weetabix any time soon. One of them could surely see that Poppy wasn't smiling, yet but it didn't stop her asking about it.

My experience was nothing like theirs. There was no comparison. I was just happy that she was alive. Glad to get through each day, but I was struggling, and each day was more challenging than the last. The dietician at the hospital set a target of sixty mls of milk every three hours but that was so hard to achieve. I noted down the *times and amounts in a diary and had to ring the hospital every few days to let them know how she was getting on. One day I phoned with my worries and they said, 'Bring her in for the day and we'll work out where you're going wrong.' I wanted to scream. I wasn't doing anything wrong. I couldn't help it if she was struggling to feed, if it was taking fifty minutes to drink twenty mls when according to them it should have taken ten. But at the hospital the nurses took over and managed to feed her a reasonable amount. Why couldn't I do the same? The nurse looked at me as if I was stupid. 'She's feeding very well,' she said in a smug tone. Why wouldn't they believe me when I told them it was taking all day to feed her and that sometimes she cried throughout the feed? I had been recording the amounts she drank each day and it was going down. Each day she drank less. 'But she has doubled her weight,' they kept repeating.*

I didn't want to read their reams of information - leaflets on how to position the teat in the mouth, instructions on posture. I just wanted them to fit a gastric nasal tube. Surely that was the answer? 'She'll lose the ability to suck,' one nurse told me. But how could that be when she loved her dummy? The nurse went to find the doctor and together they agreed to admit her overnight for observation.

The following day, I took Sophie round to Mum's so that she could take her to nursery. I wanted to get to the hospital early so that I didn't miss the all-important ward round which could happen from eighty-thirty onwards. Several people gathered around her cot: a senior house officer, the registrar and several trainee doctors. 'I was looking through your notes,' the senior registrar said, 'how long have you suffered with Carpal Tunnel Syndrome?' I looked down at my hands, massaging them, pulling the fingertips and rubbing them together. The pain in my hands had been keeping me awake for weeks. It started soon after Sophie's birth and had never gone away. Some nights were worse than others. I had a cortisone injection which was horrendously painful and screamed in agony when the needle was pushed through my hand, but the cortisone worked for a few months, then the pain returned.

'I think we may have cracked this feeding problem.' She smiled and nodded to the doctors, happy with her simple diagnosis. My hands have been burning and tingling for weeks and were particularly bad when holding things - like bottles. 'You need a break.' She thought I gave up halfway through a feed. I could see her mind whirring. 'Are you squeezing too hard on the teat when you feed?' She thought I was in too much pain to feed Poppy and tried to get it over with quickly. 'She could aspirate. It could be dangerous. Never force her to drink.' Force her? What does she take me for? Of course, I wouldn't. 'Go home, have a rest, pick her up on Monday and go and see the doctor about those hands.' I was furious. Her feeding problems had nothing to do with how I held the bottle.

On Monday the team gathered around her bed. 'There's definitely a problem,' the nurse on duty said. The senior registrar peered at her notes, frowning, then took a deep breath. 'I think I've cracked it. As she grows, her hair lip grows too. She can't get a good grip.'

'But that doesn't explain why she's so breathless. Until the surgeons can fix her heart, she needs a gastric tube,' I said.

'Erm.' Silence while she thought. More frowning, more staring at the notes. 'I'm going to book her in to see the cleft palette team in London. She should be seen quickly, hopefully tomorrow or the day after.

Poppy stayed in hospital and I went home, grateful to have the time with Sophie.

'Why is baby Poppy poorly?' Sophie asked as we baked cookies together.

'She's got a lot wrong with her. That's just the way things are sometimes.'

'Why can't you send her back to the big bird?'

Confused, I'd no idea what she was talking about. 'What big bird?'

She got down from her pink stool and ran to the lounge, returning with one of the baby congratulations cards that were still on the mantelpiece, despite the fact that Poppy was now three months old. It had a picture of a stork on it carrying a baby.

'Can't the big bird make her better?'

I laughed, sat her down on my knee and explained where babies came from.

THE APPOINTMENT CAME QUICKLY. We were told to come in early the following day and a volunteer driver would take us and Poppy to London.

'I'm sorry, Dee but can you go on your own? I can't take any more days off. The kids' learning is really suffering with all this time off. They hate having supply teachers. I'm worried about the GCSE students. The exams are just weeks away.'

I suppose it's only for one day, I could cope. Sophie would have to go to one of our mum's houses though. I'd no idea when I would get home.

I coaxed Sophie from her bed early the next day. 'I don't want to get up,' she moaned. She curled her legs up, stretching her nighty over her legs. I experienced a flurry of impatience, then felt bad about it. I reached out for her small hand, closed it up in mine. I did my best to keep my cool, planting a kiss on her cheek, smoothing her soft hair from her sticky warm forehead. I lifted her from the bed, still clutching Blar in her arms. Sophie sleeps with Blar, her fluffy blanket, beside her head on the pillow. We named it Blar because that was what Sophie called it. She couldn't say blanket. She sucked at it, twisted it between her chubby fingers. Every few weeks I stole Blar away to wash it. When it was returned to her, fresh and clean, she always insisted that it was different and didn't smell the same.

I wished I still had the time to just sit and watch Sophie sleeping, to savour those special moments. To be constantly amazed that I'd had a hand in creating such a sweet and beautiful child. But life was now so rushed and centred around Poppy and her needs that I felt as *if in the blink of an eye Sophie would soon be at school and I'd find myself asking how had that happened?*

I hurried round the house, picking up dirty laundry, making myself sandwiches to take with me. There was only so much a three-year-old could do using their own initiative and I ended up barking at Sophie to find her shoes, while Jay ate toast without a plate dropping crumbs onto the carpet as he stood watching the news, oblivious to my efforts to organise Sophie.

'Come on Soph, I'll take you to Grandmas on my way to work,' he said.

I was reaching down to pick up my bag when Sophie launched herself at my feet, her legs spread across the carpet, she grabbed my ankles and wouldn't let me move. 'Not letting you go,' she said through pouted lips and let out a laugh which under normal circumstances I would have found endearing.

'Get up, Sophie,' Jay said in his teacherly tone, leaning to grab her arm and pulling her away from me.

'You hurt me, Daddy.' She rubbed her arm. 'I want to go with Mummy, why can't I go?'

Jay picked her up but by the time they reached the door she was kicking him and screaming, pummelling his chest with her little fists. Rivers of snot cascaded down her red face. It was at this point that I bypassed all the usual bribes: ice cream at Sally's café, a visit to Turner's Farm to watch the goats trip trapping across the wooden bridge, pineapple pizza for dinner. I went for the jackpot, the jugular, I did the unthinkable, I mentioned the D word - I promised her a trip to Disneyland. Jay stared at me, open-mouthed. Disney was the one theme park he'd always said under no circumstances would he visit. Kids went missing there, he once told me. He hated long queues snaking round posts, standing on his feet for hours, 'for some silly ride in a teacup, or worse, a roller coaster.'

Sophie slid from Jay's grasp and rushed towards me. 'Really Mummy, really? When? Now?'

'No not now, but if you're a good girl we might think about it.' I looked at Jay hoping he'd agree but he shook his head in disbelief as he opened the front door.

A RETIRED MAN in a clapped-out old blue Ford Fiesta picked us up from the hospital. It was lovely that he was doing voluntary work. A whole day of his time to take us all the way to London, through heavy traffic. I hope they paid him good expenses and his petrol of course. But he'd bought his little grandson with him and sat him in the middle between Poppy and me and he wriggled for most of the journey and kept asking 'are we nearly there yet' and every five minutes his granddad passed him more sweets to placate him.

We were close to the hospital, maybe still half an hour away. The traffic was heavy. Poppy was crying. It had been four hours since her last feed. I couldn't feed her in the car, as we drove. She would have been sick and she wouldn't drink it cold. We had to get there, but the traffic wasn't moving. I wanted to be next to her. Why did he put his grandson in the middle? Silly thing to do. And shit, I took my eyes off Poppy for a minute and the kid was touching her face. Why weren't we there yet? The boy fidgeted, elbowed me, couldn't stay still. He was bouncing. But Grandad didn't tell him to be still. Maybe the boy needed the loo. I willed Grandad to drive faster and wished Jay was with us. I really needed him. He took his job far too seriously. Surely family should come first? I was annoyed with Grandad, boy and Jay.

I stretched my back hoping to see the traffic ahead but there's a white van in front. Was the traffic moving? It was hard to tell.

'What's wrong with her mouth?' the boy asked.

My head shot round. There was foam around her mouth. It didn't look normal. It wasn't clear in colour. It was rusty. Blood? Had she cut her lip? Had the boy done something to her while I'd been concentrating my attention on the traffic?

'Should we stop at the next phone box, call ahead for an ambulance?'

'We're nearly there, one more street.'

I dabbed at her mouth with a tissue, but there was more rusty-foam. My heart slammed in my chest. Please get her there quickly. I wished I was driving. I wished we were in an ambulance. I felt as if I were sitting on a train track with a fast train approaching. That feeling of powerlessness took over.

What was wrong with my baby? Was this serious?

WE ARRIVED at the hospital ten minutes before the appointment. I rushed in through the entrance, carrying Poppy in her car seat, leaving Grandad and his son to park the car having arranged to meet them in the hospital's café after the appointment. There was no more foaming from Poppy's mouth, but she was screaming, in a right state the poor love. Probably very hungry. Waiting to be called in, I offered her a bottle and she fed greedily, gulping it down. I'd never seen her feed so well.

We were called in to see the consultant. It was a large room and there were nine doctors gathered in a semi-circle, too many to introduce each one. All eyes were fixed on Poppy as I put her car seat on the floor. Then their faces switched from mild interest to alarm. One man asked, 'Is she normally that colour?' Her cheeks were pink minutes ago, but then, as I peered down at her, I could see that something was wrong. I shook my head solemnly. Her face was white, growing paler by the second and worse, her lips were blue-tinged. She was rasping for breath. Everything then seemed to happen in slow motion, like in a movie. I stood, it felt as if I were falling. Someone linked their arm in mine, people were moving in every direction. I was vaguely aware of us all rushing along a corridor, a sign above, cardiac wing, another sign, intensive care.

19

'Stay calm,' someone told me, 'she'll sense your anxiety.'
Questions, more questions, doctors reading notes, nurses flurrying around, a room was set up. I was a shadow watching them work like ants in a nest. My baby girl was lying with her head in some kind of box. There was an oxygen tank, a tube. Then I remembered Grandad and boy were still downstairs. I had to tell them to go home. I found the café where they had agreed to wait for us and scanned the sea of faces. He was drinking tea and chatting to the boy. I explain what had happened.

'The wife will enjoy that story,' he chuckled without care or concern. This was just a day out for him. He may as well have taken the boy to the seaside and for fish and chips. 'Most of the time I don't have any stories. I just taxi people back and forth to different hospitals.'

I couldn't bear to talk to him any longer. Horrible man. Who did he think he was? A journalist? My child was dangerously ill. And as for being a grandad, what sort of grandad takes his grandkid on this sort of day out?

Jay rushed up to London, bringing overnight bags for both of us and Mum was again looking after Sophie. Jay told me that Sophie had kicked up a fuss wanting to come to London too but when he left her, she was happy snuggling on Granny's lap with a book.

We sat outside Poppy's room waiting, pacing up and down, making coffee. Every so often we asked the nurses what was going on and what was wrong with her. But they couldn't tell us anything yet. The blind was down so we couldn't watch what they were doing through the window. At midnight the doctor told us he thought she had pneumonia and we should get to bed, some rest and if anything changed somebody would call us. They'd given us a bedroom in a section of the hospital where parents could stay over. It was a basic bedroom and there was a communal lounge with a kettle, sink and microwave and a shared bathroom.

In bed Jay and I didn't talk, we just clung to each other and cried as if we were sinking in a broken boat. His t-shirt was wet from the tears I'd shed. I turned, pulling my legs up into a fetal position but it was hard to sleep. I felt so helpless and so worried. I stared at the artexed ceiling, seeing shapes and figures in the twists and turns that played out above my head. I drifted into a disturbed sleep, waking at around six to the phone ringing somewhere near but not in our room. It rang off. Thank God, it wasn't for us. But then it rang in our room; there was a phone by the bed, I hadn't noticed.

'I'm afraid she really is very poorly indeed. You can come up now and see her. The doctors have finished.'

Panic set in. They'd been working on her all night. Shit, this was serious but she was still alive. My heart was pounding as we fumbled for our clothes in the darkness. Where was the light switch? Where did I put my socks? Got to get up there, got to see her. My baby was poorly. Not sick or ill. Poorly, because that's the word doctors and nurses always use when things are really, really bad.

When we arrived on the ward and went into her room we couldn't believe how bad things were. My brain stuttered for a moment as my eyes took in the scene, every part of me went on pause.

'Oh God.' My heart was breaking into a million tiny pieces. She was hooked up to tubes and wires. There were different drugs going into her veins and there was a ventilator taking over her breathing. My hands flew to my face. My baby couldn't breathe without machinery. The apparatus was keeping her alive.

The nurse looked at us gravely. 'Overnight she nearly lost her leg. While we were inserting the syringes, her leg went into spasm and was nearly paralysed. We're keeping a close eye on it and giving her drugs to stop the blood from clotting. We're pumping her with dopamine, a feel-good hormone.'

I couldn't bear to sit and watch. I needed to get out of there, anywhere. I looked at Jay and he'd pulled a chair up at her bedside.

'She's going to die,' I whispered.

'Oh lovey,' the nurse said in a Mancunian accent. She came over to me and put her hand on my shoulder. 'She's a little fighter, it's not going to happen.'

'You never look on the positive side. Always negative with you,' Jay said in a sombre tone. I was taken aback. He'd barely said a word since last night and now was not the time for a dig. We sat there in silence until I couldn't bear it any longer. I couldn't be there; I needed to escape. And I needed breakfast.

'I'm going for a walk,' I told him. 'I need some fresh air, you coming?'

'No. I'm not leaving her. She needs me.' His face was frozen, his eyes turned away from me, fixing on Poppy.

I left the hospital and walked down the street until I found a café. I ordered a coffee and a croissant. Afterwards I left the café but didn't know where I was going. I just needed to put one foot in front of the other, see normal life...pretend this was not happening. The underground station was ahead of me and I ran down the steps, bought a ticket, went down the escalator. Warm air rushed at me, a sea of faces heading in the same direction, everybody cramming on, grabbing seats, standing close, packed like sardines. Where was I going? I didn't even know, I didn't care.

Knightsbridge. Harrods. That's where I would go. I bustled

through the doors of the famous store wandering through the ladies' jewellery section gasping at the prices, on into the food court. I bought a sticky baklava eating it from the bag as I gazed at all the chocolates choosing my favourites, lemon, caramel and raspberry, again baulking at the price as I handed over the money. On the way out of the store I browsed round the hair accessories and chose a pretty slide with dainty flowers. It was a heck of a lot of money for a silly hair-slide; thirty pounds. Why was I even bothering? I could go into Clare's and pick one up for fiver. But I fumbled in my purse and handed the money over with a grimace. This wasn't like me. I was normally quite frugal. Where I should be right now was the toy department choosing something for Sophie. I considered this thought for all of five seconds, then turned and scuttled out of the store, pretending that thought hadn't occurred to me.

With my shopping fix satisfied, I headed back to the ward. The ghastly images of Poppy hadn't left me. I could have shopped all day but there was no escape. I needed to confront this. I shouldn't have left her.

I plonk my handbag on the floor beside the chair where Jay was sitting. His eyes fell to the open handbag, fixing on the Harrods bag tucked inside.

'A shopping spree,' he said coldly without looking at me.

'How is she?' I asked. I couldn't meet his eyes; the guilt I felt was eating away at me. He still didn't look at me, his eyes were now fixed on Poppy. Fatigue was engraved on his face. His eyes were glassy, sadness seeped through them. I'd never seen him like this before. It was heart-wrenching to watch.

There was a low keening from somewhere outside the room. Another parent going through the same agony.

I heard the rubber squeak of shoes in the corridor. The nurse appeared. 'Back again?' she asked coming into the room. I didn't want to tell here where I'd been. It was enough that Jay had condemned me for leaving. 'Now that you're both here, I wanted to put you in the picture. The doctors have been discussing her treatment. They'll be doing an x-ray later of her lungs and if the phlegm isn't dislodged by tomorrow, they will put her on a high- pressured ventilator - an oscillator. Hopefully that will work. If we do then she won't be on it for long, twenty-four hours at the most. Because it's high-pressured, to remain on it for too long would damage her lungs permanently. But hopefully in that time the antibiotics will begin to fight the infection. Her lungs are very blocked.'

'She's going to die, isn't she?' I blurted out.

Jay glared at me through angry eyes and I could see his exasperation towards me. The needle on his internal gauge was swinging towards the red zone. Something inside me turned cold, despite the heat in the room, it was like splinters of ice spreading and branching down my spine. I was right; he knew it, he didn't want to accept it.

TWENTY-FOUR HOURS CAME AND WENT. We sat and watched our daughter fight for her life with the aid of drugs and the oscillator. I flitted in and out, escaping for walks along the corridor and out into the fresh air but Jay wouldn't leave her bedside unless he needed the loo. I took him sandwiches and cans of drink. Unless I prompted him to eat, I don't think he'd have bothered. 'How can you keep leaving the room?' he asked me. 'She needs us.'

'I can't keep watching. Nothing's changing. She's getting worse. Can't you see? Each day they add a new drug. Her face is yellow, her eyes are bulging, I can't watch her suffer. I want this to end.'

'I'm not leaving her,' he said with a stiff expression on his face.

X-rays over the next four or five days showed no improvement. They tried to drain her lungs with a tube and managed to remove some of the blockage, but in doing so the space around her lungs filled with air and this had to be removed as well. Both lungs were now blocked. She was still on the oscillator which was much longer than expected. Throughout the week they gave her several blood transfusions because her blood saturation level had dipped.

. . .

ON THE NINTH day one of the nurses asked us, 'How do you honestly feel about all this?' The unspoken word, death, hovered between us and on her lips. I ignored her and Jay stared at Poppy. I went over to Poppy and did the one thing we'd been able to do for her all week; I dabbed her eyes with cotton wool and sterile water to keep them moist. And I whispered near her ear, 'Mummy's here, Daddy's here, we're not giving up on you little one, fight on.' She couldn't hear, she was heavily sedated. She couldn't fight, we were making her fight.

At the end of the ninth day the doctor came to speak to tell us. 'If we can't bring down the pressure on the oscillator in the next twelve hours her lungs will be permanently damaged. And even if we can, she only has a fair chance of survival. Her organs are failing.'

THE FOLLOWING MORNING, Poppy was considerably worse. Her face and body looked bloated, her skin had yellowed, her eyes were puffy. The tube in her side draining her lungs was oozing blood staining the bandage and a hand-knitted yellow chick that sat beside her. Her legs were spotted with blood clots and sores. I stared at the monitors, not really understanding what they meant, but they were the indicators on the dashboard of what was happening.

The doctor arrived and took us to see the latest x-rays, pointing out the damage to the lungs and showing us an x-ray of a healthy baby's lungs.

'I'm very sorry, there's simply nothing more we can do.' The oxygen saturation levels were going down. The ventilator was one of the best in the country, but it could not do what it needed to do. 'When we put her on nitric oxide two days ago, really that was the end. We used it as an experiment, but it hasn't worked for her.'

The doctor left us with the nurse who asked if we wanted her christened. Jay shrugged. 'Maybe, yes,' I said, but what did it matter? It wouldn't change the situation.

The vicar arrived and looked so out of place on the hospital ward. He reminded me of Christopher Lee - creepy looking, scary even. I was living in my own horror movie and even had the actor playing the part. His eyes were hollow, his face boney and he showed no compassion.

'I received a phone call about fifteen minutes ago, but I don't know why I'm here,' he said.

Jay and I looked at each other, confused.

'I don't know why I'm here,' he repeated.

I was puzzled. What did he want me to say? Something religious to indicate I had a faith? But I didn't have a faith, neither of us did. 'We want God to look after her, we would like you to bless her.'

'But I don't know why I'm here,' he said again. I wished he would go. This was a mistake. I just wanted to be alone with Jay and our baby. His presence was creeping me out.

'She's going to die,' Jay said.

'I didn't know that. The nurse didn't say.'

The brief christening was over. I was glad because it felt macabre and I hated every moment of it. It was of no comfort whatsoever and I wished we'd not gone through the ordeal.

The machinery around her bed was dismantled. The tube in her side was removed and rough stitches were sewn to seal the hole in the side of her body. The drugs were removed. The only thing that now kept her alive was the oscillator.

'How long will it take for her to die? What will she look like?' I was panicked. I'd never seen a dead person. It was nearly midnight and in a few moments time it would be Mother's Day.

'She'll be at peace, lovey.'

Jay opened his rucksack, pulling out a Mother's Day card for me and a box of chocolates. A card of a cute bunny. Inside Sophie had squiggled her name in large writing and Jay had written Poppy's name. Tears spilled down my face and onto the card smudging their names. Jay was clutching me, sobbing unceasingly; only pausing for short recovery breaths.

The nurse leaned over Poppy and removed the mouthpiece. Silent tears streamed down my face as I watched. The nurse brought her to us to hold, gently putting her in my arms. She tucked the yellow blood-stained chick in beside her. Through a fog of tears, I watched her body change colour. She was less yellow, but paler. Sickness rose inside me; I couldn't be here, I couldn't hold my dead baby. I passed her to Jay but clutched the chick in my hand. Sobs ripped through me, punching my gut. Dad was standing in the doorway, his face crumbling. When had he arrived? Who had told him? I collapsed into his arms and he guided me to a nearby chair. We were just outside the room but I glanced up, and in that moment Jay turned to look at me. His face was full of grief, loss and devastation. Everything around me blurred; was this a coping mechanism? Muffled sounds, smells, a smudge of oblivion, my head was spinning. I buried myself into Dad's shoulder and howled.

TIME DISSOLVED INTO ITSELF, as shapeless as the rain. How long had we been sitting here, somewhere in the hospital, just Dad and me? I was staring into milky tea; Dad's arm around my shoulder, when Jay appeared in front of me and out of breath. His tears were gone, his face was lit up. What had happened? She was dead... wasn't she?

'Dee, you need to come,' he said with urgency, reaching for my hand for me to get up. 'She looks beautiful, our daughter, our Poppy.' There was warmth in his eyes and an aura of serenity about him. I was compelled to go with him.

I tightened my grip around Jay's hand as we walked along the corridor, but inside I was shaking, shivering, nervous. 'But she's dead, our daughter is dead,' I told him.

'But she looks so peaceful, you need to see her.'

I didn't know what to do. Our daughter was dead, why did I have to see her?

'She's dead, isn't she?' He stopped, cradled my face with his hands, planted a kiss on my forehead and looked into my eyes. 'Yes, she's gone, but you must see her. We mustn't remember her rigged up to wires, her body all puffy and yellow. She wasn't our baby. They've done such a lovely job, the nurses. This is our baby.' He pointed to a door. She was beyond the door, our dead baby.

Jay opened the door and smiled, encouraging me to go in. I looked around and gasped. It was like some kind of religious shrine. A temple. Beautiful, like a nursery, but creepy like a ghost-house in a theme park. Soft lighting, mint-coloured walls. A crib with frilly broderie anglaise draped around it, a white shawl tucked neatly around our baby to keep her...warm? It could have been the film set of a dark fantasy film. The Wizard of Oz. In a moment the window would blow in and hit me on the head and the room would be sent spinning off. I wanted to laugh, this was so absurd.

A cot-mobile hang above the crib. Why? For her entertainment? This was white-washing the horror of the scenes earlier on, glossing over her death, trying to erase those images; wiping away my grief, but how could we ever forget? I peered into the crib, pulled the shawl away to see her face. Her cheeks had been rouged and there was a light touch of lipstick to pinken her eyes. It wasn't right that a dead baby should be in a cot, looking as if she was alive and well - no sound, no movement. Underneath the shawl her little body was covered in stitches, bruises, mottled skin.

'My first instinct was to put a little bonnet on her head, to keep her warm,' Jay whispered.

'This isn't natural. It reminds me of when I went to Moscow and queued up to see Lenin in his mausoleum.'

A TREMENDOUS RUSH of love hit me when I saw Dad in the corridor, hunched over staring at a piece of paper. He'd driven all that way. And it was now two in the morning. The journey hadn't fazed him, he was there for us, for me, when it counted. Like he'd always been there for me in a crisis. He hadn't thought twice about coming. He knew we needed him. Like the time I rang at three in the morning from university. 'Dad I can't do this; I'm going to fail my exams, I've not revised hard enough.' And his reply, so wise, so calming. 'Do your best love, that's all you can do.'

'What's that, Dad?'

'From the nurses; her footprint.'

'That's amazing,' Jay said.

Dad handed me the piece of paper and fumbled in his pocket, pulling out a lock of hair in a small plastic container. Together with photographs and numerous medical notes these were all I had to remind me of Poppy's existence. They seemed so inadequate but with passing time, I knew they'd become more precious. Jay's words sliced through me, niggled me because right then this wasn't amazing; it was just adding to my sense of loss. My heart was torn in two - they were rubbish consolation prizes.

∼

I CAN'T READ any more of my diary, the section about Sophie's death. It's just too awful. Poppy had so much wrong with her, the doctors did all they could. But Sophie's death was perfectly avoidable. That was my fault.

20

Returning the diary to the box, I head down the winding stairs. Pippin is curled up on the landing carpet waiting for me. She gives me a sad look, she's missing Dad. There's someone in the field. I step closer, peering out of the window over the back lawn. My brain stutters for a moment. It's Jay. He's holding flowers, bending to put them at the foot of the oak tree, like the woman had a few days ago. He's talking to Dad's neighbour, Jill at a safe distance.

It's seems strange to be standing here watching him from a safe distance. He was always the one to come up behind me, when I stood at the bedroom window, claiming I was always nosy, people-watching, fascinated by the comings and goings of the neighbours. Now, here I am spying on my own husband. But there's something unfamiliar about him. Time has shaped him into someone I don't quite recognise. My Jay would never have worn a black leather jacket, they were for bikers and men who were hard. I wonder how long he's adopted this new style. And ripped jeans. My Jay wore chinos from Debenhams and a faded khaki jacket with a broken zip. What's happened to him? He's not the man I used to know.

Jill is heading away in the direction of her cottage. Now there's a woman running towards Jay. She's carrying a bunch of tulips. She kneels and puts them next to Jay's flowers. As she gets up, Jay puts his hand on her shoulder, pulling her into a hug. Who the hell is she? But why am I bothered? Stop it, Dee. It's been over twenty-five years. His life has moved on. He's obviously in a relationship. I don't know why Pandora and Lyn didn't tell me he was with someone. Trying to protect me again, no doubt. Like my bloody family. This is getting silly. I don't need protecting. Jay and whatever her name is - they look so close. She's pretty, younger than him. Something gnaws away in my stomach. Young enough to have children? I'm not sure. I move away from the window. I don't want to know about his happy life. How, unlike mine, he actually has a life.

I lie on the landing, spreading my arms like wings, feeling the softness of the thick beige carpet. It's a technique that Helen taught me as a way of taking control of the mind so that it becomes peaceful, and to stop the mind rushing about in an aimless stream of thought. I breathe deeply, focusing my energy on tightening my inner thighs. Pippin sits and watches. She has that look about her when she's puzzled. I pull my legs up, reaching out to stroke her head. 'You missing him? Poor little Pippin. Do you want to be my therapist?' She stares at me, those sad brown eyes, and shivers. 'What shall I do, Pippin? Should I ask him for a divorce? Talk to him? Find out why he left me? It's not nice is it?' I stroke her ears. 'You missing Dad?'

I stop talking, just lie here stroking Pippin. The quietness grows deeper and I hear my own steady rhythm within. I miss the constant clamour, the occasional plane in the sky, cars on the road. The world has stilled, this is life on pause and I'm not sure I like it. I don't want to hunker down, live in fear behind closed doors, scared of others, viewing them as potential deadly disease carriers. What I need is a hug. Such a simple human gesture. I need the warmth of someone's body next to mine.

The silence sings in my head. I miss the clatter of Ruth in the kitchen, her mop swishing across the floor in great sweeping strokes and the hum of the Hoover. I never thought I'd miss the sound of household appliances, but I'm not about to switch the Hoover on just for company.

I pull Pippin into my arms. At least I have her. I need her warm silky body and she needs me. My face is buried in her fur when the phone breaks the silence. She jumps from my arms and runs downstairs barking, with me at her heels. I'm relieved to hear a nurse's voice at the other end. News of Dad.

'He's had a comfortable night but is disorientated. At the moment we aren't allowing visitors to come into the hospital to reduce the risk of infection due to the Coronavirus, but what we can do is connect you both via Facetime, this afternoon at three?'

A sense of panic constricts me. I've never used Facetime, I hate technology. But I have to do this. The reason why Dad doesn't recognise me is because we never did Facetime or Skype when I was in Australia. It always seemed easier just to phone. But with this lockdown everybody, it seems, has taken to video-calling. After putting the phone down, having agreed to Facetime at three, I am determined to master this. Dad needs me. I open every drawer until I find his ipad. I turn it on and locate the Facetime icon. I probably need to ring Andrew to ask him how Facetime works but if I can figure it out myself that would be better. I don't want him chiding and belittling me with comments like, 'Oh for God's sake, Dee, don't you even know how that works? I can't believe you've never used it.' And worst, Emily in the background laughing at her auntie's ignorance. Taking deep breaths, I calm myself and test it out by ringing my own number. I smile to myself and do a little jig around the kitchen when I find it's surprisingly easy. If I could give Pippin a high-five I would. Why ever did I put this off for so long?

At spot on three, I dial the number the nurse gave me. She's standing next to Dad who is lying in bed in a white gown. His face looks drawn and his nose redder than normal. Dad, what's happened to you? The transformation in him is cruel. He's holding the bedsheet and watching him for several seconds I see that he is making pleats in the sheet with his hands, fiddling like he did at home with every used tissue in sight. His vulnerability hits me in the gut, realising how much his illness has taken its toll. How childlike it's made him, lying there, helpless. I try to erase all visions of him dressed as a woman. I don't want to believe what Andrew told me. That wasn't the dad I knew, the one I want to commit to memory after he's gone.

'I can't see who it is?' Dad says, frowning.

'We can't see you,' the nurse says directly into the camera.

I can see them. Why can't they see me? I should have known this wouldn't work. I can feel my patience levels waning. 'I can see you.'

'Turn the screen round,' the nurse says with hand gestures that look like a driving instructor teaching a new driver to do a three-point turn. I tilt the screen. 'All we can see is the ceiling.' She's losing her rag, only slightly though. Probably has lots of patients who all need to speak to their loved ones. How time-consuming this must be and how amazing that the hospital are up for doing this. 'Now we can see the floor.' I can't get to grips with this. I wish Andrew was here. 'That's better, we can see you now.' Thank God for that. My face is in the corner of the screen, I look a mess. No make-up and my chin looks baggier than normal. Do I really look this bad? Now I remember why I don't do Facetime.

'It's your daughter,' the nurse says looking from Dad to the screen. 'See, how clever is this?'

'Oh, it's her,' he says in a flat tone. I catch the disappointment on Dad's face.

'What do you mean, *her*? It's your daughter,' the nurse repeats pointing to the screen. 'See.'

Dad raises his eyebrows, tuts and looks away, with an expression that tells me he's sick of playing this game of recognise-the-daughter. 'My daughter lives in Australia. That's not her.'

'I don't think she's in Australia. Stop fiddling with the sheet and look at her,' the nurse coaxes. Dad has the attention span of a small child. His eyes are darting all over the place and it makes me sad to remember how years ago he sat for hours with his nose in hardback biographies of politicians like Harold Wilson and Ted Heath.

After several minutes, I'm secretly pleased when the doorbell rings, giving me an excuse to end the call. I carefully put the ipad back in its case and head towards the door, wondering who it could possibly be.

When I open the door, I find an older woman, dressed in a flowery Joules rain jacket and matching wellies standing in the middle of the drive.

'Hi, I'm Pat, I live in The Old Stables,' she says in a loud voice because she's standing so far away from me. She waves a beautifully manicured hand in the direction of her house. There's a snooty air about her and she's poshly spoken. Rivermead is teeming with Pat-types, I can spot them a mile off. Busy bodies, curtain twitchers who like to keep an eye on what's going on in the road, as if they are gatekeepers on an estate. They're always quick to redirect groups of walkers onto the correct public footpath. 'I heard you were back from Australia,' Pat says. 'I couldn't help noticing an ambulance late last night. Is Dad okay?'

I'm surprised she noticed the ambulance. After explaining about Dad being in hospital and how difficult it's been since coming back, I ask how she is. 'I expect you're in self-isolation. Who does your shopping? I'm happy to get anything for you.'

'Oh goodness, darling. I know I'm over seventy, but the government aren't going to shackle me to the house. I shall be taking my morning stroll down to the village shop each day for provisions and hopefully this jolly nasty virus will go away just as fast as it arrived. Those wretched Chinese, they have a lot to answer for. I run an Airbnb, but I'm expecting they'll advise us to shut up shop very soon. It's a frightful business this virus. Anyway, keep me posted on Dad, must fly, chow for now.'

Ghastly woman, I hope she doesn't call again. As I close the door, a pang of sadness washes over me. I'm missing something. Is it Dad, Ruth, Andrew...not being able to be with other people, not going to the pub with Lyn and Pandora while this lockdown is in place? Or am I missing something deeper than that? My head is a tangled mess. It might be the not knowing how long this will go on for. Life is in limbo. But as I walk towards the kitchen, I realise that I'm missing Australia and the life I had. Drinking margaritas at lunchtime, barbecues on the beach, the hysterical laughter of my friends. I stop, breathe in the silence, capturing it all in my head. I can't just step on a plane and go back. And if I could, if it were possible, I'd have to be quarantined in a hotel room for fourteen days before I could go anywhere. I don't like this new feeling of powerlessness. I didn't vote for this to happen. We are all being goaded along by The Science. The Science is now ruling the world. But I must be grateful, I tell myself. I am safe, I am healthy, and I do not have the virus.

I glance over the garden and Jay is still there, with the woman, hand-in-hand walking away from the oak tree back towards the village. I watch her smile up at him and there's warmth in her eyes. Is it love? It's so tender, so sweet. I look away, but her smile is imprinted on my mind. Something constricts inside me. It's the same sadness I get when I see happy couples choosing food together in the supermarket - the small moments that are best filled with a partner. I take several deep breaths but can't stop my eyes from watering. I so need someone here right now, to share these empty lockdown days with. I want to be content on my own, and I should be, this won't last forever, but I miss the way love and companionship gave meaning to my life. But what is it about these middle-aged men? I'm thinking of Jay and the young woman and Glen and his young tart. Is my body so unlovable? I feel about as attractive as an upturned trolley in a canal. It's just not fair.

I head to the kettle and make a strong coffee. Bloody woman, slinking around the village with my husband. My husband. Did I really just say that? Dee, he's your husband in name only. You've not been together in years. I shake my head, feeling like a fool.

I'M JUST WATCHING Boris's daily briefing at five when Pippin's ears prick up and she jumps from my lap, pulling a thread of my jumper with her claws. There's a soft knock on the front door. She rushes towards it barking, wagging her tail, expecting Dad to be home. Another knock, louder, faster this time. My heart sinks as I follow Pippin down the corridor. I hope it isn't that ghastly woman from The Old Stables.

When I open the door, it takes one or two seconds to register who is standing on the doorstep. It's like every neurone in my brain is trying to fire at once. I'm so shocked, I can't form words.

'Dee.'

It's Jay.

21

Jay takes a few steps back. I can't believe he's here, on my doorstep. He has a shadow of stubble and doesn't look as if he's shaved in a while, so unlike my Jay. His hands are in his pockets and although he's trying to be casual and relaxed, I just know that he's fizzing with nerves. 'I just wanted to call round, find out how your dad is. I heard that he's in hospital.' His mouth twists and he doesn't look directly at me. He'd rather look at anything except me. Nerves. Embarrassment. That's what it is.

'Thanks, nice of you to call round. Who told you?' I'm careful to keep my tone and my face deliberately cold. I don't want to come across as too friendly. I'm not letting him off the hook.

'News travels fast in a small village, you know how it is.' He rubs his stubble and I sense that he's wondering what to say next.

'Thanks for calling, I'll tell Dad you were here.'

'Nice seeing you, Dee.' He pauses. 'Take care of yourself.' Before he turns to go, I remember his dad, killed in the field by the cows. I can't not mention it.

'Jay, I'm really sorry about your dad. Andrew only told me the other day, what happened. It's just dreadful.'

'Yep, it was pretty awful.'

Part of me wants to reach out and give him a hug. I still can't get over what happened in that field.

I sense a portcullis slamming down over his eyes. It's as if our families are pitted against each other over this. I can certainly see that he doesn't want to talk about it. Yes, a definite family rift, but it didn't stop him coming here and thinking of Dad. So maybe this rift is all in my imagination. 'Well, I'll be seeing you,' he says.

Closing the door on him I slide to the floor and I let out a sob. I wait for the wave of emotion to pass. It's fine. I am fine. I will cope. Every time I see him, it's hard. I need wine, that will help. I scour the kitchen but find only vodka. It's stronger than wine, the medicinal tonic I need right now. I pour myself a generous glass, not bothering to add a mixer. It slides down my throat like a serpent and slithers around my system. After another glass, smaller this time, I am almost knocked over by the wave of euphoria that follows as the alcohol sings in my head. It's the crutch I need.

～

A FEW DAYS LATER, I'm in the village shop holding Dad's discount card at arm's length, standing as far back from the cashier as I possibly can in order to swipe it through the reader. After several attempts she looks at me through despairing eyes. 'Turn it round, no, the black strip goes in that way, no the other way,' come her snappy orders. What's her problem? It would be easier if she just did it for me. After all, she is wearing plastic gloves and there's a bottle of disinfectant sitting by the till. Everybody is paranoid about getting this virus. The woman behind me is standing on the yellow floor strip which marks two-metres between each customer. She looks like Horrible Grandma on *Friday Night Dinner*. She sighs heavily and calls to the cashier, 'You should chuck her out. She's holding up the queue *and* she walked round the shop the wrong way.' There are arrowed markers along each aisle so that customers walk in one direction to avoid people bumping into each other, but I didn't notice until half-way round the shop.

I turn to the customer. 'I'm very sorry I've held you up,' I say, 'but I don't know this store and it took me a while to find everything.' Give up, Dee, you're not going to win this battle. They're all staring at you as if you're mad.

Apologising to the cashier, I ask her if she can swipe it through the reader. 'You're hardly likely to catch the virus from a plastic card,' I tell her.

Somebody is standing behind me. My heart sinks. The store's security man is about to remove me, but when I turn, it's Jay. He has a bewildered expression on his face. The same expression he had years ago when I accidentally dyed his favourite t-shirt pink in the wash.

'Yes, I could,' the cashier snaps. 'They're mucky, filthy things.' She screws her face up in disgust. I want to tell her not to be so daft, but what's the point? I don't have the science to back up my claim. I'm not Professor Neil Ferguson, the expert on all matters Covid-19. I've got to use this shop again and I don't want to get a bad name for myself. In any case Jay has appeared out of nowhere to help. He turns the card round and asks me to enter my pin.

'Some people have got no consideration for others,' the customer behind me barks. I glare at her. I'm relieved that I don't have to put all the items back on the shelves, but where did Jay appear from? I didn't see him in the store. I can sense the queue are becoming irritable. There's grumbling and snarling. I just want to get out of here, which is a shame because this is, at present, my sole legal excitement. I like to linger in the aisles. Wondering whether white eggs are as good as brown eggs can kill a few minutes. I ask for some bags and the cashier throws me a filthy look. Oh dear. I've committed a double-sin, I have totally disregarded the severity of this virus, putting lives at risk, and now I'm not considering the effects on the environment of my plastic bag usage. I should be locked up and the key thrown away. I pack the final three items and a tickle rises in my throat unexpectedly. Please don't cough, please don't cough, I will myself. But it's a nervous cough and I can't help it. Out it comes. I raise my arm to my face to catch it.

'You should call the police,' the woman says to the cashier. 'Coughing in public is an offence.'

'So is hoarding bog rolls,' I call back as she loads three packets onto the conveyor belt.' I leave the store fuming. Is this what I've come back to? To live among narrow-minded, gossipy, bigoted whingers? This type of mentality is normally kept under wraps, but given the current situation, it hasn't taken long for some people to turn into little Hitlers who think they know best. Rudeness is spreading faster than the virus. I hope I don't meet any more shouting busybodies in the coming weeks.

I head towards the bench opposite the village hall where I used to gather with friends after discos when we were teenagers. I need a rest before I tackle the hill back to Dad's. But the bench has been cordoned off with yellow tape to discourage people from sitting down and resting their legs. I think of the local news on the tv last night. A couple arrested for sunbathing on an empty beach. What's actually not being permitted is anyone looking as if they may be enjoying themselves, briefly soaking up the rare British sunshine. It's bad form these days to have a smile on your face. I pull the tape off the bench, roll it into a ball and chuck it defiantly into a nearby bin. I sit down, sweeping my arms across the back of the bench, closing my eyes against the sun. If someone wants to call the police let them. I'm happy to watch them get done for wasting police time. I feel as rebellious today as I did when I smoked a cheeky fag on this bench as a teenager.

Footsteps approach, a shadow blocks the sun. I don't want to open my eyes; I've had my dose of busy-bodies for one day. But when I open them, I find Jay standing in front of me. I wish he'd stop popping up like this.

'Thankyou for rescuing me.' I smile up at him out of politeness, but my heart sinks as I watch him dump his shopping next to the bench. Surely, he's not going to sit down? The bench isn't big enough for two people to keep a safe social distance.

'Wow, what dumb people.' He bursts into a loud cackle of laughter. 'Everybody is starting to snap and snipe at each other. Have you noticed how this pandemic is starting to change people? Suddenly everybody is so judgemental and they're all dobbing each other in to the police. Mrs Smith, who still lives next to Mom, rang the police because she saw three people sunbathing in the field.' He's picked up an American accent. He doesn't sound like the Jay I remember. The Jay I've lived with in my head for all these years. I want to tell him this, but that would lead us down another conversational path.

'I guess so.' We could sit here all afternoon exchanging our supermarket horror stories, slipping into easy banter, reconnecting as friends. The virus is the hot topic of conversation at the moment. I could tell him what happened to Pandora when she went to a shop yesterday. A grumpy security guard shouted at her, 'Just because we are open doesn't mean we are here for you to spend your time browsing around. We are designated as an essential service. We are not here for you because you have nothing else to do. We are not here for you because you feel like getting out of the house for a while. We are in a state of emergency. Every customer who walks in our doors puts us at risk.'

I'm not going to keep up a pretence and brush aside everything that happened twenty-five years ago, but I am lonely.

Apart from the people I met at the school reunion I don't really know anybody in this village anymore and even if I did, I can't meet them in the pub or café. I would dearly love to chat, to have proper human contact that isn't over Skype or the phone. But an inner voice warns me and keeps me in check. Do not let Jay off the hook. I fold my arms, determined not to get into a long conversation.

'They're all cooped up in their houses with a poor WIFI connection. Facetiming friends, emailing, staring at computer screens. Boredom does strange things to people,' Jay says.

'Yep.' I hope my short replies give him the hint to move on, but they don't appear to. I can see his mind whirling, trying to think of more things to say.

'Do you remember that time when...?' He's not going to move on. What's he going to say now? I quell an urge to let out a dramatic sigh. '...We took those two big sweetie jars full of one and two pence pieces into the bank to exchange them for euros for our honeymoon?' Jay never liked small change rattling around in his pockets and used to empty them into sweet jars that he kept at the back of his wardrobe. I wonder if he still does it but I don't ask.

I remember the look on the faces of the bank staff when we told them we'd been saving one penny pieces for our honeymoon. The same look we've just witnessed in that shop. Laughter bubbles inside me, threatening to erupt. I can't contain it. Maybe it's nerves but I let out a laugh and then I can't stop myself. My breath comes in short gasps between my unstoppable giggles and tears gather in the corner of my eyes. Catching my breath, I realise the laughter is a welcome release, a tonic even.

But then reality hits. I'm cross with myself for laughing with the man I've grown to loathe. My pulse is pounding in my temples, but I need to say something before he turns to go.

'Jay, why did you leave me, when I needed you? We needed each other.'

He looks up at the sky rather than at me and pauses for a few seconds. 'I shouldn't have left the way I did. I was a coward.'

'Yes, you were.'

'I wrote to you.' He throws his arms into the air and scuffs his shoe into the gravel. 'Many times. Did your Mum send them on?'

'What letters? I got one letter from you in all that time.' A sense of unease slithers to the pit of my stomach with the slow realisation that the people I thought I could trust - Mum and Dad - have let me down. It's as if I'm looking at my life on a fuzzy tv screen. Why didn't Mum forward the letters on to me? Or is Jay lying? Did he really bother to write?

There's a strange frozen look in his eyes, as if like me he too is struggling to digest this news. 'I poured my heart and soul onto those pages and you didn't read them. I couldn't face the aftermath of everything. Two dead daughters lying cold in the morgue, the funeral. I had to go. It was all so horrific.'

'I had to walk up that aisle following my daughter's coffins... alone. How could you let me go through all that on my own? You let me down really badly, Jay.' My heart is hammering in my chest, I can't be in his company any longer.

Gathering the shopping together I get up from the bench.

'I let everyone down, Dee, and no I don't expect you to forgive me but just because I ran away doesn't mean I haven't lived the past twenty-five years in pain, thinking about what happened.'

'I've got to go. The hospital might be trying to get hold of me.' My tone is cool, my face set like stone as I glance at him before turning to go. Referring to the woman I saw him with I add, 'Well at least you've found some happiness.'

He grabs my arms. 'What's that supposed to mean?'

'Get off me.' I shake my arm free of his grip. 'We're meant to be socially distancing.'

'Sorry.' He sighs, taking a few steps back. 'Good luck with your Dad and if you need anything... Look, Dee, I do want to talk, just think about it. Hear me out. Or find the letters first. Your Mum might have kept them even if she chose not to send them to you.'

22

As soon as I get through the door, I phone the hospital. They are planning to perform Dad's hip operation tomorrow which is a relief. I can't bear the thought of Dad being in pain and coming round from his operation confused and alone. I wish the hospital would let us visit, I feel so helpless.

After unloading the shopping, I make a cup of tea and head to the attic to look for Jay's letters, the bell on Pippin's collar tinkling as she waddles along behind me. Lowering my head, I enter the attic. Sinking to my knees I look around, wondering which box to attack first. I don't know where to start but the box where I found Mum's diary is a good place to begin. I rummage through the box, but Jay's letters aren't here. It's going to take days to open all the other boxes. I feel deflated; the drive to find them is waning. But as my hands keep delving into the box, I find another of Mum's diaries tucked at the bottom of the box and it's dated Summer 1995. I pull it out, flicking through. Sophie and Poppy's joint funeral was March 30th 1995, but this diary starts in June of that year. Why doesn't it cover the first half of the year? I pause to consider this. Maybe Mum was too upset to write about the deaths of her grandchildren. It was too dark a period to write about. Too traumatic. The first entry comes in July 1995...

JAY HAS SENT *three letters to Dee, in quick succession. I forwarded the first one to her but the next two I opened. I can't forward them on. They will make her more upset. She moved to Australia to get away from the pain. I don't want her getting all upset over his emotions. It was tough on both of them. I have to respect her when she says she wants nothing more to do with him. I need to let her move on.*

My emotions are all over the place. I miss Sophie so much. We would be picking flowers in the meadow at this time of year, pressing them in a book and making framed pictures. Or sitting by the river having a picnic. What's happened to my life? I've lost Dee too. Will she ever come back? I've tried to get her to come back, but she won't. She can't hide forever. There's a part of me that does want Jay and Dee to get back together but a part of me that doesn't, and I feel dreadful for feeling this way. I want her to meet someone new. I've never liked Jay's family. They aren't our type of people. It was embarrassing at their wedding when Jay's mother got drunk and started having a go at her husband on the dance floor.

Damn. Where could those letters be? The diary gives no indication that she kept them. She could have burned them, tossed them in the bin.

I slump against the wall feeling completely defeated. I'm not getting anywhere with this. Maybe I'm not meant to find the letters, maybe it's for the best that I don't find them.

But as I sit and stare at the boxes, anger takes hold. Goddamn it, why should I be defeated? How dare you, Mum? They were my letters. My life. It was one thing not to have told me about Dad's cross-dressing, but you had no right to keep those letters from me. I'm furious. You didn't want Jay and me to get back together. And you made bloody sure that wasn't going to happen.

WITH THE WINDOW of my bedroom open all night, I'm woken early by birdsong and the first light. I slip out of bed, dress, go down to the kitchen and with a steaming mug of coffee I open the back door, with Pippin following at my heels. All this talk on the news about getting daily exercise while in lockdown has made me realise I don't get enough.

The air smells of damp grass and is fresh and exhilarating, filling my lungs, waking me up. A haze of mist hugs the earth, a comforting blanket heralding a glorious day of deep blue skies and bright sunshine. I wish I could see into the future; where will I be? Will life be back to normal or will we be living with this wretched virus for a long time to come?

I dump my empty coffee mug by the back door and taking a public footpath at the back of the house I pass a stone wall, where clusters of blue flowers, called Speedwell trail along the cracks. Dad and I used to go for a walk each evening after dinner, when I was in my teens and he delighted in telling me about all the plants along the way. A canopy covers a section of pathway, streamers of light pour through vibrant young leaves. My trousers brush damp nettles, chickweed and cow's parsley which haven't yet achieved the creamy effect of full-flowering blooms. There's even groundsel, food for caterpillars when the time comes. I love watching butterflies.

In terms of nature there's so much here to look forward to. Except that there's nobody to enjoy it with. But a part of me likes this solitude. The white noise gone. The way people in my life jockey to be heard. I'm free of it all. At one with nature. Not a single plane to disturb the peace. The fact that I'm not techo-minded - am I cutting myself off? Should I be connecting with people on social media? I'm in two minds. I've heard bad things; people arguing and falling out, lots of nastiness. I have spoken to Lyn and Pandora on the phone though and other people via email. And Andrew rings each day. Lyn is struggling in lockdown because her bird-watching husband, Ray, has become even more introvert, burying his head in books on wildlife. Still, she has her daughter, Felicity, at home and they've been binging on Netflix. I'd be doing that now, with Sophie and Poppy. A pang of sadness hits me. Mum's voice filters through my head, countering these thoughts. Stop it, Dee, you'll drown in self-pity if you dwell. And it's clear to me now that she really didn't want me to dwell, to the point of destroying Jay's letters. Not wanting me, her own daughter to be reconciled with my husband, well, it's despicable, spiteful even.

In the midst of this pandemic, this chaos, where the future is so uncertain, reading my journal anchored me, but to what I'm not sure. Learning about who I was back then has been therapeutic. Re-living my past, the past that's been with me, like an appendage, an extra limb, for so long. Reading my journal has purged the past. I've indulged myself, wallowed, orbited my life, looked in from a great height. The pages were familiar territory, a way of hiding from the news. This virus and how it's changing things day by day is odd, an unknown landscape. Stock markets plummeting, shops and other businesses I took for granted, going to the wall. Death, or the possibility of it, just around the corner; everything we know, hanging by a thread. What's going to happen long term to the life we lead? How will we connect in any meaningful way if we have to socially distance forevermore; living in a sanitised world in which we cower in our caves afraid of illness, living an existence behind a computer screen?

But I can't think all this. It's beyond my control. I just want to control my own world. Those bloody letters. I'd dearly love to have had the chance to read them, to hear Jay's thoughts, find out what he went through. Mum has robbed me of that.

My journal helped me to reconnect with myself, but what I now want to hear is Jay's side of things. My journal told me nothing about Jay. It was as if he was in the background. I need to find his letters.

I reach a clearing. My heart sinks. The hop gardens that used to stretch across this land are long gone. I close my eyes against the green and billowing field where wheat is now growing. I conjure the past; my childhood arcadia, the sweet-perfumed air, the straggly vines snaking along poles, the caked earth. I miss how it was. The footpath skirts the edge of the field and beyond a hedge lining the field is the road. It's quiet but as I approach the gate at the end of the field, I can hear voices and see a white van through the leaves of the hedge. Panic sets in; something makes me scared. I grab Pippin, clamping my hand around her mouth so that she doesn't attract attention by barking. She struggles in my arms, her feet scratching me. We are crouched low. I make out two men, gruff voices, they're up to no good, I just know it. An old mattress is hurled into the field, followed by a metal bedframe. I don't move, hoping they can't see me. Doors bang. I lean into the hedge, straining to see the number plate of their van and repeating it in my head so that I remember it. A fridge is hauled over the fence. They laugh throatily, then they are gone. My heart is pounding in my chest. It was so hard to stop Pippin from barking, but I managed it and freeing her from my arms I type the vehicle registration number into my phone. I'll call the council later and report it. I've heard about this happening: people dumping their rubbish in the countryside because the amenity tips are closed due to the lockdown. It's appalling. Suddenly I don't feel like continuing my walk. I want to head back to the attic to find those letters. Please, please, let them be there, tucked away in a box somewhere. But at the back of my mind I have a strong feeling that Mum probably binned them. It doesn't make sense for her to have kept them without sending them. But whether the letters are still there or not, Jay wrote them. His emotions were on those pages.

As I open the back door, I feel a rising sense of desperation to hear Jay's story, but once I'm back in the house there are more immediate things to deal with like calling the police about the fly-tipping I witnessed. Afterwards, I phone the hospital. Dad has come round after his hip replacement, and is comfortable. A doctor will be ringing soon to update me.

With a second mug of coffee in my hand I head for the attic to look for Jay's letters, with Pippin trailing after me. I missed having a dog while I was in Australia. Growing up we were never without one. Pippin's lovely company and I've started to wonder if I could continue to look after her when Dad dies. I've always assumed that Andrew would take her under his wings although we've never discussed it. He's not a particularly doggy person and I can't imagine it somehow, but I'm sure my nieces would love having a dog. If I did have her, it would mean putting roots down in England. I stop mid-flight on the stairs and ponder the thought.

I plough through more boxes but can't find the letters. Feeling hungry I give up and head downstairs. Reaching the kitchen, the phone starts ringing. It's Pandora wanting to catch up. So nice to hear from a friend.

'How's your dad?' she asks. I fill her in on what's happened.

'How are you?' I ask her. 'Boring this lockdown, isn't it? I wonder how long it will go on for?'

'Covid's nailed me.'

'What? You've got the virus?'

'No, but I'm suffering because of the virus. I've had horrendous toothache, but the dentist is now closed. They've cancelled all appointments, so I had to ring the emergency dentist it was so bad.'

'Poor you, they fixed it though?'

'No. I was horrified. They told me that all they can do is give you advice - no dentists are working.'

'Oh my God, Pandora.'

'I thought shit, this can't be happening. I was up all night in agony. I wish I had the guts to pull it out with pliers, Dee.'

'Can't they at least give you painkillers?'

'They offered me antibiotics which I picked up the next morning with the single mindedness of a crack addict.'

'Didn't they work?'

'I'm onto my second course of antibiotics and I've got clove oil and throat spray.'

I don't like to tell her that people have died from toothache. I'm sure she already knows.

'Oh Dee, it's taught me some lessons. Never to assume that everything is just going to be there. You can always go to a dentist, right? Wrong. And it's so exhausting scheduling your life around pain management.'

'You poor thing. Makes me appreciate everything we had in our lives before this virus came along.' I'm sure she'd be able to go to A&E. Why suffer?

I put the phone down and immediately it rings again. It's the hospital. They're good with their updates. I thought they'd be rushed off their feet and short staffed because of the virus. It's not good that Dad fell out of bed though and broke his hip and that nobody knew how this happened. But these are difficult times; I've no desire to sue. That wouldn't be right at all.

The doctor tells me that Dad needs specialised care rather than returning home. 'His hip operation went well. His recovery is likely to be very slow after the fall and given how poorly he already is, he will need to be transferred to a nursing home, but that won't be for another few days,' the doctor explains.

'A nursing home? But we've tried our best to prevent him having to go into a nursing home.'

'It's the best place for him. He needs specialised care.'

'But which nursing home? We weren't expecting this to happen.'

'I've made enquiries and there's a room available at Twyford's. But if you want to make your own enquiries, please feel free to.'

'What's it like there?'

'I think it's the best place for his particular needs. Patients in similar circumstances to your father have gone there.'

I'm flustered and not sure what to do. I tell the doctor I'll call him back, then I phone Andrew to run it past him. We both do some research and a few hours later I ring the doctor back. We decide to go with the doctor's opinion. Twyfords it is.

Maybe this is for the best. Get him out of hospital and into a safer environment where he's less likely to pick up the Coronavirus and receive more intensive care. This has to be the right thing to do for Dad. Ruth and I would never cope if he came home. He'd need two carers to get him washed for starters.

Ruth, I better ring her. We won't be needing her any more.

'Not to worry, love,' she says, after I've explained that Dad needs to go into a nursing home. 'He's in the best place, that's all that matters.'

'What will you do now? Difficult to start a new job in the middle of a lockdown.'

'I'm happy to take a few weeks off. I need a break, I've been working flat out. I'm going to enjoy some time in the garden.'

'Well you take care, and thank you for everything. You've been a star.'

THE FOLLOWING morning after phoning the hospital to check Dad's progress, I'm desperate to scour the attic for Jay's letters, one more time. Reaching the landing, I stop, heart slamming in my chest as I peer out of the little window onto the garden and field beyond. Jay and the girlfriend are standing by the tree again. I stand to one side and watch them. They aren't holding hands this time. She's beautiful, he's struck lucky. Huh, at least he's got someone. Someone to snuggle up on the settee with, and at night in bed. I take a step closer. A flash of something sweeps over me... What exactly? Jealousy? Surely not after all this time? My fists clench and as I study her my muscles tighten. I pull away. I can't watch any longer. So much time has passed between us. Good for him. Least he's happy. And yet we are still linked, legally he's mine. 'Start the divorce,' comes a voice in my head. It's time you dealt with this, Dee, once and for all.

23

It's early morning, a few days after I saw Jay. The sky is deep indigo. I pull on my trainers, Pippin excited that we are going for a walk. Outside I breathe in the sweet, musky spring air. Each day more flowers seem to be exploding into bloom. In the distance the fields are cloaked in a pearly veil. The path I choose takes me under a canopy of oak trees. Shafts of sunlight filter through the young leaves making them appear lime in colour and illuminating their veins. The verges are thick with nettles, brambles and a tiny pink flower called Herb Robert. Deeper into the wood the boughs crowd in but the sun still finds its way through, lighting up the spongy floor thick with moss, broken twigs, rotting wood, a few stray bluebells. Further ahead is the most incredible wildflower spectacle, something I've not seen in so long. It's breathtaking. The wood is carpeted with the violet glow of bluebells. I stop to listen to birdsong, a bubbling mix of chiffchaff rattle, the cheery whistle of a robin and blackbirds singing a melody. I love the bubbling mix of churrs and warbles.

I amble further into the wood, twigs crunching underfoot. There are more bluebells and now I'm surrounded by them.

The dappled light drifts across the near-purple blanket. I gasp as I look about me. It's magical, a heavenly sapphire hue and makes me think of Cicely Mary Barker's *Flower Fairies*. Those stories of different flower fairies enchanted me as a child. The drawings and fairy images were bewitching and because I loved those books so much, I kept them, to read to my own children. I let out a sigh of sadness, lean down to pluck a bluebell examining it between my fingers.

I sit down, propping myself against a tree to admire the scene. I want to drink it in and savour it, for it won't last; it'll be gone in a few weeks. Like Poppy, here for one season, then gone as fast as a puff of smoke. She bloomed, she withered. When we came back from London after Poppy died, our main concern - beyond our own grief - was how to break the news to Sophie. I stressed about what to say, wanting to get the words just right. She was only three, how could she understand death? I wanted to believe she was in a better place, but I didn't believe in God and still don't. Not believing in God or heaven has made it hard to focus my mind on where she is. Under the cold earth? Mum, said, 'Just tell Sophie she's now in God's care.' I know Mum tried but she came from a generation that didn't talk about death. Dad came up with a great suggestion. 'Use an analogy with the natural world,' he said. 'Not all flowers are destined to unfurl...' And that's what I did. I brought Sophie here, the day after Poppy died, and we picked flowers and talked about how some flowers survive the rain and some don't. I'm not sure whether she understood.

Mum and Dad both meant well in their own ways. But they were so different. I always found that Dad's wisdom made more sense. His approach was always softer, kinder, less harsh. I'm glad I came back to be with Dad. But Mum... why didn't I come back for her, at the end? Was it simple logistics? Everything happened so fast. Or was there more to it? I know that grief isn't something you can simply fix by turning an eloquent phrase. I didn't expect Mum to be a walking Hallmark card and maybe she just didn't know the exact right words to say to me after Sophie and Poppy's death. But there was something cold behind her demeanour, her lack of compassion, her steadfast resolve to just, 'Put it all behind us and move on.' And worst of all, 'You can always have more children.' In her desperation to create a silver lining she held onto whatever she could think of, but it would have been better to have said nothing. I'll never forget Mum saying after Poppy died, 'You still have Sophie.' She was right, technically speaking. I did still have Sophie. But only for three more days.

I get up, brushing the damp bark from my bottom. I need to keep moving, it's easier to walk when painful memories are flooding my head. It helps to unscramble the past. Beyond the bluebells, I emerge out of the clearing in the wood into a field of sheep. They are like walking clouds or demented white spuds boiling in a pot and I watch them for several moments. The lambs are close to their mothers, some are feeding, but some are jumping in the grass. So cute. So adorable. And then it comes to me. I remember how I explained to Sophie why Poppy died. We were in this field, or a similar field, skirting the edge marvelling at the lambs when we saw a lamb that was different to the others. Maybe his leg was broken I'm not sure, but he looked sickly, not destined to live for long and we stopped to watch him, and it was then that I talked about some babies being weak and sick and some, like Sophie, were fighting fit and healthy. I told Sophie that her sister had a poorly heart and she was too weak to drink her milk like that little lamb. 'But you, Sophie, have always eaten well and look at you now, a big girl.' She looked up at me and elongated her body, stretching on her tippy toes and pointing up, her chest pressed forward. She crinkled her face. 'Can we go home now,' she'd said, and repeating words that Jay often said, 'I'm hungry, I could eat a horse.'

I look up at the sky. Maybe my children are up there somewhere, playing in the gauzy clouds. I close my eyes against the sun. Oscar Wilde once said, 'To lose one parent maybe regarded as a misfortune, to lose two looks like carelessness.' Losing two children though is awful. But we expect to lose our parents, at some point in our lives. The depth and the breadth of the pain, losing a child, is pain like no other. It will never go away. There will never come a day when I don't think about my children. There is no end. There is no moving on, or getting over it. There is no fix, no solution to my heartache, no glue for a broken heart. For as long as I breathe, I will grieve. Grief lasts forever because my love for my children will last forever.

And the feeling of guilt will last a lifetime too. It's like a fire raging deep in my gut. Nothing anybody can say will ever extinguish those flames of guilt. I have to live with it. For several months after Sophie's death I had palpitations every time I got into a car, and my heart still misses a beat when I cross the road. The memory is replayed in my head on loop. I wish I could take a pair of scissors and cut that part of the reel. Rewind to the best parts of her short life, not the ending when I heard the screech of brakes, saw her body move in slow motion through the air, hitting the bonnet of that red car, tumbling to the road, the crack of her head on the tarmac, blood streaked through her curls. It was my fault. It will always be my fault.

I head back to the house but instead of going inside I sit on the bench in the garden. The driver of that red car is out there somewhere, leading his life. I have a fleeting image of the man who was driving, the look of horror on his face, the seconds it took for him to make a decision, stop or carry on. He killed a child but drove off; a coward who couldn't face what he'd done. I often wonder about that man. What he does for a job, is he married with kids of his own? Does he have counselling? How does he live with what happened? I hate him. I hate him so much. I want him to rot in hell. Fire to lash at his body. I hope life has brought suffering. Time and chance - that's all it took. I close my eyes, but the memory is there, tucked behind my eyelids. It will never fade.

I tried to keep busy between arranging Poppy's funeral and phoning everybody to tell them that Poppy had died. It was a mistake to walk into the village; it was too soon, and I was bound to bump into people I knew, and I'd have to tell them and recount all the details leading up to her death. But life had to carry on, for Sophie. I couldn't hide away and wallow in my grief. I was a mummy, I'd missed out on my daughter growing up, so much time in and out of hospital, with Poppy and Sophie spending more and more time with Mum. She needed me - the old cheerful mummy - and on that particular day, three days after Poppy died, Sophie wanted to go to the village to buy sweets from the shop, feed the ducks in the village pond and play in the park on the swings and roundabout. She was helping me to take my mind off the baby I'd lost and the plans for the funeral. If only we hadn't stopped to talk to Mary. If only I hadn't let Sophie stroke her Irish Setter. But Sophie loved dogs. We couldn't have seen what was coming. It happened so fast. The dog spotted another dog on the other side of the road, tugged on his lead, Mary lost her grip - she was suffering from arthritis - and Sophie flew after him. Why? What made her forget the road safety rules I'd drummed into her tirelessly, reinforced by the nursery school staff?

I can keep asking these questions, but bottom line it was my fault. No wonder Jay left me. How could he face me after what I'd done? I was unfit to be a mother. Putting him through so much pain, so much agony. I get up and walk to the house. I want to find out what happened to Jay after he left the village. I will find those letters he sent; I need to know what he went through. This is not just about my pain, it's about his pain too. And I will talk to him. And then I will get on with the divorce. It's time we both moved on.

24

The phone is ringing. It's the 7th of April. It's the hospital and they tell me that Dad is being discharged this afternoon and will be taken straight to the nursing home.

'Can my brother and I see him? I could meet you, outside the hospital.'

'I'm afraid not,' the nurse says.

'But we'll be out in the open, in fresh area.'

'It's still not safe. I'm so sorry but I'm only following Covid-19 guidelines.'

'What if I met you in the carpark of the care home, before he goes in?

'I'm sorry, that's not practical either. I'm sure once he's settled in, they can arrange video calls.'

It's not the same. Dad will think we don't care about him. His mind is going. He'll be in pain. He's doesn't understand what's going on and even if he does, he'll forget and not realise that we do care, we do love him and do want to see him but because of this bloody virus we can't. It's all so futile. Oh God. A thought slams into me. Will I ever see him again? He doesn't have long to live. He's riddled with cancer. My eyes fill with tears. I've come all this way to be with him, to say goodbye, to spend precious time with him in his final weeks and now that's all been snatched away. He's destined to die along. How horrible. Nobody should have to die alone. And in the meantime, he'll probably be confined to living in one room, like all the other residents in the home, only seeing care assistants and kitchen porters a few times a day. They'll be busy, rushing from room to room, no time to sit and talk, unable to hold his hand or give him a reassuring hug. And because he's just arrived from hospital, they'll be extra wary, worried he might have picked up the virus on the ward and will give him an extra wide berth. He'll be treated like a leper, a plague victim. I wish I could do something. Anything to make this sorry situation easier. I wish I could sit with him in the garden of the home, but that won't be allowed either. Why doesn't anyone use some common sense? How can you get the virus in fresh air and if you're socially distancing? I sigh. No point in challenging 'The Science.' It feels as if we're all living in some ghastly dystopia, like in *Nineteen Eighty-Four*, everybody is keeping a watchful eye on each other making sure there's no hugging, and God forbide, if anybody should have a sneaky romp in the sack with someone outside their household. Ugh, I bet it happens all the time. We've all been terrorised into believing this virus will kill us. Steer clear of people. Do not touch them. Do not sit next to them. They might be diseased. And you might be diseased. That instruction, pumped out every day on the daily briefings at five pm, 'Stay Home and Save Lives' makes it clear: I am dangerous, if I go outside, I could kill someone. It's a culture of fear. We've become hysterical. It's against human nature not to have contact with others. Is life worth living? In some ways, Dad is lucky to be leaving this world. Suddenly a wave of depression hits. All my best times have been with other people, not on my own. I'm not destined to be alone. When all this social distancing is a thing of the past I'm going to hug a little tighter, hold a little longer and remember that nothing else matters than the time we spend together with loved ones. But right now, I feel powerless to help the person I love, my dad.

'What about the reason why he went into hospital? Have you given him tests? Do you know why he was bleeding?'

'It will be a symptom of the cancer. He will be seen at some point by the specialist but at the moment we are prioritising appointments.'

What the hell does that mean? I don't bother asking. They're doing what they can in difficult circumstances. Dad's going into the nursing home to die, I know he is. Nobody's said as much, but it is palliative care all the same.

Coming off the phone I immediately call Andrew to update him. He's very matter-of-fact. 'It is what it is. We just have to accept it.' How can he be like this? Poor Dad. Andrew doesn't seem to care that Dad will be in his room all day and night. It'll be worse than prison because at least in prison they get to go outside every day and see people. Why is he being like this? Is it a manifestation of their broken relationship? Andrew was always closer to Mum and this business about Dad dressing up could be affecting Andrew's attitude.

'It just seems cruel,' I say.

'Well I know, but what can we do?'

I change the subject; I'm not getting through to Andrew. 'How's the lockdown going?' I ask.

He lets out a big sigh. I can hear a door close and birdsong in the background. It sounds as if he's gone outside. I wonder why. Is there something he doesn't want his family to hear or is he disturbing them by talking on the phone? 'Things aren't easy here.' His voice drops to a whisper. 'Tracy and I are arguing all the time.' Doesn't surprise me. Can't be a bed of roses, both working from home at the moment. Bet they're not alone. This lockdown isn't easy for anybody. Must be thousands of couples arguing and screaming at each other, confined within four walls and that's not to mention the domestic abuse that must be going on in some homes.

'That can't be fun for Emily and Izzy.' Emily must be bored out of her brains. This lockdown is no life for a sixteen-year-old. And Tracy is trying to work from home and help eleven-year-old Izzy with her schoolwork.

'Emily's fed up. I've told her to order books for sixth-form college. September will soon come round. She's decorated her bedroom and cleaned a few kitchen cupboards, but other than that, she's a lazy madam.'

'Not her fault they cancelled the GCSES. So why are you and Tracy arguing?' Knowing that his life isn't all wedded bliss makes me feel that I'm not missing out by being alone. In some ways I'm lucky to be locked down with Pippin for company. At least she doesn't argue back.

'She's tearing her hair out trying to help Izzy. She's no good at Maths or Science and I don't have the time, I'm busy working. She's always disturbing me, knocking on the spare room door where I'm working, asking dumb questions.' He sighs. 'And we've got a lousy internet connection with all of us using it at once. Still, there's a silver lining. We can eat dinner in the garden every evening. Weather's been fantastic. We've taken to playing board games, although that usually leads to arguments.'

My mind fills with visions of sizzling barbecues on their decking, breakfast in their conservatory and family game nights. Lucky sods. Wish I could join them. Maybe I'll chance it and suggest coming over.

'What if I came over...we could social-distance in the garden.' I just want some company. Would it do any harm?

'No, it's not safe. I can't believe you'd even suggest it, putting everybody at risk.'

'But...'

'We aren't supposed to be mixing with other households.'

'I don't consider myself a household.'

He lets out a big sigh. 'And you'd have to use the loo. Touching door handles, taps. No. It's just not practical.'

'I hate it here on my own.' I'm surprised to hear myself say this. Maybe I'm lonelier than I thought.

'I'm sorry I dragged you over from Australia.'

'You didn't drag me. I was happy to come. If it's getting too much you could come and stay here for a few days. We haven't spent much time together.'

'You know I can't do that. We're not supposed to be driving far. And what if the police are doing spot checks?'

I come off the phone. Andrew and Tracy are arguing, but so what? At least they have each other. Someone to snuggle up to at night, someone to cuddle up with on the sofa, choosing which Netflix series to watch and sharing a bottle of wine together. It's five years since I was last on my own. I'm not used to it. I don't like it.

When it's bedtime I trudge upstairs. Pausing outside the bedroom a thought occurs to me. Why am I still sleeping in this old-fashioned room? I can sleep in any room I choose. I want to be back in my own bedroom, at the front of the house, where I spent the first eighteen years of my life. It's in the other wing of the house. I head over there.

The room feels dank and unused, but it'll be cosy with a hot-water bottle to warm the bed. Sitting down, I sink into the middle. In all this time they haven't replaced the shabby mattress. I remember now how I used to complain because the springs were going. It's too soft and uncomfortable. I'm not sure I'll get much sleep, but I can try. The walls are still daffodil yellow but the pictures adorning the walls are now filled with Mum's gold-framed sketches of sheep and oast houses. There's a pine bookcase and kneeling beside it I cast my eyes across each row. They are novels, mostly. Ones I read in my teens including my favourites, John Wyndham's *The Day of the Triffids* and Neville Shute's *A Town Like Alice*. On the bottom shelf is an old shoebox from Dolcis, a shop long gone from the high street. I take the lid off and stop in my tracks. Jay's letters, tied in blue ribbon and postmarked, New York.

25

I stare at the letters. Maybe I should just burn them, be done with it. File for divorce, put it all behind me. There are probably matches in the kitchen by the Aga. They would be gone in seconds. But no, of course I can't burn them. They were written for me to read. I've visited the grave where my children are buried, how much more difficult can reading these letters be?

I pick the first letter up, postmarked 25th April 1995, New York. A month after our children died.

D*ee*,

I'm writing from the Big Apple. I bet you never thought I'd end up in New York. You thought I was a simple village guy, content to holiday in Majorca each year for the rest of my life. Wrong. I have ambitions and there's nothing to stop me now. You've ruined my life. Sophie's life...

. . .

I can't read the rest. It's full of bitterness. I tear it in two and then into lots of tiny pieces. I should bin the lot, but I can't bring myself to do it. I open the next one, it's dated June 1996.

Darling Dee,

It's hard to explain why I just walked out that day. Everything that happened to us, and all in the space of a week. I was close to crumbling in the funeral directors, making the arrangements - to bury not one child, but two. It was like standing on the edge of a cliff. A sheer and rocky drop in front of me. I was supposed to be the strong one. But I couldn't be strong for you. I looked at you. Those eyes that used to dance and sparkle. What sort of husband would I be if I could never get you to smile again? What good would we be for each other? Your eyes were flat and lifeless. We'd both have dragged each other down into a pit. And we'd never have been able to start again. I needed to set you free, to meet a happy man, someone that would help you forget and move on.

Love Jay. X

I open the next one. Postmarked June 1995

Darling Dee,

I'm sorry it's been several months since my last letter. I feel as if I've been through hell and back these past months. I know you have too. And I know in some ways I've made it worse for you because you've lost me too. I know it's hard, I know we promised till death do us part and all that, but sometimes promises have to be broken, for the good of both of us. It's like setting a bird free from its cage. We needed to be uncaged from the horrible things that happened.

. . .

Love Jay x

THE NEXT ONE is postmarked September 1995.

DARLING DEE,

I just wanted to let you know that I often think of you and wonder how you are. I hope you're happy and have met someone new. I want the best for you, I really do. I hope you understand why I did what I did. It was about realising when something's over, even when that's not what you want. If I hadn't left, we would have been locked in sadness forever. I needed to be with people who would lift me out of the harrowing place I was in, people who had greater needs than my own. I'm working at a tough school, one of the toughest in New York. It's going well, but I miss you, I miss you so much.

Love Jay x

I DON'T WANT to open the remaining letters. On a whim I take the lot to the toilet to flush them away. It feels like an appropriate thing to do. He flushed our marriage away. But they would clog the loo, so I head to the kitchen, find some matches and burn them outside in the garden. The letters aren't helping me to understand why he would walk out on our marriage. In fact, I find his words damn-right insulting, and selfish. As far as I can see we were a good couple, we were happy. It would have been tough, but we would have come out stronger in the long run. And we had family to support and help us. It's better that I don't read the other letters. I don't want a potted history of his life over the last twenty odd years. His job, his relationships, children?

It's strange he's not filed for divorce. I stare out at the garden pondering the possible reasons why he hasn't, in all this time. It does seem very odd. But then I haven't filed for divorce either. Nobody has proposed to me, so the need for a divorce has never arisen. Most of the time I don't think of myself as a married woman. After all, it's just a piece of paper. Australians are more liberal than us Brits, at least the ones I met over the years. Formalities don't mean as much to them. I forget to tell men that I'm married. Glen was the only guy I told and even then, he didn't seem bothered. I guess he thought that one day I'd get around to divorcing.

I'm curious to meet Jay to discuss all of this, but I don't know if I've got the courage to. Finding out about his life since we parted is bound to be unsettling. I'm not sure I'm up to it.

THE FOLLOWING MORNING, I ring the care home. The nurse on duty tells me that Dad is very weak and not eating much. 'Can I visit?' It's worth asking even though I know the answer will be no.

'Sadly not. We have to consider the well-being of our residents, but we can arrange for you to have a video chat with him. Can you ring back later, after tea and we'll sort something out?'

'Ok. I'm worried that he'll be very distressed and disorientated. I couldn't visit him in hospital. He won't know where he is.' It seems so unfair to put a blanket restriction on all visitors. Dad has felt alone for the past few years, since Mum died. This seems like cruelty taken to the extreme. If Dad had a choice between not seeing his family or risk getting the virus, I wonder what choice he would make. Is it even legal to ban visitors? Surely, he has a right to family and private life? If I had the symptoms of the virus then of course I wouldn't visit. But I don't. I'm perfectly well.

'Just to reassure you, he is comfortable. We've been chatting to him, but he is very weak and needs to rest.'

When the phone call ends, the house is silent apart from the continuing marking of time; the Swiss carriage clock chimes on the hour and Pippin scurries to my feet waiting to be let out for a wee. I open the back door for her, return to the kitchen to make coffee before joining her outside.

Outside it's a sunny morning with a deep blue sky and gauzy clouds but there's an erratic, nervy wind. It's too chilly to sit outside and so I let Pippin do her business before calling her back in.

The phone rings again. It's Lyn, my school friend.

'I heard about your dad,' she says, 'so sorry. It must be very lonely stuck out there on your own. But just to reassure you, it's no better being married. Ray's doing my head in.'

'Oh dear, well I did warn you when you got back with him.' Her husband Ray is an obsessive twitcher. Can't be easy to live with a man like that. 'Because of the lockdown he can't get out. He's stir-crazy having to birdwatch almost exclusively from the back-garden.' They live on the outskirts of Tunbridge Wells. 'He's set up his equipment in the garden. Says there are all sorts of rarities flying into people's gardens with human activity grinding to a halt. It's taken over the whole lawn. There's no room for Brett to play football and he won't let me do any gardening. What I am supposed to do with my time? I'm tired of making banana loaf.'

'Oh dear, makes me think I'm better on my own.'

'Do you want to hear something funny? I'm dying to tell someone.' She chuckles before launching into a story. 'A man passed our house wearing,' she pauses for effect, 'what looked like a plastic greenhouse.'

'No way! Some people will go to extreme measures to protect themselves from the virus.'

'I kid you not.'

We laugh.

'You couldn't make it up. His ankles and feet were the only part of himself on display. The greenhouse covered most of his body. And several Union flags were stuck on the outside of the greenhouse.'

'That's very funny. You've brightened my day with that one. It's so quiet here.'

'Do you want to hear another one?

'Go on, cheer me up.'

I pull over a stool and prepare to be entertained. She's making me realise how much I'm missing human contact. It's a shit situation we're in, not being able to meet in a pub or café. Not at all how I'd imagined my trip to England would be.

'A friend of mine has been chatting to a guy on Tinder. They planned to meet but then the lockdown came along and they couldn't. They got fed up of chatting online so decided to risk it and met up in Godstone. They planned to go for a long walk by the ponds and out into the fields. She put on her frumpy walking shoes, hoping he wouldn't notice. She filled a flask of tea but was a bit worried knowing of course that there would be no toilets open. He wasn't at all what she was expecting. He was sitting on a bench waiting for her and looked much older than his profile picture with a big paunch and he'd dyed his hair specially, would you believe. Before they'd even said hello, he looked down at his feet and said, 'I'm terribly sorry, but I've not been out in two weeks and I've left my slippers on.'

'Oh my God, Lyn! That's priceless.' I start laughing and don't stop until my belly aches. I might wet myself if I laugh any longer.

When the laughter dies down, Lyn asks me if I've seen Jay since the school reunion.

'It's hard to see anyone, given the lockdown, but I did bump into him in the village shop.'

'I don't suppose you had the chance to talk. I've noticed shop assistants don't like their customers lingering in aisles at the moment. We're goaded in and goaded out like a herd of school children.'

'Don't even go there, Lyn. The cashier got a bit stroppy with me. But yes, I did get to talk to Jay, outside, just briefly.'

'And?'

I let out a heavy sigh. 'Jay said he wrote to me. Soon after he arrived in New York, in the mid-nineties. I found a bundle of his letters. Mum never sent them onto me, Lyn. What sort of mother would do that?'

'A controlling one. I'm shocked that she'd do that, Dee, but I'm kind of not surprised.'

'Really? Why?'

'Your mum was always a bit controlling. Don't you remember the time you caught her reading your diary? We must have been about thirteen.'

'I don't remember that. I know she was always obsessed about keeping tabs on my period. When it was due, if it was late, that kind of thing. But I never had her down as a controlling mother.'

'I don't think she really liked Jay. She made some derogatory comment about him to me once. After he left you, she probably hated him. We were all confused, worried for you, worried for him. None of us could understand why he would just upsticks like that. But you were our main concern, Dee, we were all rooting for you. He wasn't there to support you. As far as we were all concerned, he was an utter bastard. That's probably why she decided not to send them. She was probably angry.'

'Angry or not, they were my letters. My life.'

'I guess. What did the letters say?'

I pause, thinking. 'Do you know Lyn, I don't actually know. They didn't really say very much at all. Outside the village shop, when he mentioned that he'd sent the letters, he said he'd poured his heart and soul onto those pages. But he hadn't. I think he was just excusing himself for what he'd done. There wasn't much remorse tucked behind his words.'

'You need to meet up with him probably. Sounds as if there's a lot you need to get off your chest and you both so need to put it all to bed and move on.'

'Yes, I will do, once I've worked out what I'll say to him.'

26

I spend the next couple of days bumbling around the house trying to get stuck into different activities: bagging up stuff to take to either the tip or the charity shop, cleaning and even gardening. Anything to pass the time till lockdown is over, till I can start living again, properly. The jobs do need doing, but there's so much for one person to tackle. Andrew is stubbornly refusing to come over to help. 'We can't break lockdown rules. The house can wait. Estate agents aren't open, we can't put the house on the market even if we were ready to. Just relax, sit in the garden with a book. Make the most of this nice weather. It won't last.'

Typical of my brother. I don't think he trusts me to sort everything on my own. I remember how Mum and Dad used to treat him when we were kids. He was the golden boy. I always felt as if he was more useful, to Mum and Dad than I was. He could chop wood, milk the goats, charge a car battery, lift heavy boxes. They didn't trust me with any chores and belittled the way I tried to help. 'No, let Andrew do that. He's better at that,' they'd say. I was strong and tall and capable of lots of things. When they couldn't think of an excuse they'd say, 'You've got no common sense.' I didn't have a role at home. They even paid for Andrew to go to private school. Why? For no other reason than he was a boy and his education mattered more than mine. When I failed my maths O Level Mum humoured me. 'We can't all be clever, dear,' she said. Maybe all of these factors were at play when I decided to leap across the world to Australia.

Every now and again I stop what I'm doing, pondering whether to call Jay. He slipped me his number when we met outside the village shop. 'The letters explain everything,' he'd said. But they don't and I want to tell him that.

I'M in the middle of sorting through the airing cupboard, folding sheets and towels. I hurl a towel across the landing and sink to the floor, my face in my hands. I can't stand it anymore. It's been five days since I read those bloody letters. Why should he get away with it? I've been silent for long enough. I'm going to confront him, have it out with him once and for all. He walked out on me. Let me suffer alone.

I rush down the stairs, grabbing my phone from the kitchen table, about to call him when the landline rings out. 'What now?' It's probably the nursing home. What am I doing, thinking about Jay all the time, when Dad is ill? I should have phoned the home yesterday, but I forgot. Jay doesn't deserve my thoughts.

It's the senior nurse at the home and she tells me that Dad is very weak. He's not eating and is running a temperature.

'Do you think he's got Covid?'

'Well...' she hesitates. 'I don't think so, he's not coughing, although we can't rule it out. He may have picked the virus up while in hospital. I think it's far more likely that he has a urinary tract infection. The doctor's prescribed a course of antibiotics, so we'll have to see what happens. We'll keep a close eye on him.'

'Can I speak to him on Skype again?' I don't enjoy these online conversations but it's necessary, to let him know that I'm here and care about him. I was so shocked at how he was I couldn't bring myself to repeat the experience in a hurry. It's frustrating. There's nothing I can do to help and seeing him on video just makes me more upset. Video chats don't seem to bother Andrew. He's phoned Dad a few times.

'He's asleep at the moment. We'll let you know and if we think he's up to it...'

After the phone call, I open the back door, letting in the spring air and decide to go for a walk across the fields. I set off towards the public footpath and coming to the brow of the hill I stop and gaze at the view. The countryside stretches before me like a great rolling quilt of squares held together by the thick green stitching of the hedgerows. It's like a giant ocean dotted with animals. Occasionally there is a wood, a farmhouse, barn or oast. I can see the next few days mapped out for me, rambling through pastures and over stiles, forgetting about Jay, about Dad, about the dilemma of my future, embracing God's garden, lapping up its beauty, just enjoying being here. Living in the moment.

Further along the path two people dressed in running garb are heading towards me. A man and a woman, I think. I hear their panting breaths, giving it their all, feet kicking up tiny stones. I pin myself against the hedge giving them a wide berth but don't watch them as they approach. In this pandemic everybody keeps a distance from each other, nodding politely, doing the awkward pavement dance to avoid getting too close to strangers, and taking their place in long, fractured queues outside supermarkets. As they approach me they slow down and only then do I turn my head. It's Jay and his girlfriend. Shit, what am I going to say? Why can't they run on the other side of the village where I'm less likely to bump into them? Everything that man does is selfish.

The woman is slightly behind him. She's nauseatingly pretty. Her blonde hair is tied back, her face is flushed and sweaty. Jay says, 'Hello Dee,' before turning to, what exactly? Introduce me to his girlfriend? I hope not. Her foot catches in a rut as she slows. She tumbles, crying in pain, brushing her grazed hands. She's probably twisted her ankle. She inches her bottom onto the soft grass. I can see what's going to happen next. He's going to ask me for help, because we're near to Dad's house. Groan, sigh. I really don't need this.

I watch as the woman continues to wince in pain with Jay now kneeling to look at her ankle. I can't leave them here. I'll have to help them. But I don't want to. I'd much rather walk away... like he did twenty-five years ago.

'Can I help? What can I do?'

The woman glares at me. I've only offered to help. Silly cow, what's her problem? Or is it just a look of pain rather than a glare? I really am getting paranoid these days.

'Would you, Dee? Thanks so much. Mel's probably twisted her ankle. Mel...He's not even bothered to introduce us.

'Can you help her along the path, and I'll drive as far up here as I can, then give you a lift back to your mum's,' I suggest. This is against lockdown rules. It will mean we're within two metres of each other. I'll grab something from the house to wrap around my mouth and nose and bring a bottle of disinfectant and a cloth. 'I'm assuming that's where you're staying at the moment?' I'm irritated by the situation. I shouldn't be compromising my safety, but of course I must help. I ignore this Mel woman, and address everything through Jay.

'Yes, we're staying at Mum's.'

'Okay, I'll run ahead and get the car.'

JAY HELPS Mel into the back of Dad's car, and I hand her a bag of peas. She's doesn't say thank you but glares at me through the mirror. I wasn't mistaken then. But why's she so cross with me? The look on her face could kill. She doesn't know I'm his ex and I'm helping her, for God's sake. I feel like throwing the pair of them out of the car, but I don't. I bite my lip and keep my cool.

'You need a new pair of trainers,' Jay tells her as we drive along.

'There's nothing wrong with these trainers.'

'I did warn you they aren't strong enough for paths like that, full of potholes.'

'You're such a know-all, always right, nothing changes.' I glance in the mirror as Mel folds her arms, looks out of the window, in full sulk.

I'm subjected to a minor domestic for the next few minutes and am glad when we arrive at the bottom of Summer Lane. I wish I hadn't bumped into them. He's welcome to her. Whinging little madam. He left me to be with women like her.

'Wait there a minute, Dee,' Jay says to me as they get out of the car. She hobbles into the house supported by Jay as I turn the car round. I haven't got used to driving Dad's Jag. It's heavy to turn, especially in small spaces.

Jay is waiting for me and I open the window to speak to him.

'Thanks for helping, Dee. I really appreciate it.'

'It's nothing.'

'Did you find my letters?'

'Yes, I've read them, most of them.'

'And?'

I shrug. 'What do you want me to say?'

'Can we meet? To talk?' His brow is sweaty and there are droplets of water in his hair.

I let out a heavy sigh. 'Do we have to?'

'Not if you don't want to.'

I hesitate. 'Okay then. We need to discuss divorce at some point.'

I catch a slight sadness in his eyes and quickly look away. He can't be sad though. He left me. He decided he wanted nothing more to do with me.

'I'll text you in a few days. Dad's in a care home. He's not well. When things calm down...'

'I'm really sorry. Yep, text me when you're ready.'

27

It's the day after I gave Jay and Mel a lift. I'm about to take Pippin out for a walk when the manager from the nursing home calls. Dad's been on a course of antibiotics for three days now. 'He's not rallying, I'm afraid. He's taken a turn for the worst. He's still got a temperature, he's cold, clammy, isn't eating,' the manager tells me.

'Can I...?' I'm about to ask if they'll make an exception, if they'll let me visit. Things don't look good. He's fading. But I don't have to finish the sentence. She talks over me.

'I think you need to come in, spend time with him. I'm so sorry to ring you with this news. He hasn't been here long, but we all think he's such a sweetie. A lovely man...'

I try to think of something to say but my mind clouds over. My stomach goes into freefall, my throat constricts. Is this it?

'How soon can you get here?' she asks.

'Twenty minutes.'

'Ring the bell, then wait at the bottom of the steps, at least two metres from the door. Someone will come out and provide you with PPE - an apron, gloves and a mask to wear. If you can make sure you've been to the loo before you arrive, only we can't let you use the loo or make a cup of tea. We'll guide you straight to his room.'

EXACTLY TWENTY MINUTES later I pull up on the gravelly driveway in front of the nursing home. I've not had time to call Andrew. I feel bad, don't want to exclude him. Should I send a quick text? Better not, I'll call him soon as I've seen Dad.

The house is Georgian and looks like a two-tiered wedding cake. It's in need of a good lick of paint, but the gardens are well-tended. The lawn - laid out to the side of the house - is immaculate and so are the flower beds. I ring the doorbell, step well away while I wait for it to be answered. A nurse in blue-shirt and black trousers opens the door, inviting me to come in after I have put the PPE on that she puts on the step, two metres between us. I tear open the plastic, commenting to her what a strange way of life this is. 'Necessary though,' she replies.

She leads me into a hallway where she asks me my car registration number so that she can enter it into the visitor's book, before heading through a very pleasant communal area where there's a fireplace, a mismatched assortment of armchairs and a huge chandelier hanging above. It's the middle of the day but the chandelier is throwing bright light across the room. Passing the kitchen, I'm hit by the smell of boiled veg, then we head along another corridor to a wing that's been added onto the house. Yellow sacks wait outside the resident's rooms, waiting for disposal. I catch a whiff of wee passing the sacks and wrinkle my nose.

The nurse opens Dad's door, standing back to let me go in. 'I'll leave you with him. Take as long as you like. He's high on morphine, he may not wake while you're here.'

My hand flies to my mouth. I can't believe how poorly he

looks. He's wasting away. There's no flesh on his shoulders and his cheek bones, now visible, have changed the appearance of his face. Tears prick as shock hits. This isn't my dad. He's a corpse with buttery flesh stretched over bones, like clingfilm over a sandwich. He's asleep, so I pull up a chair. I don't know if I want him to wake. He might be alarmed. He hasn't recognised me so far. And a sudden thought hits, he's less likely to now. I don't look like myself with a mask covering half my face. Behind the face-covering he won't be able to see me smile. I wish I could pull it off, but a nurse might come in. I don't want to risk getting chucked out. A golden ticket got me in here. These care homes have become like Fort Knox. I take Dad's hand, but it doesn't feel right that I'm wearing plastic gloves, spoiling the intimacy, the only link to my dad. The glove is a barrier between us, some of the connection is taken away. But I'm lucky to be here. So many other families can't visit their relatives because of this dreadful virus. And at least my dad doesn't have Covid. He won't be one of the statistics on today's daily briefing.

I'm sick of listening to those sombre daily briefings, waiting to hear how many have died of the virus. It's become a number game with graphs and charts across our tv screens. Our lives in the hands of the government, depending on their actions to bring those figures down. It's hard looking at him and thinking about the man he was. Dad was a civil engineer. He built power stations all over the world. He gave people power, brought light into people's lives, and corny though it sounds, he brought light into our lives. And now the light inside him is fast fading.

His great career seems like an age ago. There's nothing in this room and there's nothing looking at him now to indicate who he was. A man who had a great desire to learn, who'd travelled widely, who knew stuff that so many people didn't. He had been there, seen it, done it, lived it. His work spread far and wide. Fleeting memories filter through my head as I sit here. The wonderful stories he told us when he came home from his travels.

For about an hour I hold his hand, watch his face, his half-open mouth, the crust in the corners of his eyes, patchy skin, tumultuous eyebrows. I strain to listen for each breath. Sometimes I can't hear it, it's so slow, shallow and indistinct that I wonder if he's quietly slipped away. I move closer, watching, waiting, and then there's a sudden intake of breath, like a calm sea lapping at the shore.

Another hour passes and I'm bursting for a wee. I'm not allowed to use the loo, I'll have to go home but if I do, I can't just pop back. I'll have to ring, organise for someone to hand me PPE at the doorstep. It's too complicated. I try to forget about my groaning bladder by crossing my legs tightly like I did when I was a kid on a long car journey. 'Hold on,' Dad would say as we headed up the M1, 'not long till the next service station.' It's easier for men. They find a way, as Dad did on one occasion when the traffic ground to a halt on the M1, he jumped out to relieve himself on the grass bank, along with a row of other men all doing the same.

I can't hold on any longer, I'm bursting. Silently willing Dad to open his eyes it's as if telepathy is at work, when he magically opens them. He can't see my smile, but I try to communicate love through my eyes and actions, squeezing his hands. His own eyes are blank and it's as if I'm gazing into big dark black holes.

It's a strain for him to talk but he manages to form words, but they aren't the words I want to hear.

'What's your name?' I stare at him, the hope I had of him recognising me at this late hour, gone. His words splinter inside me. He must think I'm just another carer. It's a question he shouldn't have to ask, and I shouldn't have to answer. Under normal circumstances it would be an innocent question. Two people meeting for the first time.

'My name is Dee, I'm your daughter.'

His eyes soften, a gentle smile spreads across his face. Maybe he does recognise me, at last. Surely my name is engraved on his soul. According to Mum he adored me as a small child and couldn't get enough of my company. Rushing home from work to read bedtime stories, taking me swimming on a Saturday, then to BHS to buy me whatever clothes I wanted, including a fluffy pink jumper I loved to bits.

With his simple but heart-breaking question comes a moment of truth. I lost my dad a long time ago.

BACK AT DAD'S after visiting the care home I rush to the loo and am barely finished washing my hands when the phone rings. I have an ominous feeling as I scoop it up and press it to my ear. It's as if I already know.

'I'm sorry...' the nursing home manager says in a soft voice. 'After you left, he took a turn... He's gone.'

She's still talking, but my mind goes numb. I know I've been expecting this, for days, weeks, but still, it's a massive shock.

Panic begins when I come off the phone. It's like a cluster of spark plugs in the abdomen. I pace up and down the kitchen, tears flowing. Every thought inside my head tangles. Both my parents, dead. This might be the natural order of things, but its inevitability is no cushion to the pain and the feeling of being rudderless. I slump to the floor, head bowed, legs pulled up as tears fill my eyes. Lying at the very core of my being is regret. If only I'd come back a few years ago when both of them were well. So much time lost. There's a horrible emptiness inside me. Time we could have enjoyed, talking, eating together... I wish I could have made it up to them both. But now it's too late.

I realise now that I've not severed the emotional tie to my parents, even though I cut myself off, banishing myself to the ends of the earth, refusing to return. And now that I'm finally back it's to mop up, sort out all the practicalities. A funeral to organise, a house to clear and sell.

I must phone Andrew, let him know. Wiping away my tears I get up and walk over to the phone.

'He's gone. Slipped away a while ago.'

'Well...we were expecting it,' he says, matter of factly. He lets out a sigh. 'What now? Can we even have a funeral given the current situation?'

'I think we can, but the numbers will be restricted. And I guess there'll be no hugging and no reception to organise.' Under normal circumstances Dad's funeral would be a big occasion. He knew lots of people: from his working life, the golf club, close friends, villagers and even old school friends would come along.

'Is there much point in having a funeral? Why bother?' Andrew says flatly.

'Of course there is. We owe that much to Dad.' I can't believe he's even suggesting this.

'But why? If it's only you, me, Tracy and the kids? We know his life story. We don't need to hear a eulogy.' There's a certain weariness in his tone, as if his own father's death is too much effort.

'What would Dad want? This isn't about us. We need to respect his last wishes.'

'I never asked him. I've no idea what music he'd want, or poems.' He goes quiet. 'We just didn't talk about death.'

'You must know...did he want to be cremated or buried?'

'It might say in his will. You'll find it in the bottom drawer of his desk, left side. Go and check, I'll ring you back in a few minutes.'

The will is easy to find on the top of papers in the drawer. I hold it in my hands, staring at the words on the front page. I can't believe that Dad has gone. I scan each page and there at the end is our answer. He wants to be cremated and his ashes scattered by the river beyond the back field. Dad loved spending time by the river, especially when we were young. We'd take big picnics and sit on the bank.

Andrew and I resume our discussion and it's then that I realise something. There's no emotion in his voice or his words. It's as if he wants this over with quickly, that it's an inconvenience he'd rather not have.

'Sis, I'm sorry,' he says. 'I just don't see the point in a funeral, given the current circumstances. Can't we just arrange for a cremation and at a later date have a memorial service?'

'I'd like a funeral,' I insist, trying not to let my voice wobble. Already I'm feeling as if I'm grieving alone. 'If we put it off till a later date, will we even bother? It's got to be now or never. The current situation isn't Dad's fault. We need to make it a special day, in his honour.'

Andrew sighs. Clearly, it's too much effort for him. I can't believe my own brother being like this. I need to take the reins. 'Let me organise it. You don't have to do a thing.'

When he replies the tension is gone from his voice. Maybe I've misread the signals. It's not that he doesn't want a funeral, more like he doesn't want the hassle of organising one. 'Ok then, sorry,' he says. He's probably struggling in his own way. He's not a man to emote and it's coming across that he doesn't care, but I know he does, he must care, despite the ups and downs of his relationship with Dad. 'There's a folder in the same drawer with all the paperwork in it that you'll need when you ring the funeral director.'

'Are you sure you don't want to be involved with the arrangements?'

He hesitates. 'You'll manage. You're probably right, we

should have one. I'm not sure I'd want a memorial service at a later date. At least this way it'll all be over.'

Putting the phone down I realise exactly why Andrew doesn't want a memorial service. He's scared of who might attend and what might be said. Dad's friends... who were the men that went away each year to explore their feminine side?

28

Eight days after Dad died, on a cold, bright day, the hearse pulls up at the crematorium. I follow in my car alone parking it behind the chapel. There is space for around a hundred cars but today there are only four cars parked. The death toll from Coronavirus continues to rise. In the last few days it's been around eight, nine hundred a day and yet these places are empty. Any gatherings of people are restricted, for fear of spreading the virus.

Outside the chapel I wait for the six pallbearers to step out of the hearse. My eyes are drawn to a sign staked in the grass. 'Following advice on social distancing, please do not approach or talk to any of the crematorium staff.' I step to the side of the chapel door as they hoist the coffin, decorated with spring flowers, on to their shoulders and I watch them carry it to the catafalque. Vaughan Williams, *The Lark Ascending* is playing. One of Dad's favourites, reminding me of springtime.

All the arrangements for Dad's funeral were done over the phone but Andrew and I had a Zoom meeting with the vicar a few days ago. Andrew didn't look well, he kept mopping his face with a tissue which worried me. Is he coming down with the virus? No, he'd said firmly, as if the virus was a dirty affliction to be ashamed of. The vicar told us we were lucky. Some local authorities have banned funeral ceremonies in crematoria and cemeteries and if we'd requested a church service that wouldn't have been possible. But I don't feel very lucky, I'm here alone. Last night Andrew called me to say that Tracy had symptoms of the virus and the whole family were now having to isolate. Convenient I wondered? Was he just looking for an excuse not to come? I guess that's something else I'll never know. But he'll have the option of watching the ceremony from home because it's being livestreamed. I was told yesterday by the crematorium staff that the platform had its limits: no more than twenty people can log on. My list of twenty people was soon whittled down to below twenty because of the number of people who couldn't figure out Skype. Or don't want the bother of finding out how to work it.

I stare at the coffin. I want Dad to be surrounded by a big crowd of mourners who loved him and with the comfort of kind words, hugs and handshakes. None of this feels right, it's not how the end is supposed to be. But although nobody will be here, I take a fragment of comfort knowing that there's a generalised sense of grief across the whole world right now, collectively for everybody lost and for the loss of the way we live our lives. Not a single person is unaffected by this pandemic. It's grief upon grief, so many layers, for so many different reasons. Each family has its own story to tell. Knowing this makes me well with sadness but it also gives me strength.

The funeral director is standing respectfully at the back. He nods and indicates with a wave of his arm that I can sit wherever I like. In front of the funeral director are three of the pallbearers. Are they standing in as proxy mourners? Between the pallbearers, the funeral director and the vicar standing at the front are rows of chairs. Every single one is empty. Dad's friends are like him, elderly and therefore self-isolating. There are relatives who would have come, but most of them live miles away and because of the Coronavirus restrictions they cannot travel. Everybody, up and down the country, has had the message drummed into them. Stay at Home. Protect Lives. Save the NHS. It's a successful message. Nobody dares venture out unless it's essential.

The music fades. The vicar is about to begin the service and the funeral director steps towards the door to close it. In that moment somebody rushes in. The funeral director whispers to them and I hear feet moving towards a seat but don't turn to see who it is. Maybe it's Ruth. Nice of her to come. I focus on the vicar's words and smile at all the lovely things he has to say about Dad, my eyes wet by the end. It's only when the final music, Samuel Barber's *Adagio For Strings* begins to play and I stand up to go, do I turn and see who the mourner is. My husband. Jay.

My inner peace is felled in one blow, replaced with anger. Why is Jay here? Not a bloody word from him in twenty-five years. Now he's popping up everywhere. And today of all days. Here, in the midst of my grief. He has no right to be here. Given the current situation you don't just turn up to a funeral uninvited. He's not close family. He may have loved Dad at one time when we were together. Dad was good to him and they were friends, but that was a lifetime ago. He's not family anymore. Barely even an acquaintance. Damn it, he's so not welcome. How dare he invade this special day? And knowing how angry I was at the school reunion. Why would he risk another scene? Count to ten, Dee, focus on Dad, filter him from your vision. Poor Dad, I don't want to be angry, I'm here for you. Calm, Dee, calm. I must control myself, mustn't let the same thing happen again that happened at the school reunion. Good grief, I'd never forgive myself.

Out in the open I cover my face with my hands. Having contained my emotions for the past twenty minutes I can't any longer. Salty drops fill my eyes. My chin muscles tremble like a small child. The funeral director sweeps past me as I'm dabbing my eyes, placing the floral tribute on the grass next to a stand with Dad's name on. I go to stand by the flowers; they are something to focus on. Everything in my life feels so raw.

After thanking the vicar and the funeral director I hurry away. I don't want to linger too long. Jay will come over. Shit, he's calling my name. I turn but don't smile.

I'm all flustered and sweat is building around my neck. 'You shouldn't have come. Please go.'

He's wearing a suit. He backs away, his hands flying up. 'I don't want to upset you.'

'You must have known that your being here would upset me.'

'I just wanted to pay my respects. Be here for you.'

I stare at him. 'Be here for me?' I hiss. 'You can't be serious?' I almost laugh.

'Meet me by the river bridge tomorrow, at four. Dee, please... I don't want to fight with you. I want us to talk.'

'Okay, alright, if it means you go... now...please...just go,' I snap, pointing my finger in the direction of the carpark.

I watch him walk back to his car. Good. Gone. I breathe a big sigh of relief. Shit, I can't believe I've arranged to meet him.

IT's the day after Dad's funeral and I set off along the footpath leading towards the village to meet Jay. My stomach's been tied in knots all morning with nerves and worry. It feels as if butterflies are dancing round my stomach. I'm completely panicked at the thought of meeting him. I only agreed to meet him to get rid of him at the funeral. What am I going to say to him after all this bloody time? Daft as it sounds, I almost wish I'd prepared a script to learn beforehand because I feel so on edge. I know I'm going to be tongue-tied.

It's another beautiful day. I take a deep breath welcoming the fresh air and as I start to walk, I feel calmer. Clouds brush stroke against a faded blue sky, which looks like the knees of an old pair of jeans. Entering the tree-canopied pathway a woodpigeon startles me rising up from the undergrowth, the sound of its wings like gunshot. After the sombreness of yesterday I welcome the sounds and smell of nature. Clusters of primroses I'd like to pick, hedges leafing with green springtime and I delight in pausing to watch lambs in the field.

My phone ringing in my pocket interrupts the peace and beauty of my surroundings. It's Andrew. I felt so let down by his absence yesterday that I didn't bother to call him. Seeing his name flash up I'm tempted not to answer but do.

'I'm sorry I wasn't there yesterday.'

'Andrew, Jay was there. I didn't notice until the end of the service otherwise I would have gone into meltdown. I've no idea how he found out about Dad's funeral and why he found it acceptable to just turn up.'

Andrew goes quiet.

'Andrew... you didn't tell him?'

'I mentioned it on a whim, on Facebook. Dee, I felt really bad about not being there and he was the only other family member around. He wants to make things right with you.'

'Make things right? After twenty-five years? What the heck, Andrew? I can't believe you'd ask him to step in. And he's certainly not family. You make me sound needy. He's the last person I wanted to see at Dad's funeral.'

'They were close, you forget that.'

'Were. It's all in the past.'

'I'm sorry. I didn't think. I didn't want you to be alone.'

'So, you thought, let's invite your sister's ex. Andrew, I saw him at the school reunion. I ended up slapping his face.'

'Oh, I didn't know that.'

'I'm getting sick and tired of you deciding what's right and wrong for me. No more interfering, all right?'

'Sorry.'

Andrew changes the subject with a cheery tone, something he always does when he knows he's in the wrong. 'It was a lovely service, sad though. And strange watching it on-line. Can't believe the old bugger's gone.' He doesn't sound particularly sad. His voice is upbeat.

'Me neither. The house feels so quiet without him even though I've been on my own for weeks now. Doesn't feel right my being here.'

'Not much we can do right now, not till lockdown's over. With planes grounded you can't go back to Australia and with estate agents closed we can't put the house on the market. But this won't go on forever. Think of it as a temporary blip.'

'I hope not. Feels like life's on pause.' I've come full circle, living back where my life started. 'Anyway, how are you? Are you better now?' I'm not convinced that Andrew is ill. I think he couldn't face going to Dad's funeral.

'Tracy and I both have dry coughs. Other than that, we feel okay. We had Covid tests this morning. It was a right palaver. It was a drive-through at Gatwick. Tracy was more interested in the line-up of soldiers than reading the leaflet that explained what we had to do. They get you to swab your tonsils then your nose. Made me gag.'

'Shit, you had Covid tests? You're okay though, other than having a cough?'

'We feel okay.'

'What about the girls?'

'They're absolutely fine.'

'Look after yourselves. Things can turn very fast.'

His absence from the funeral was genuine after all. 'I did wonder if you were deliberately staying away from the funeral.' Maybe he's faking being ill. I wouldn't put it past him, not after what he said in the garden a few weeks back when we'd been talking about Dad's cross-dressing. His tone had been vicious, and I could see in his eyes he'd come to hate Dad.

The fact that he doesn't immediately answer me suggests there is a grain of truth to my statement.

'I would have found it really hard.'

'All funerals are hard, Andrew. He was our dad. We've lost both our parents.'

'Look, Dee, I don't want to colour your memories of Dad. I know you loved him very much, but...'

'Things were different for you? But you still loved him.'

'I could never get over seeing him in a dress that evening in Brighton. It changed everything. I went through the motions, sis. I was there for him like a good son should be. But it put a distance between us. Our relationship was never the same after that.'

'That's very sad.'

'I'm sorry.' We're silent for a moment. 'I should have kept it all to myself.' He coughs again.

'I want to remember Dad in my own way.'

'I've got to go, Dee, I need to cough.'

By the time our conversation has ended, the speed camera at the bottom of the hill comes into view. I spot Jay. He's leaning over the bridge peering into the river, his back to me. I stop and stare at him. My husband. The word sounds alien. He's not a husband, he's a stranger, a ghost from another lifetime. I hate him, I hate what he did to me. I head down the hill towards him with mounting nerves. He needs to know how disappointed I'd been on reading his letters. They were all about him. His needs, making himself feel better. He didn't stop to consider my feelings and his duty, his loyalty towards me. When I think of poor Mum, sticking by Dad. That generation didn't bail out on each other. They supported each other through thick and thin. God damn him. Jay has no idea about commitment. He needs to know what it was like for me after he left. Just what he put me through. As I walk closer, I'm beginning to think should I even be here? I should just pick up the phone and ring a solicitor to start divorce proceedings.

Jay still doesn't turn around. But as I draw closer somebody else waves at me from the other side of the bridge. Jay. The man staring into the water still doesn't move, and I realise now why I thought he was Jay. He's a younger version of my husband. More like the image of Jay I've held in my mind for so long. The man I fell in love with. How silly of me, I've seen Jay several times now in the past few weeks; I should have known. How disconcerting.

At the sight of Jay walking towards me, something inside me constricts. Something heavy and foreboding and linked to loss.

29

'Hi,' Jay says. There's a vague hint of a smile on his lips. He looks scrubbed from a recent shower, his hair damp around his face. I catch a whiff of pine. He regards me through wary eyes, as if I'm a Jehovah's Witness caller to his front door. I sense a steel girder, like an aura around him and it makes me wary too. 'I'm sorry for just turning up yesterday to the funeral. Andrew was worried about you. I only wanted to help.'

'Help? How could *you* possibly help?' I feel my anger mounting and we've only just met. Jeez. Why does he make me feel like this? 'It was a shock, seeing you there. You must have known I wouldn't have wanted you there. What's wrong with you? You seem to have developed rhino skin.' I'm all nervy and on edge. I don't like how I am right now, but God he deserves it.

'How are you? I'm really sorry about your dad.'

I grind my teeth and feel like exploding. He has a clever way of diverting the conversation and not getting riled by the things I say.

'I'm okay,' I say stiffly. If he was a friend I'd open up and tell him how sad I feel about losing Dad.

'Shall we?' He points to the path by the river and we cross the road in silence, stepping over a stile and into the field. 'We shouldn't really be meeting as we're from different households. There's a lot of snitchers around, bored with lockdown and nothing better to do than ring the police. So rather than risk that happening, I'll walk ahead. Safer we keep a distance anyway, either of us could have the virus. Once we reach the wide part of the river we can find somewhere to sit and talk.'

Who gives a flying fig? The man's paranoid. He seems to like big distances between us, in fact the bigger the distance the better, escaping from his marriage all the way to New York. But this idea of everybody watching what everybody else is up to is a tad over the top. Typical Jay, he's got it all worked out. Likes to follow rules for the sake of it. Always has a plan. Little sparks of anger start to fizz. Bailing out on me all those years ago must have been a carefully calculated plan.

As we begin to walk, I'm suddenly grateful for the current situation. If it wasn't for the lockdown we might have arranged to meet in a pub, sitting opposite each other twiddling our hands and fiddling with beer mats. Awkward or what?

I follow Jay's feet across the field as they kick the earth. He's wearing a pair of black-and-white old skool Vans trainers and tight-fitting black jeans. So different to the Debenham's style he wore in the nineties. I like this new style, suits him. He's very with-it for a man of fifty-five. But he's got a much younger girlfriend; I guess he has to keep up.

We reach the part of the river that widens into a bowl, where, as kids, we used to lower ourselves from the bank onto a beached area dipping our toes in the shallow riverbed, and if we were feeling more daring we'd plunge into the murky waters for a swim. Despite the damp grass, Jay sits down on the bank, his legs dangling over the river.

The unease between us slips up a gear. He fiddles with his hands and stares into the river before pulling out his phone to check for messages. There's always been something slightly gauche about Jay, as if he struggles to connect, as if he's in the room but not actually in the conversation. But the connection was there, between us once, surely? Otherwise we'd never have married. It's hard to remember back to those early days together. The loss of our children is a blanket that smothered everything that happened before.

'You want a divorce?' he asks.

The question takes me by surprise in its bluntness with no build-up. 'You do too, surely? It's something we should have done long ago.'

'I guess it would bring closure.'

'I can give a solicitor a ring, if you like?' I try to sound upbeat even though inside I feel so let down. I don't show any emotion on my face.

'Yeah, might be a good idea.' His casualness is starting to piss me off. Or maybe, like me, he feels too nervous to think what to say.

'I found your letters. I read a few of them - but had to destroy the rest. Quite honestly, I wish I hadn't read them. I found it all too upsetting.'

'I'm sorry. They were supposed to explain everything, why I did what I did.' He glances at me. He gives me a half-smile and I notice his eyes are blank. He looks distressed, shrivelled like an unwatered plant.

'Oh, they explained all right,' I say throwing him a sardonic look. 'Made me see you for what you really are. A complete bastard. What came across was that it was all about you. What you wanted. Moving on. Forgetting about everything because it was easier. But when you left, my whole world collapsed around me like a house of cards. And blaming me for Sophie's death.' I pause, take a deep breath. 'I'm still broken, Jay,' I find myself crying out. 'I can't accept they're dead, even now, years later. I just can't grasp it. Why we'd lose two children. Time's made no difference. I still want our children so badly sometimes it makes me almost sick.' I've never said this to anyone before, not even to Helen and my words feel hot and dangerous. But as soon as I've spoken them, I wonder why I've waited so long. Maybe these words have been stowed away and I'd known that one day I'd pour out my feelings to Jay. But I'm worried now because Jay isn't a big talker. He doesn't wear his heart on his sleeve. I'd forgotten that until now. He's a man of few words. Is he really likely to fully open up to me, tell me exactly what was going through his mind?

He doesn't speak, just stares into the river, like an obstinate teenager. He pulls a blade of grass and winds it round his fingers. He's uptight, I can see it in his posture. He's floundering, so am I. It's as if we are inarticulate.

He looks over at me and fleetingly, as our eyes connect, I see the blame, it's still there. Raw and painful.

The longer the silence goes on, I want to reach over and shake him. Demand to know, why are you still accusing me after all this time? I close my eyes and go back to that day outside the café when Sophie ran into the road. The day that changed our lives.

Someone called for an ambulance, someone else rang Jay. The sequence of events is a haze in my mind. As if the surroundings were covered in gauze, everything was distorted including the voices around me. It was as if my body was floating above the scene. A passer-by wrapped a coat around me. I shook, every part of my body trembling. I sat crumpled on the pavement, my head jerking, hysterical. I couldn't stop shivering. I felt so cold, colder than I've ever felt before. A small group of people gathered to watch, witnessing me at my most vulnerable.

And then Jay arrived. To see my husband, the one I loved always so in control of every situation, so distressed, it was disturbing. Screaming, yelling with a rawness I've never seen in a man before. Then slumping to the ground, thick lines of spit looped in a lacey bib round his mouth. It would have pulled at every thread of my body and I would have rushed to comfort him, but I was rooted to the spot quaking inconsolably.

'You can't keep blaming me, Jay.' With heat rising to my face I fight tears. 'I had to take Sophie out that day. You had a pile of homework to mark. You needed to catch up. I thought we'd give you some peace and quiet and I wanted time alone with Sophie. I'd spent so little time with her, because of being in hospital with Poppy.' But I know that no matter how hard I try to justify my actions, I will never be able to convince myself. It was an indisputable cast-iron fact that if I'd not dropped Sophie's hand that day, she would still be alive. I think it's being here with Jay after all this time, but I suddenly realise now that I'm tired of the fight that goes on inside me.

He turns on me, catching me unawares. '*You* wanted time alone with her? What about me? Did you stop to think what I wanted? I didn't give a flying fig about work that day. Work could wait. What did you think, that I could just switch back into work mode after losing Poppy? You gave up your job, remember? You had the luxury of not working. All the time in the world to sit around wallowing in your grief.'

His harsh words slice through me. 'That's not fair.' My voice falters. I'm close to tears.

'I had no choice. It was straight back to the chalkface for me, to face a bunch of teenagers. Someone had to work,' he says in a defensive tone.

'You could have taken extended bereavement leave. You didn't have to walk out on me. But instead you left me to pick up the pieces.'

'I wanted you to read all of the letters.'

'I couldn't. It was as if you hated me.'

'It was hard enough writing them. It took me ages to find

the right words. I don't blame you. Not anymore. But I did for a very long time. It was my escape route.'

'What changed?' I'm not sure I believe him. We've been apart so long that it's hard to read his body language and the subtleties in his voice. But I want to believe him because this blame-game is eating me up. For so many years I've imagined him taking me in his arms, stroking my hair, kissing my head and whispering to me, 'You weren't to blame.' Simple words I needed to hear. So important to me. Words that would have gone some way to heal my soul.

'I met someone.'

'Someone?' I look at him and frown.

'A woman. She helped me to see things differently. That it was an accident. She'd lost a child. Did enough soul-searching of her own.'

'Poor woman.'

'People come into our lives for a reason. They're meant to cross our path. There's a role for everyone we meet. Each person we connect with brings a unique perspective on life. And for every person I've met over the years I've learned a bit more about myself. She had her role, she helped me when I needed help, but in the end, we wanted different things.'

Wow. This is the most eloquent thing I've ever heard Jay say. The only time I remember him speaking in such a profound and relaxed way was after a few jars of beer or drinking sangria in a bar next to the Med'. Most of the time his conversation centred around daily routines. He wasn't a relaxed person now I come to think of it. Always a stickler for time, doing things in his words 'properly,' getting cross and agitated if things didn't go to plan or went off-balance. And when our life tipped off its axis big-time, he couldn't cope. He had no logical explanation for what happened other than to blame me. It was an easy thing to do. Maybe the tough challenges he's faced in New York have given him a wider perspective on life. But I don't agree with him. We don't have roles. People don't come in neat packages. Life isn't theatre, it's more improvisation.

I'm hit in the gut by a bomb of emotion. 'But if that's the case and things happen for a reason then our children were meant to die, like it was a test for us or something, and I don't want to think that, I can't think it.' I let out a sob. 'It's simple. I should have stayed at home that day rather than going out. It was my fault. Why didn't I listen to you? Sophie didn't need to go out. If only we'd played in the garden instead.' There's static in my head and my eyes drip with tears.

We turn to face each other and at the sight of forgiveness shining in his eyes something in me twists. I want to reach over and hug him. Thank him for forgiving me even though he's not spoken those words I crave to hear but that would involve showing my vulnerability. It feels as if I'm swimming in a deep cloudy soup. Has he really stopped blaming me or is the blame a coin waiting to be flipped?

'It was that bastard that killed her.' There's anger and a tinge of purple in his face. 'If he'd been driving slowly it might not have happened. He robbed us. And the shit is out there, somewhere, leading a normal life. I'm sorry, there was no way I could have stayed. How could I walk into the village every day and be reminded? Looking at every car, wondering if it was him? I blamed you, but mostly I blamed him. Reckless bloody driver.' He spits the words and with one hand on the grass he stumbles to his feet, faltering. With his fists clenched he shouts, 'And not to stop. What sort of a human being would do that?' He walks away from me as if to deal with his anger alone, returning moments later to sit down again. He fiddles with his hands. I wish I could grab his hands. I wish I could grab him, pull him into a cuddle. I need to do it, but I can't, I won't, it's not appropriate and would be weird after all this time. His face is set, stone-like. He's still that stranger. And a hug in any case would be breaking lockdown rules.

'The guilt never goes away. I've had to live with it. But I didn't need my husband blaming me too and leaving me. For God's sake, Jay, how could you walk away, just like that? We'd known each other since we were at primary school. You were my first love. We got together when we were sixteen. You were my world, the only world I knew. All those years, all those shared experiences, memories. Did they count for nothing? Was it easy just closing the door on it all? It doesn't make sense.' My hands fly in the air in frustration and I realise I need him to explain everything. 'Didn't you care what happened to me? How could you just switch off? Or maybe you didn't love me at all. Maybe it was all a horrible lie and me being a fool couldn't see it.' I scramble to my feet and walk towards the bridge. The way I feel right now I wish it was a tall bridge like the Clifton Suspension Bridge. I'd hurl myself over.

He gets to his feet too, wiping soil from his bottom, in true Jay style. He hates any dirt on his jeans.

'I couldn't think straight,' he screams, clutching the sides of his head with his hands.

I scoff. 'Your mind was straight when you took yourself to New York and started a new job there.' His actions made no sense. It was a massive change in lifestyle, and I know that Jay doesn't do change. He resists change. Jay had no desire to even visit America, let alone live there. Once we were married he was content to spend the rest of his life in Rivermead in the same house, sitting on the same bar stall in the King's Head every Friday evening and holidaying at the same resort each year,even if he'd spent the previous holiday complaining about the food or the beach and other things that weren't right. He was inexorable, wouldn't consider a different resort. The mere suggestion of a different pub would be out of his comfort zone making him freak.

'I had to get away. It felt as if I was being suffocated.'

'I didn't do that to you.' My face feels flushed I'm so worked up.

'I know you didn't. It was just me. It was all in my head.' He jabs his head with his finger. 'I was messed up, Dee. Good and proper.'

'You could have told me you were going,' I screech back.

'How could I tell you? Mike did everything for me. If it hadn't have been for Mike I wouldn't have had the guts.'

'Head of department Mike, your boss? If I'd known he was behind it all I would have gone round to his house and given him a peace of my mind. Wasn't he at some Christmas do I went to? He made some patronising comment to me, remember? What was it? Oh yeah, he said I'd never make much of my career unless I taught A levels and only very bright people can teach A levels well.'

'He was brilliant.' Jay's shoulders slump and I think how pathetic he looks.

'I was in no fit state at that point. He booked the flight and even came with me. He's American, from New York. We stayed with his folk. We had a week of sightseeing and then he took me to the school, introduced me to the head and I was given a limited timetable to start with. I'm a teacher and I shouldn't say this but it's not what you know, it's who you know. It was just luck that Mike had contacts. He thought I could do with a new challenge. It was just what I needed.'

'Sightseeing? How the hell could you go sightseeing when our children had just died?'

'I don't know, Dee, I don't know what was going through my head at the time, but it helped. A change of scene. Escapism, just to pretend that nothing had happened.'

'I can't believe I'm hearing this,' I shout. I'm putrid with anger as I grip the railings of the bridge. Lucky the railing isn't Jay's neck. I'd wring it right now. And there was me having thought all along that he'd suffered a nervous breakdown.

Clearly, he hadn't. His head was screwed on tightly, as tight as a duck's arse. Bastard.

'Alright,' he shouts up at me, 'I'll tell you the truth. You won't like it though.'

'Maybe not, but at least it'll be the truth, or will it?'

'I was shit scared. I thought I was going to do something silly, like hurt you.'

Stunned, too shocked to speak, my hand flies to my mouth. I stare down into the murky river water wishing it would rise up and sweep me away. My head's gone all fuzzy, I need to sit down. Turning away from Jay I head over the bridge to the other side and plonk myself down on the grassy bank, the river separating us as we face each other in mortal combat.

'It's the God-damn truth, Dee.' His voice has gone husky as he shouts across. 'You were broken. I was broken. I was angry. I don't know what I would have done, but I didn't trust myself. And even if I had controlled my temper there would have been hurtful words, dark thoughts. How could we have ever moved on from what happened? It would have always been there, a dark cloud hanging over the marriage, swallowing us whole like some vile ugly creature. It's not a tunnel any relationship can come out of.'

'You were always the optimist. It was my job to be the pessimist. You thought Poppy was going to survive, remember? But I prepared myself for the worse.'

'I accept the pain I caused you and I'm sorry, but escaping was the only way I could deal with it all.'

'You didn't give a flying pig what I was going through. The hell I lived through day-in day-out, processing it all alone.'

'I'm sorry. I can't say it enough. At the time I probably thought well, you had your mum.'

'Mum?' I hobble to my feet. Dazed and with my hands on my hips I stare at him dumbfounded. He knows I wasn't close to Mum. She wasn't the type of mum who would have carried me through such an horrendous time. She did her best but she retreated into her own shell, grieving for her grandchildren alone, never openly showing her emotions and never asking how I was, probably because she thought it would make things worse. 'You knew what she was like. A cold fish.'

'Can't you see, Dee, we couldn't be together. We would have destroyed each other lingering on our dark thoughts and hurtful words. We needed to be thousands of miles apart. It would have swallowed us whole.'

'We might have had more children and recovered.'

'Replacement children? You can't replace your children, Dee. Like a Hoover or a washing machine. After Sophie and Poppy, I didn't want more children, not with you, not with anyone. It didn't feel right, to deny their existence and move on.'

'I know you can't replace children. I'm completely stupid and heartless. But at some point, couples do move on. They have to for their own sanity.'

'It wouldn't have been the same. I wanted Sophie and Poppy. Without them life wasn't worth living.'

'And what about me?' I scream. Clutching my chest, I say, 'They died. I didn't. I was still there. I was there long before they were conceived. I wasn't going to leave *you,* however hard things got.'

'We can keep going over this, Dee, until we're blue in the face. I made some dreadful mistakes.' Jay makes some strange facial gestures as he looks across at me that I'm not familiar with. He reminds me of the actor Jim Carrey. God knows what's going through his mind.

'And so did I. I've re-played that day so many times in my head. I'm not going to keep beating myself up over what happened. I tried to be a good mother. Just one brief lapse, that's all it took. Jay...' I look across at him and our eyes connect. 'We loved them so much. We were good parents. I've been up in the attic looking at photos. Do you remember the time when Sophie was covered in spag bol?'

Jay's face relaxes and he smiles. 'In Tenerife?'

Then we begin to talk about Sophie and Poppy. The dam has burst and we interrupt each other in our eagerness to share memories of our children: how Sophie loved broccoli but hated sweetcorn, playing hide-and-seek, singing nursery rhymes to Poppy late at night to stop her crying; the delicious way they smelt; Poppy of milk and Sophie of spun candy and their soft chubbiness as each gained weight and how we'd loved to blow raspberries on their bellies.

We laugh briefly while we embrace our sorrow, and it's as if they're still alive and all we are doing is reflecting back on their early lives. And then it's as if we're jolted back to reality. Their lives ended. The memories stopped. There are no school photos, no holiday snaps, no prom pics or wedding albums. All we can do is dare to imagine how life might have been.

'What would Poppy have looked like?' Jay asks with a thoughtful expression on his face.

'I often wonder what sort of work Sophie would have done?'

There are tears welling in Jay's eyes. 'Who would they have been if they'd lived? Oh Dee, we'll never know.'

I'm about to answer but am distracted by the sound of music. I glance round wondering where it's coming from. We're in an open field, there aren't any trees or bushes nearby. Jay looks at me and frowns. 'It's coming from the pillbox,' he says.

There are pillboxes dotted along the river. Built in the Second World War they are small concrete buildings with holes through which to fire weapons. The wartime government expected the Germans to invade by coming up the river. That never happened, and they weren't taken down. Very much part of the landscape, our forgotten past, some are covered in nettles or ivy. As kids we used to play in them or stand on the top to survey the view, pretending to be pirates. And as teenagers Jay and I had a few snogs in pillboxes, long before we snogged in the comfort of his Ford Escort. Gosh, Jay and I have known each other for an age. The thought makes me shudder.

We walk towards the pillbox, Jay in front. 'Careful, Jay, you don't know who's in there.'

He ducks his head and goes in while I wait outside.

'Sorry to disturb you,' I hear him say.

'Jay, come out. Have you forgotten about social distancing?'

'Dee, come here.'

Dipping my head I go in, crunching over empty crisp packets and other rubbish. These buildings are small and hexagonal and there isn't much space because there's usually a pillar in the middle taking up most of the space. This one doesn't have a pillar.

Ivy covers the gun ports that crown the building choking the light, but my eyes adjust to the gloom. My noise wrinkles as the smell hits - urine, body odour. Somebody has been living in here.

30

A man is curled up in a sleeping bag on the concrete floor surrounded by his worldly goods, several bags and a radio pumping music anaesthetising his desperate situation.

'Go away.' His voice is sharp. I feel as if I'm trespassing, invading his privacy. This is his home. We have to no right to be here. He lifts his head from a pillow that's seen better days, it's yellowy with black mould patches. Such a pitiful scene. How did he come to be here? I glance at Jay and can see the same questions ticking around his head. Why here and not in a town where he can beg and get support from the homeless shelter? But maybe this is safer. He won't be discovered or get attacked. But food and drink, how on earth does he survive?

'Ok mate,' Jay says backing towards the opening. The weather is good at the moment but when it starts raining again the wind and rain will gust in. It won't be pleasant.

'I recognise you…you're Pandora's brother, Jules. You used to live next door to us, I say.

He doesn't reply but inches into a sitting position before

looking at me for a moment. 'Yeah, you're Dee? Back from Australia?'

'For a while. And you remember Jay?' I turn to Jay who's stepped back in.

'Yeah I do. Thought you too had broken up years ago.'

'We have,' I say. 'So why are you here? If you don't mind my asking. It's not a pleasant place to pitch up.'

'Long story.' He's a wreck. His hair is dishevelled, and his face is stubbly. 'Pandora's told you about my problems?'

I know everything. She keeps me posted. He can't kick his gambling habit. He had a wake-up call a couple of years ago when his girlfriend, Amanda announced she was expecting but it didn't take him long to return to his old tricks. Hard to change people. It's a nasty habit. 'I'm sorry. I heard that you're still struggling. Can't be easy.'

'My girlfriend kicked me out, just before lockdown.'

His addiction is going to destroy him sooner or later. 'How are getting by though? Food? Drink? And other stuff?' Jay asks. 'Anything we can get you?' Jay's words snag in my head. It feels as if we are in this together, a couple. Like me, Jay doesn't seem worried about catching the virus. Jules needs our help. His desperation calls for the rules to be dropped, for us to show kindness and compassion rather than worrying that Jules might have the virus. It's a risk we must take, and it doesn't cross my mind that we should keep a safe distance.

'I'm fine, but if you're passing, I'd appreciate a coffee. Two sugars and milk.' I smile. It's unlikely we'd just be passing, out here in this field but I want to help him.

'I can come back tomorrow. Anything else you need?' I ask.

'Some more batteries for my radio. It takes three As. If you've got any.'

'How are you feeding yourself?' Jay asks.

'I get by.'

Jay and I look at each other confused. Jules is hardly going to survive by foraging for berries in the hedgerow.

Seeing our confusion, Jules elaborates, but there's wariness in his eyes. 'The pub's still doing takeaways. I know one of the blokes that works in the kitchen. He leaves a meal outside for me every night.'

PROMISING to Jules that we'll come back to see him, we continue our walk along the river. Discovering an old friend pitched up in a dirty pillbox was a massive shock. Our focus has shifted to Jules. We want to help him. There's an explosion of questions, each one teasing thoughts and opening new conversations. Now that we've finished hurling accusations at each other it's as if we're learning to ride a bike again. Our chat is wobbly at first but soon the words flow. 'What can we do to help Jules?' It's refreshing to talk about someone else's problems. And, 'Isn't it a shame that he can't turn his life around?'

But there are times when a small stone of sorrow sinks to the pit of my stomach when Jay shows me snippets of his life. It feels as if he's spent the past twenty-five years cheating on me, leading a furtive existence. Silly, I know. And then, as we start to relax, it's as if our time apart has been an interlude and that we are here now to make a go of it again - which of course we most definitely aren't. And then my mind plays out different scenarios, imagining how things might have been if we'd stayed together. Between conversations, when there's silence, I ask myself, can I ever forgive him for leaving me? Do I really understand why he left? And I realise I'm still having a hard time grappling with his reasons, still not understanding. But I'm trying to. I want to see things from his point of view. I can't carry this heavy grudge in my heart forever. I have to accept that he had his reasons, I have to let the burden lift.

He's picked up a slight American accent, it's quite sexy,

makes him sounds more worldly, less insular. 'You should see New York, it's full of homeless people, carrying their stuff in supermarket trolleys, but you'd love it, Dee, have you been there?'

'Yes, it's the same in Sydney. Lots of homeless. No, I've not been to New York, but you'd love Sydney, have you been?'

'No. What made you go to the other side of the earth? Not exactly easy to get back to England.'

'I went to stay with my Auntie Edna and Uncle Reg in Brisbane. They were lovely. They helped me get settled and then I found a job and met new friends.'

'I thought they lived in Leicester.'

'They emigrated to Australia.'

'Wow, that's a surprise.'

'Their son, my cousin Steve and his family were out there. They wanted to be close to their grandchildren, but I think he misses his garden. It was his pride and joy.'

'You needed a change too? You can understand where I was coming from then?'

A shadow seems to fall between us. We are back there, dealing with the issue that's caused me so much pain. Jay leaving me. He's explained and in detail, but I realise now that no, I still don't get it. Maybe I never will. If he'd loved me, he wouldn't have gone. 'Jay, you bailed out on me. Without a word. It was totally different.'

Jay turns and stares at me and stepping closer he places his hands on my shoulders, a soft look on his face that I remember from years ago.

'There's only one thing you need to know. Dee, I never stopped loving you.'

Even though I see the love burning brightly in his eyes and I feel a flutter across my chest, I look away. I'm not falling for this. They're just words. It's easy to use the word love, it can be turned on like a tap; it's a convenient get-out clause because it shuts the other person up. And after all, what can I possibly say in reply? I feel myself melting inside. That's what he wants. Am I supposed to be flattered? I'm no fool and I won't be taken for one. So much time has passed. He's found love, he's lost love. We both have. We've moved on. He takes his hands from my shoulders and looks away, embarrassed.

Having felt weak hearing the word love, my strength is back, my head is in control. 'You could have come back, but you didn't. You started a new life.'

'I didn't think you'd want me, not after what I'd done. But I kept writing to you hoping you'd understand, hoping you'd ask me to come back. But you didn't get the letters.'

'Look, Jay, we both found our feet again. I'm sure you've had lots of relationships over the years. I know I have. I've thought about you, of course I have, but the pain of losing you...well it did get easier. I found love again several times. Neither of us are weak people. We're strong and even though we'd been together for so long, we did find love again. I don't want to know all about in ins and outs of who you've shagged and shacked up with over the years and I'm sure you don't want to know the gory details of my life either. But life didn't stop just because we broke up.'

'Did you try to contact me?' He asks with a vulnerable expression on his face.

'Yes, at first, of course. I'm not going to flatter you by telling you I didn't stop loving you and searched the whole of New York for you. For Christ's sake you left me.'

'I know. Stop reminding me.' He's angry now. I see it in his eyes and taut face. 'I feel a complete shit. I've felt a shit for years. If I could turn back the clock I would.'

'Just stop it. What's done is done.' I start walking again and he follows.

'Have you been back here often?' I sense he wants to move the conversation on. It had become stagnant, stuck.

'This is the first time I've been back to England,' I tell him.

He stops walking and looks at me with a puzzled expression. 'Why so long?'

'Like you I had to escape. I went to book a flight several times, but I couldn't. I'd get a panic attack and start hyperventilating. It was very hard. I missed my family so much. I didn't want to face the memories back here of us and our children. And like you, I didn't want to live in fear of every car passing through the village wondering if it was that bastard driver.'

He holds my gaze for a few seconds, long enough for me to feel something pass between us. I quickly look away feeling my cheeks flush. Was he about to walk over and hug me? Maybe it was just a look of understanding that we both share the same fears, nothing more.

By the time we reach the road leading back to the village to complete a full circuit, we've covered lots subjects. On the road, walking along the verge it becomes difficult to chat, with him two metres in front, keeping a good social distance. After a while we give up talking and walk in silence. The next time he speaks we are nearly in the village. No cars have passed at all. Turning to check for traffic, Jay steps into the road walking beside me instead, at a safe social distance. We pass a row of cottages where a child is playing hopscotch along the pathway. Two cottages have children's rainbow paintings taped to the windows and the third cottage has a banner saying, 'Thank you NHS.' During the Coronavirus pandemic the rainbow has become a symbol of support for NHS workers on the frontline. The trend was started by a nurse who wanted to create a sign of hope for patients and staff in hospitals across the country.

'Pretty cottages,' I comment. 'It's so quiet. I can't remember the last time I saw a plane in the sky and isn't it nice with no cars on the roads?'

'It's like how it was when we were kids. As if life has rewound back to the seventies,' Jay says.

Passing another cottage, again the scene is idyllic. A mother is sitting in the front garden peeling potatoes on her lap, her gurgling baby lying on a rug at her feet. My heart does a flip, and Jay on seeing the scene, quickly looks away with a sad look on his face.

Reaching the apple orchard, we stop and lean over the gate.

Conjuring memories of walking through these orchards together on damp, misty late afternoons, the dank smell of autumn in the air, I ask, 'Do you remember scrumping apples?'

'Apples right off the tree - they taste so much better. No chemicals, no plastic packaging.' Jay is so much more relaxed than he was a while back.

I'm enjoying the view, the twisted boughs of each tree, the buds in their vibrant hues belonging in the spring air, all of nature's potential in those buds, as much as the birdsong and the fluffy white clouds.

'What can we do about Jules?' I ask.

'I had an idea just now when we were walking along the road.'

I laugh. 'I hope it doesn't involve him coming to live at Dad's.'

'Nothing like that. The government wants people off the streets during the pandemic and so councils have been given government funding to move rough sleepers into hotel accommodation. Thousands are being helped through the scheme. They're even being offered counselling support over the phone while staying in the hotels. In Brighton every rough sleeper is being offered accommodation.'

'Why though?'

'It's a public health emergency. They want everybody inside and safe. I guess it's all part of the stay at home message. Talking of which, we've been out for hours. We should be getting back. We're only supposed to go out for a short daily exercise.'

'Who's to know?'

'You never know who's watching. Anyway... my idea. I was thinking we should ask the landlord at the King's Head if he'll take Jules in. They're a hotel as well as a pub.'

'Brilliant idea. We can but ask.' I turn to him and we smile at each other. It's a comfortable, warm smile. Helping Jules is something we both feel passionate about. Something's changed between us. It's only small, but noticeable. I wonder if he feels it too. I'm not sure what it is but something is starting to click back into place. I'd like to see him again, just to talk, tie up loose ends, ask questions in my head that might still be niggling, but above all it would be nice to have company on a walk. But he's with Mel and she'd find it strange if he arranged to meet his ex. And she'd be right; maybe it is.

We resume our walk. Rounding the bend, the bus stop comes into view and next to it the small housing estate where Jay and I lived together. Six homes face the road with magnificent views over the fields and down to the river. They were built as council houses but from the late seventies they began to be sold off. As council houses, they were drab and uniform, with identical front doors and plain gardens. I don't want to stop to reminisce. For this is where our problems started. It's where Sophie and Poppy were conceived, where we spent our married life. Jay stops and I realise it's not to take stock of memories. Front doors are opening. Families are spilling into front gardens. It's eight o' clock - the time when we, as a nation, applaud the NHS. The sound of clapping, cheering and wooden spoons hitting saucepan lids fills the street. A little boy leans out of an upstairs window playing a flute and people are waving across their gardens to each other. Our clapping hands join the thunder of gratitude which resounds across the village, eerily hushed for most of the day. It seems odd to be here again, in this special national moment, heavy with emotion and I can't help myself, my eyes fill with tears. Is it the wonderful communal atmosphere, or am I struggling like everybody else to absorb the huge changes of the past weeks as well as Dad's death or the emotions of meeting Jay again after such a long time? How many times have I imagined this? How many versions have played through my mind - the angry, the passionate, the blasé versions? Here we are, we've struggled, we've both moved on. I wonder what he notices in me. Have I changed? Am I a better person? He's guarded, he's kept his thoughts close to his chest but over the past few hours I've seen every emotion: anger, sadness, regret.

As we clap, an old man dressed in full Scottish attire steps onto his doorstep and raising a bagpipe to his mouth, makes a loud noise. Jay and I look at each other and burst out laughing and in a few brief moments it's as if everything between us flutters to a rest, like feathers after a pillow fight. With aching hands having clapped so much, I give up, turning to watch the sun melting behind the trees in dusty amber shafts, the colour of fire hearths and tangerines. It's a magical moment, like the first stab of love and it's almost as if we are meant to be here, sharing the spirit of the clap, and now this blaze of colour, together, because it's healing and restorative. Neither of us is keen to reach for our phones to capture the sky; we're too mesmerised by its beauty. Everything else pales into insignificance. It's humbling, a religious moment of sorts, making me think of greater and deeper things than the narrow world of Jay and Dee. We're just a dot on the landscape of time, but the forces of nature are stronger. Glancing at Jay I think he's feeling the same, though I can't be sure. I'd give anything for him to touch me right now. But we've travelled too far down the road of separation to swing round and make grand gestures of regret and longing. Our relationship is severed. Today is the start of our goodbye journey, putting everything to rest.

Darkness gathers and with sadness in my heart we continue into the village. The pub is lit up although it's closed. There's a notice pinned to the door about remaining shut for the foreseeable future and a phone number to order a takeaway meal.

'Shall we go round to the back, see if we can catch anyone?' I suggest.

At the back of the pub the fire door is propped open with a chair. 'Anyone there?' Jay calls.

A young chap in a white apron comes into the corridor. 'Can we speak to the landlord please?'

After waiting for a few minutes, a burly guy with a grey beard, also in a white apron comes out to speak to us. He wipes his wet hands on his apron and asks us how he can help. I know from his expression that he's expecting a complaint about his food and when we explain why we've come, his face changes to one of curiosity.

'I'm a hotelier as well as a publican. My job is to look after people. A very long time ago I was homeless. I understand their predicament. People like that need a safe haven during this crisis. A pillbox, you say? The poor bugger can't sleep in a pillbox. I'd like to help, but it's a difficult situation, we don't know how long this whole thing's going to go on for.'

'I think the council are providing funding for hotels to house the homeless,' Jay says.

The landlord's thoughtful. 'He could be useful in the kitchen. I've just lost my odd job boy.'

'He wouldn't give you any trouble. He's not an alcoholic. I grew up with him. I can vouch for him,' I say.

'Let me take your number and I'll give the council a ring in the morning. I can't promise anything mind.'

After the conversation, Jay offers to walk me home because it's now dark but I don't want him going out of his way, and walking home alone will help me reflect on the day.

The awkwardness between us returns when it comes to saying goodbye. Neither of us knows what to say and I'm not sure what, if anything has been resolved. Down by the river he said he'd forgiven me. Was that what I wanted to hear? But then I saw anger in his eyes and in his words, a flash of bitterness. But clapping together and watching the sun go down felt special and relaxed. Do I want to see him again? Or am I just yearning for company?

'Thanks for hearing me out, Dee. Let me know when you want to get on with the divorce.'

His cold, matter-of-fact words slice through me. So, this is it? It's over. But Dee, I chastise myself, your marriage was over twenty-five years ago. What were you expecting? A tearful reunion?

I'm about to turn away from him to head up the hill when our attention is caught by Mel waving from across the road. My belly clenches at the sight of her. She's so beautiful, her skin is flawless, and worst of all her stomach is flat, like mine used to be before children. I don't want to talk to her, I know my words will be coated in resentment and she'll pick up on it. But it's too late, she's coming over.

'Hi, Dee,' she says, looping her arm through Jay's.

I smile through gritted teeth. 'Your ankle better now?' I ask coldly.

'All good now isn't it, love?' Jay says looking lovingly at her. How cringey, he never used to call me love or any cute pet name. And the way he's looking at her. My insides twist remembering how Jay and I used to be - just like them. I can't wait to escape.

'Thanks, Dee, for giving us a lift the other day. I know it was risky, but I appreciate it.'

'No problem, see ya,' I say rushing away. I hate that woman, Mel and I don't think she likes me either.

31

Last night's glorious sunset brings a beautiful day. There's not a single cloud in the pale enamel blue sky as I saunter round Mum's herb garden mid-morning, smelling the chives and rosemary, listening to blackbirds while contemplating all the weeding that needs doing. The other day I rang a few gardeners but they all said they are in lockdown.

Sitting on the bench in the afternoon, I ring Pandora to tell her about her brother, Jules.

'How are things with you?' I ask.

'Good thanks, I'm managing to keep busy in lockdown, doing exercises against the kitchen worktop, watching *Killing Eve* and I've sorted out my shed. I'm missing friends though. Such a shame you came back during this awful time. I was hoping we could do a pub crawl, visit all our old haunts. How are you?'

'It looks like I'll be stuck here for a while so I might as well get used to this solitude.'

'Oh, for God's sake... Sorry Dee, I'm just looking through my net curtains. That's the fifth person I've seen go through the neighbour's door. Would you believe it? They must be having a party.'

'Really? Some people ah? Think the law doesn't apply to them.'

'Shall I call the police?'

'I wouldn't bother wasting police time. The police are probably inundated with similar calls from pious, holier-than-thou twats, killjoys and do-gooders.'

'I think I will do in a minute. I feel like I should be a good citizen. It's disgusting. Yesterday when I was out, I saw a big table of about twenty people around it in someone's garden. Just because the weather's so nice doesn't give them an excuse to flout the law. That couple opposite though, they've had visitors to their house for two days in a row. Am I missing something Dee? What part of "stay at home to save lives, protect the NHS" is difficult to understand?'

'I wonder what the police would say?'

'They could all get fines but it's a shame we haven't adopted the tough Spanish policy. Immediate on the spot fines, simple but effective.'

'Well, anyway, there we are... I was ringing because I saw Jules yesterday.'

'Where is he? Mandy kicked him out a few weeks ago, I know that much. He wanted to come here, but if I'd let him, I'd never get rid of him.'

'Yeah, it's tough. He's been kipping in a pillbox.' I don't tell her that Jay was with me at the time. 'In a field by the river. I found him there when I was on a walk.'

'Strewth.' It's silent while she digests the news. 'What about food and how is he washing?'

'Scavenging in bins, so he says. Washing in the river?'

She sighs. 'Well at least he's managing to get by. He just needs to get his life together. He's got a small daughter. You'd think that would be enough incentive.'

'Yeah, you'd think so. I actually dropped by at the the King's Head to ask the landlord if he can stay there, at least till lockdown ends. I've heard that some hotels in London are taking in homeless people while this is going on.'

'That's really kind of you, Dee. He's not a bad person...'

'I know.'

'The doorbell's ringing. Probably my Amazon delivery, got to go. Stay safe, ring me later, tell me what happens.'

'You too,' I reply before ending the call. Stay safe. It's something that everyone now says to each other, but to me it always sounds as if the recipient of such a warning is planning to do something dangerous like get tarted up to walk along a dark and dangerous alley where there are likely to be drug dealers and other dodgy characters.

I close my eyes and stare at the sun. Being here really isn't so bad - until the weather breaks. That's the cynic inside me. Fingers crossed it lasts for weeks. British weather is so unpredictable. There's a comforting feeling knowing that everyone else's life is on hold right now. Each day merging into the next, a daily regime of quiet solitude and reflection, pausing to appreciate life's simple pleasures rather than dashing around at full pelt, never achieving very much apart from headaches, agro and a wage packet to fritter away on rubbish we don't need.

But I'm alone, trapped on my own hamster wheel heading nowhere. With my marriage about to be finally turned over to the lawyers, the next chapter of my life is a work-in-progress.

IT'S mid-afternoon by the time I get the phone call from the landlord. His name is Rich and he tells me he's run the pub for fifteen years.

'Can you tell your mate he can move in, only temporary mind.'

'That's wonderful, thank you so much.'

'If I can do a good turn I will. Fetch him over. He'll be useful so he will.'

After the call I immediately ring Jay. He's delighted. 'That is good news.' Hearing this phrase takes me back and I smile. That was always Jay's standard stock saying to pretty much everything positive that happened. 'Probably best we both go. We can tell him together, then help him over to the pub. Wish we could drive him there, from where the field meets the road, but it's not far to walk and probably best not to drive given the lockdown.'

'Yes, quite. Can you meet me by the river bridge then, in say half an hour?' I suggest. I sense an eagerness inside me to see him again and quell it. Stop it, Dee.

MEETING JAY this time feels hurried as if he wants to get it over and done with and get back to Mel. He sets a pace and I have to run to keep up. Silence folds across the field and he doesn't seem keen to disturb it. Slowing to climb the stile into the next field he stops, catching his breath, taking a moment to survey the landscape as if noticing it for the first time.

'Hasn't changed much has it, the village?'

'No. Very little new housing or other development since...' I'm about to say since we were here twenty-five years ago, but I stop myself. It might lead us into a repeat of yesterday's tortured conversation. I glance at him. A flicker of pain darts across his eyes for the briefest of moments. I wonder what he's thinking, dwelling on the past maybe.

We continue along the field, our trousers brushing cow parsley in the shaded part of the field. So abundant at this time of year and on into the summer. I love the simple spray of white frothy flowers. When we were teenagers walking these fields, we'd pull sprigs and sieve the tiny flowers through our fingers.

We cross the bridge where yesterday's argument became heated and head over towards the pillbox. When the small concrete structure comes into view I stop. Something doesn't feel right. I can't hear music or any other sound of human activity. I have a bad feeling about this. Jay carries on walking and I resist the urge to pull him back. If Jules is dead, I'd rather that Jay discover the body. You hear harrowing stories all the time about corpses being found in derelict buildings. Jules looked awful when we found him crouched on the cold floor. Pandora said he could only have been there a few weeks but how can she be sure? He may have been struggling to survive for longer than that.

Ducking his head, I watch Jay disappear into the pillbox. Taking a deep gulp of air, every muscle in my body taut, I wait for voices before expelling my breath with relief. They're talking for a while and I begin to worry. Maybe Jules doesn't want to leave. But why would anyone want to live in a pillbox? He won't survive the winter. He'll need plastic sheeting around the firing slits and insulating boards to line the floor and something to cook on. At some point he'll be discovered and shunted on.

Jay emerges first, followed by Jules. I gasp at the sight of him standing here in the open. He's gaunt, unkempt, his clothes are filthy and I wonder if I should take him home first so that he can clean himself up. He can even wear some of Dad's clothes. There are piles of trousers, shirts and jumpers that will only end up at the charity shop. Rich, the landlord might change his mind if he sees him in this state.

'I'm okay here,' he says. 'It's nice by the river, safe and quiet, better than being in a town centre where you can get set alight or pissed on.'

I frown at him. 'Jules, it won't be nice when the weather turns bad.'

'I wanted to see what it was like to go off grid, a free man on the land. That pillbox was my castle.'

'Take the landlord up on his offer while you can, please. It'll give you a chance to think and maybe even salvage your relationship with Mandy.'

Jay looks at me with warmth as if he's silently telling me that I'm a kind and caring person. But I could be wrong. His face is a map of shifting expressions I'm unable to read.

Jules gives a morose shake of his head. 'She won't have me back. It was her way or the highway.'

'You'll get some good food over at the pub. A full English breakfast. Imagine all that sizzly bacon,' I coax.

I watch Jules's mind ticking over. There's a twinkle in his eyes. It's too tempting an enticement to miss. Would be for anyone. He gives me a wide open-mouthed smile revealing teeth that look like dirty pebbles and without saying anything adjusts his battered rucksack on his back, flings his dirty sleeping bag over his shoulder and starts to walk in the direction of the road.

Nearly at the road, Jay pushes brambles from the stile so that we can climb over.

'Do you want to come back to my place first, Jules? You can have a bath and change into fresh clothes. Dad died a couple of weeks ago. There's a whole wardrobe of clothes.'

He turns to look at me through eyes that look like cold, hard bullets and it's as if a storm cloud has passed over his face. 'No,' he says.

'It's not a problem, only a suggestion.' I'm embarrassed, shouldn't have said anything.

Jay looks puzzled. 'Dee's only trying to help, mate.'

'I'm not wearing a dead man's clothes.'

His harsh words hit me like an axe. With tears springing to my eyes Jay smiles at me in sympathy but he doesn't rush to give me a hug. I hate this feeling of being a leper, that I could have the virus. That any of us could have the virus so we've all got to be careful. It's doing my head in. I just need a damn hug.

'All right, calm down. It was just an offer,' I say. Shocked, I'm barely able to speak. I reach out for the stile to lean on.

'Dee,' Jay says in a calm voice, 'I'll take Jules to the pub, I'll come back in a bit.'

'No, don't bother, I just want to be alone. I'll make my own way home.'

32

I spend the next morning mooching round the garden, then in the afternoon I lie on the grass staring up at the clouds scudding across the sky. In the evening I settle down to watch *Normal People* on BBCiplayer, but I soon lose the thread of the story, my concentration interrupted by loneliness invading my head. I'm simply staring at the telly aware that the only heart beating in this house, other than the dog's, is my own. Next to me are the empty spaces where Mum, Dad and Andrew once sat. When I sniff the air, I can smell their lingering ghosts. I close my eyes and pretend we're all here: Dad is stoking the fire, Mum is still wearing her apron and Andrew is reading a novel by Neville Shute. I long for a hand to hold or an arm about my shoulders. To break the spell of social distancing that's been imposed on us, the cruel cage of self-isolation and shielding - just to feel the touch of another human being, but friends and loved ones feel like paper chains fluttering in the breeze. I'm existing and I'm breathing, like the strum of a guitar. I mean nothing to anyone and out on the street I'm a pariah, just another potential carrier of the virus. I may as well wear a sack and carry a bell. Alone I sink deeper into my own music of grief.

In bed my mind churns on in the darkness like a motor. While others embrace their dreams, I toss and turn, my brain on overdrive. For most of the past twenty-five years a rage towards Jay has burned bright, curled inside me like a coiled spring, reminding me I was rejected, tossed aside, my feelings didn't count. What did he expect, that I'd just pick myself up, dust myself down because I'm a woman, it's what we women do, we're strong? You were wrong, Jay. This woman was frail, she crumbled without your support, without you beside her at night. Lost in a sea of grief, no lighthouse to guide me back to shore. I stare at the ceiling and ask, how could a man leave his grieving wife?

Cutting into those deep-rooted thoughts are fresh one catching me unawares. Jay deserves my forgiveness. Am I really thinking this or is it just middle-of-the night confusion? I saw pain and sadness in his eyes yesterday. People don't put that on. It was real. I know he regrets what he did, I know he forgives me, is deeply saddened. And the knowledge that he tried to contact me, pouring out what he went through in letters. How hard must it have been for him to write them? Jay deserves to be heard, he deserves my forgiveness, just as I deserve his. We're frail creatures, we lost both of our children. And I expected too much from him. What made me think he was strong? I had no right to think that.

I spread my arms, feeling the cool cotton sheet. Something seems to lift from my chest. Have I finally conquered the burden of anger I've carried for so long?

'THOUGHT I'D RING you to let you know how yesterday went with Jules.'

Sweat's pouring down my back, I'm desperate for a bath,

but there's no hot water. I rang the helpline number pinned to the boiler to be told that because of the Coronavirus lockdown, they are only attending emergencies. A man with a thick accent tried explaining how I could fix the problem, but I couldn't understand him. I've wasted most of the morning peering up into the gloom of the boiler's undercarriage wondering which lever to push but too scared to try in case it breaks.

'Can it wait? I'm trying to fix the boiler. Not having much luck though.'

'The boiler's broken? I might be able to help you.'

'No, you can't. You've got your elderly mother to think of. We shouldn't be mixing with different households. That's the rule.'

'That's true.' Jay breaks off, 'What, Mum? I can't hear Dee and you at the same time. I've only got one pair of ears. Yes, her boiler's broken...no, I'm not going round there to fix it.'

He sighs in my ear. 'She's insisting I help you. Hang on a minute Dee...what now Mum?'

'What's she saying?' I ask.

'Stuff you've heard before. How her family's home was flattened by a doodlebug but luckily Nan had a premonition and took the family to the street shelter that particular night. How she survived the bitter winter of 1947. Basically, Dee, she's not at all worried about catching this virus. She refuses to stay in. Every morning she's up the shop joining the queue for a good old natter, laughing and joking.'

'The good old blitz spirit.'

I try to imagine his mum twenty-five years on. We didn't stay in touch over the years. I liked her feisty ways. She was always busy helping others and unlike my own mother, she didn't judge people. Jay's mum never minced her words and if she didn't approve she'd make it known, but my mum would quietly disapprove, then gossip behind your back. When Jay left, his mum took my side, telling me, 'I don't know what's got into him, dear. He needs to come back and look after his grieving wife.'

'Hang on a minute, Dee, she's saying something else.'

I can't hear them talking, Jay must have pressed the mute button. A minute later he surprises me and says, 'I'm coming round,' before hanging up without saying goodbye.

When the doorbell rings my stomach swills with nerves. Pippin starts barking, following me, her tail wagging as we approach the door. I play out in my mind how Jay will react, coming here after all these years. Not much has changed. The same paintings hang on the walls, the furniture hasn't changed and even the kitchen's not been updated. But the house is Grade II listed and even without a fresh lick of paint, like an aging film star or a retired ocean liner it can never lose its beauty. But the memories don't fade with time. If I close my eyes and concentrate, every room evokes something: the lounge where one New Year's Eve Jay cracked open champagne and the cork broke a lamp. Mum sitting at the helm of the long oak refectory table in the dining room apologising because the quiche she'd made was too soggy, and Jay accepting a big portion onto his plate out of politeness. Jay and me watching the first episode of *Eastenders* together. And the last episode of *Dallas*.

I pause to glance in the hall mirror, realising what a sight I am today wearing an old baggy shirt and crumpled linen trousers. Having worn make-up pretty much every day since I was fourteen, I've hardly worn a scrap of make-up during the past month and am starting to forget to put it on. All-in-all lockdown has made me care less about my appearance, until now that is. But it's too late.

When I open the door, I find Jay gazing up at the roof. He's had a haircut. It's very short at the sides and seems greyer than yesterday. His hands are tucked in the pockets of stone-washed ripped jeans and his shirt is untucked. Jeez, each time

I see him he's mutton dressed as lamb. That'll be Mel's influence.

He gives a hesitant smile through the small gap in his front teeth and looks me up and down. Oh God, I wish I'd changed. He's probably thinking I've turned into my mother. She was always scruffy around the house and about my age when he last saw her.

'Hi. You've had a haircut. But all the barbers are closed.'

'It's not what you know,' he says, tapping the side of his stub nose, 'I have my very own Covid coiffeur. Mel bought a pair of clippers on Amazon.' Ugh, does he have to keep mentioning that woman's name? Twisting the knife. Forcing me to imagine them draped over each other on the sofa whispering sweet nothings into each other's ears.

I let him in, pinning myself against the wall to give him a wide berth before going outside to check if anybody saw him come into the house. Knowing my luck that noisy woman next door will be poised to report me. 'That's okay,' I chuckle, 'bit worried about the neighbours.'

'I didn't notice anyone,' he says, not appearing to care.

'You're right to worry about your mum, but hopefully I'm not carrying the virus.'

Instinctively, like I would any other guest, I lead him into the kitchen. It would be odd if I took him straight upstairs.

'Strange to come here after all this time,' he says peering round.

'Has been for me too. I feel unhinged and restless. I don't know how to make this place feel like home even though it was my home for many years.'

'It's a beautiful place, you were lucky growing up here. At least compared to growing up in a council house like I did. I always loved spending time here. It was an escape from the madhouse.' He goes to stand at the window and looks out over the front garden. 'I remember Sophie...oh never mind.' His voice trails off and silence descends between us. I stare at his back wondering what he's remembering but he doesn't share his thoughts with me. He sniffs, turns round, his eyes glazed over. 'Where's the boiler?'

'Upstairs.' He follows me up the stairs, his big feet heavy on each step, making me recall my annoyance when he used to come to bed late after marking homework and wake Sophie. Jay can't do quiet. He stomps, thumps and scrapes.

As I open the door to the boiler, Jay hovers behind me. He's too close. How easy it is to forget social distancing. His warm breath and woody scent jar me, reeling me back to a different time. Turning slightly, I clock the hairs escaping through his open shirt, the perspiration on his neck and quickly I step aside breathless, a tight band moving across my chest.

I watch him bend down, turning to lie on his back peering up at the controls, the bulge in his trousers, his shirt slipping up to reveal just a small flash of tanned flesh. In that moment I realise something. My body still yearns for him. It's raw and primal. I'm caught in a purgatory of attachment; he's not left my heart. What's wrong with me? Stop it, Dee. I look away.

'Simple. It's the middle lever.' There's a whooshing noise as the pressure readjusts. 'Check the water,' Jay orders.

Snapping from my thoughts I go to turn the tap on in the bathroom.

'All good,' I call to him. I'm suddenly struck by an unsettling feeling of déjà vu or a glitch of the brain. We've been here before, many times fixing appliances when we were together in our own home.

Why do I have this sudden longing for him? Maybe it's just loneliness. I can't help it. I should still be feeling angry towards Jay. He left me. He didn't care about what happened to me. He moved on. I didn't matter. But my anger, where's it gone? It's as if it's fluttered away. All I've been thinking about are his words. I've never stopped loving you, Dee. When he'd said them, I'd been transfixed, spellbound, horrified even. Maybe he hadn't meant it. Perhaps it had just gushed from his mouth without thought or consideration for how I'd feel. But I've had time to daydream, replaying the words in my head. And I do know one thing. I like him. I like him a lot. I'd forgotten how much. When he'd expressed those feeling I'd felt a bolt of tenderness touch my heart. But Dee, it doesn't matter what I feel, he's in a relationship with Mel.

33

After Jay fixes the boiler, I make him coffee and we take our steaming mugs into the garden. Heavy duvet clouds drift across an azure sky and a cathedral of birds sing from the branches of the old oak tree in the field beyond the garden. Jay digs his hands into his pockets and his posture seems to stiffen as we walk past the tree - the site where his dad was killed by the herd of cows. It went to court and there was a formal inquiry. Dad wasn't found to be negligent.

'Andrew told me what happened. I'm really sorry.'

'I was living in New York. I didn't put in the complaint, just so you know. And I've never harboured a grudge against your dad. It was a terrible accident. But my brother Simon and my sister Sam are bitter to this day.'

'A freak accident. Cows seem such docile creatures,' I say. 'You miss him I expect?'

'I missed everybody when I left for New York.'

In the silence that follows I feel a prickle of hurt as I wait, giving him this opportunity to tell me that he missed me too.

'You've got lots of friends in New York?'

'Yes, it's a great city. One of the coolest places on earth. It's exciting, there's so much to do and see but it's also overwhelming. I like coming back here for a rest. It's a much slower pace of life, less frenetic.'

'You're going back, when lockdown ends?'

He pauses. 'Actually, I'm not sure. Being back has made me realise how much I've missed my folk. It's been such a great family bonding time. Half the family have been stranded at Mum's. There are bodies everywhere. Three in one bedroom, two sleeping in the lounge, one in a tent in the garden, luckily the weather's been good. We descended on her because of my niece's wedding which was cancelled because of the lockdown. My niece hasn't seen her fiancé since March.'

Such a different experience to my lonely lockdown experience. 'Your mum must have loads of grandchildren.' Jay is one of six.

'Yeah, twenty.'

So many. Makes me wonder if his mum has long forgotten about Sophie and Poppy.

'I was really looking forward to Mel's wedding,' he says.

'Mel?'

'My niece, Mel. You met her.'

I look at him, stunned. 'I thought Mel was your girlfriend.'

He laughs. 'I'm very flattered, Dee. Have you any idea how old she is?' He's beaming at me, his eyes are twinkling.

'No idea.' My cheeks are turning pink. I can't believe what an idiot I've been. 'I thought the new look, ripped jeans, Vans was to appeal to your much younger girlfriend.'

When his laughter dies there's a strange moment of stillness. Something inside me soars. It's as if the whole world has stopped, leaving just the two of us alone to sort out our futures. 'So what about you?' Jay asks in an upbeat tone. 'You're heading back to Oz?'

I sit on the bench overlooking Mum's herb garden and Jay stays standing.

'I'm not sure either. Australia is all I've known for so long. Yep, I'll probably go back at some point. But not yet. I'm happy here indefinitely.' I'm surprised by my own words. I thought I'd decided to stay. Maybe I haven't at all. 'I caught my partner, Glen, in bed with somebody else which kind of sucks. Now he's out of the picture I don't have a specific reason to go back.'

'Jesus.' He gives me a sympathetic smile. 'That's something you can't accuse me of doing. I would never two-time.'

I can't resist it, so I ask, 'How do I know what you're capable of, Jay? You were capable of leaving me.'

He stares at the brick path under his feet kicking at a weed sprouting through a crack and says nothing.

'And in terms of work,' I plough on, not wanting to dwell on tired ground, 'I'd just been promoted in Australia, but it's the sort of job I can get anywhere. I've got to stay until the house is sold. That could take months.'

'You're a teacher still?'

'God no, I haven't taught for years. I've not had a career since well…the kids.'

'But you were a good teacher.'

'No, I wasn't.' I stare at him in shock. 'I couldn't cope. The brats were determined to bring me down and they did.'

'You taught in a very challenging school. I couldn't have done it. I admired you so much. It wasn't easy.'

'I didn't know you admired me.'

'Well I did,' he says frowning.

'But you made me stay in that job.'

'No, I didn't. I encouraged you to stay because it looked better on your cv to stick it out for a whole academic year. Believe me I hated seeing you suffer. You used to come home crying every night.'

'Did I? I don't remember. I thought I hid it from you. You were doing so well in your teaching job. I was jealous.'

'Jealous? Dee, what the fudging Nora?'

I'd forgotten, until now his avoidance of swearing. He's sworn so much though each time we've met. 'If I get into the habit of swearing,' he used to say, 'I might do it in the classroom by mistake and end up losing my job so I try hard not to swear.'

'That's the trouble when a married couple do the same job. There's bound to be competition.'

He stares at me, an incredulous look on his face. 'Well I can assure you there never was with me.'

A thought hits me. We've shared our lives but not shared what is really going on in our heads.

I don't want our conversation to turn into a series of recriminations, we'll only argue so I ask about Jules. 'Anyway...how did it go yesterday?' I ask. 'You were a while in the pillbox. He took some persuading?'

'His head was all over the place. At first, he was worried about catching the virus, then I lured him out by suggesting he could have a nice hot bath at the pub. Seemed to do the trick.'

'And I planted the idea of a cooked breakfast.'

'He'll be fine at the pub. What an idiot though to risk everything.'

'Gambling's a nasty addiction.'

'Yep. It's not easy to quit.' We sit down on the lawn and Jay pulls a blade of grass.' 'I can blow louder, let's have a contest.' He takes a sharp intake of breath, his cheeks filling like a hamster, making me laugh.

Fleetingly we are teenagers again - that lovely time in our lives when there were no responsibilities or worries and the future held only hope and promise of good things to come. Jay falls onto his back to stare at the sky and as he does so, several small balls covered in powder fall from his pocket.

'Are they what I think they are?' I ask.

'They certainly are.'

'Oh my God, it's years since I ate a toffee bonbon.'

'They still sell them in The Black Kettle. Probably the reason why I've got so many fillings.'

'Me too.'

'Here, open your gob,' he says, 'let's see what my aim's like. I play basketball and I'm pretty good.'

'Are you suggesting my mouth is a basket?'

'Stop talking, close your eyes and open wide.' I do as I'm told, my mouth watering as I wait. This is the type of thing we used to do long before we were married, but back then it was a sign of our intimacy. I'm not sure what it means now, maybe it's a symbol of lockdown boredom.

True to his word Jay aims well, and my mouth closes around the sweet toffee ball sucking hard but not chewing for fear it will get stuck in my teeth.

'Told you I'm good,' he brags, 'even from two metres away I can do it.'

'Try it further away this time.'

He inches back and closing one eye lines up his target. This time it's hard for me not to giggle. It falls into the grass and as we scramble to retrieve it my hand lightly brushes his. The back of his hand is tanned and lightly covered in hair. He's wearing a silver ring on a finger and he has a leather band around his wrist. There's something sexy about his hand. When a nervous tingle shoots through my body it's as if I'm seventeen again anticipating our first kiss.

He's tossing the bonbon between his hands. 'How much is it worth?' he teases.

'No, you have it,' I say pouting my lips and pretending not to care.

He pops it into his mouth with a cheeky grin and gets to his feet. 'Let's go down to the river again.'

'Don't you have to get back?' I ask.

'Nah, what's the rush? My life's on pause. I don't have a care in the world.'

Getting to my feet I brush my trousers and say, 'Race you down there.'

When we reach the river he says, 'Come on,' unbuttoning his shirt. 'You need some fun. You over-analyse everything.'

'What on earth are you doing?'

'Going for an alfresco dip.' With his shirt off I stare at his tanned, toned chest. He's really not at all bad for a guy of fifty-five. When I think back to all the men I've slept with since him, they've all been pretty ropey.

'You're mad.'

'Come on, get your kit off.'

'It'll be freezing. Somebody died in there once from ingesting something nasty.'

'We'll be fine.'

But although I'm trotting out excuses I'm nearly down to my bra and knickers and Jay has already jumped in wearing just his boxers. 'It's lovely,' he calls up.

'You never used to be adventurous, Jay.'

'Well I am now.'

Teetering on the edge of the bank I clamp my nostrils with two fingers and plunge in before I change my mind. Like him I have a sudden urge to be young and carefree again.

'Freezing, freezing, freezing,' I scream. The temperature doesn't seem to bother Jay, he's splashing around laughing. The cold is wrapping around me. I'm chilled right through to my bones, but I'm enjoying seeing Jay having fun. 'This is a really bad idea Jay. There are probably blood-sucking leeches and ticks which cause Lyme disease.'

He laughs at me and sweeps his arms through the murky water. 'Stop worrying.'

'I'm getting out.'

'Chicken.'

I swim to the shallow beached area, desperate to get out of the bitterly cold water, my feet connecting with shingle and thick slimy mud, pushing through reeds and gripping the bank to hoist myself up.

I'm still shivering moments later when we're both on the bank struggling into our jeans over wet legs.

'I think you were right, Diesel,' he says. 'It is too cold.'

'Diesel? You used to call me that at school.' Funny how a pet name survived into our early twenties but was dropped when we had kids. Why?

'It's a cute nickname.'

He's shivering too but offers me his pullover, which had been slung over his shoulders when we'd walked across the field, too warm to wear. He's making me remember all the small acts of chivalry like opening the car door for me and walking on the outside of the pavement. I don't think any man has ever done that since. But would a true gentleman walk out on his wife without a word? Oh God, I'm done with all this analysing, it's doing my head in. He's explained, that should be enough, he had his reasons. Maybe I'll never fully understand. I'm enjoying his company though. This isn't what I expected to be doing at all when I returned to England.

'Do you want a shower at Dad's?'

'That would be great,' he replies.

Back at Dad's, we shower in different bathrooms. Afterwards he joins me in the kitchen and I make bacon sandwiches.

Finishing his sandwich and pushing the plate away he says, 'That was delicious. What now?'

'I've got apple pies if you fancy one?'

'I didn't mean food.'

He's got a devious look on his face as he swipes ketchup from the corner of his mouth. Heat rises to my cheeks, visions of his toned chest filling my head and making my heart flutter. Is he trying to seduce me? No, don't be silly. I quickly get up turning my back to him so that he can't read my thoughts.

'I was just wondering...'

When I turn to him, I feel my face flush. He has a sheepish grin on his face.

'About building a treehouse,' he says.

'A treehouse?' I feel so stupid and hope my face isn't burning.

'Yeah, why not? I've always wanted to.' This isn't the Jay I thought I knew. Apart from leaving me in a hurry, Jay doesn't do spontaneous, but today he's glorifying his adolescence, determined we should form a 'Kids R Us' pact.

I stare at him perplexed. 'And how are you going to do that?

'I expect there are tools and old bits of wood in your dad's garage,' he says taking his plate to the sink.

'Jay, when did you become so bonkers?'

'I think it's lockdown fever. It feels as if we're back in the 1970s, kids again. What else have I got to get up for in the mornings? I want to sit in a treehouse with a beer and a bag of Walker's crisps. Come on let's do something crazy for a change. What's stopping us?'

'A treehouse is a massive project.'

'Okay, well let's get a bottle of wine and sit by the river. We can start planning how to build it.

'If you say so.'

We could see if the rope's still hanging from the branch further along the river.'

'You're not getting me swinging on a rope.'

I think I like this new Jay, the reckless one, not the one who always used to be bothered about job progression and paying the bills on time. As we run down to the riverbank clutching wine, glasses, snacks and a large picnic rug, I realise something refreshing and emancipating; we're living in the moment. I feel liberated. We're not thinking of the consequences or planning for tomorrow. We can do what we like, we're not beholden to anyone. And neither of us has to prove anything to each other. We're not trying to get back together, we're just passing time till lockdown's lifted. Life is on hold, tomorrow doesn't matter. Neither of us can go anywhere, we're confined to the village. But I'm not sure why he wants to spend time with me. Maybe he's trying to smooth things out, make sure there's no lingering animosity between us before we head for the lawyer's office. Afterall, it's always better to part on good terms.

After a couple of glasses of wine, the alcohol starts to sing in my head and soon the conversation is buzzing and flowing. It's the crutch we both need, and I find myself daring to ask all the questions burning in my head. 'What are American schools like?' 'Do you prefer living in America?'

'Have I changed?' I ask when we've exhausted sharing our stories.

'Not really.' He pulls a blade of grass and is thoughtful. 'But you're bigger.'

'Hey.' I push him.

'In the right places.' He chuckles, squinting against the sun.

'Cheeky.'

'Those too,' he says glancing towards my bottom.

'Come on, be serious. But what about my personality?'

He frowns and considers the question. 'You're still as lovely as you ever were.' He smiles. Our conversation seems to have given way to playful flirting and I'm not resisting. Today I'm going to let my guard down, I'm doing the impossible, I'm here with the one man I thought I'd never see again, let alone spend time with. As we relax I begin to wonder what might have been if we'd stayed together, but I'm not brave enough to talk about these thoughts with Jay.

'You've had too much to drink.' The wine has gone to work on both our bodies. The conversation is easy between us - slowed as if by mutual consent.

'Want some more?' He lifts the bottle.

'Yep, why not?' Today I feel free, crazy and reckless. I don't care how much I drink and whether I have to stagger home.

'Why aren't you settled down with someone?' I ask.

'I've ridden every horse on the carousel.' He laughs, looks over and winks at me. There he goes again, the playful flirting. I quickly look away. This time he seems childish. I don't want to know about his conquests.

'I guess I was looking for some template woman that didn't exist. I did live with someone for a few years, but she cheated on me. Other than her there was nobody I really connected with.'

'Sounds like you've played the field.' I can't look at him. My husband has shagged the whole of New York. I can't help myself; I feel mildly disgusted. But what did I imagine, that he'd spent the past years living the life of a monk?

Jay swigs more wine. 'This is the life,' he says, throwing his empty glass into the bed of buttercups and daisies. Such hardy early summer flowers. Trampled by the weight of our bodies as we lie here staring up at the clouds brush-stroking across a sapphire canvas. The flowers will spring back to life when we get up.

'I don't get it, Jay. Why would you want to spend time with me, your ex?' And why would I want to spend time with him?

He pulls himself up and turns to look at me through drunken eyes, his pupils dilated. 'Because, Dee, I'd forgotten what nice company you are.' It's a shame he didn't realise that twenty-five years ago. It's as if he can read my thoughts because he adds, 'I can't blame you for feeling bitter. I've been torn apart ever since I left. What I did has weighed on my conscience all these years.' I see anguish in his eyes. 'Have you any idea how heartbroken I was? But the longer it went on and with no replies to my letters it became impossible to find a way back to you.'

'Sometimes two people head too far down the road of separation to swing round and turn back.'

'That's how it was.' There's a pause and as I glance at him I can see the thoughts ticking away in his mind. 'Do you remember how we used to finish each other's sentences? How we used to talk long into the night? There was a deep connection between us. But the connection was severed the day that Sophie died.'

I sit up. I don't want to go back to that dreadful day in my mind. I open a bag of Wotsits, shovelling heaps into my mouth because they're so mouthwateringly yummy. Then I wash them down with more wine.

'You don't change.' Jay laughs. 'You used to eat crisps in bed and crumbs would jab me in the buttocks.'

We laugh and he looks at me. 'Here, let me,' he says pulling a tissue from his pocket and dabbing my face. 'You've got an orange rim round your mouth.'

Heat rises to my cheeks. The gesture is so simple, so intimate that my heart tightens. Our eyes connect and something faintly unsettling seems to happen. In a split second I see the possibility of falling in love with him all over again. I know he's going to kiss me and I'm not going to push him away. I want him, I need him. I'm crying out for human contact, for things to be alright between us. It feels so naughty to be breaking lockdown rules, but I don't care, I'm caught in the spell. Tension crackles in the air, butterflies dance in my tummy as he reaches for my head, gently pulling me towards him. I don't resist, I melt into his arms under the warmth of the afternoon sun.

His kisses are soft at first but grow more intense and my desire for him makes my head spin. The kisses are fraught with all sorts of undercurrents and memories. A husband's kisses are supposed to be different, devoid of magic and longing leaving us as familiar as siblings. But this is like a first kiss, the kiss of a passionate lover. I never imagined Jay could kiss like this, leaving me with an intoxicating sensation of a hundred tiny bees' wings tickling the walls of my belly. I can hear his heartbeat, fast and steady against mine, a whiff of Nivea soap on his skin and as tiny jets pulse through me, more than anything I want to take him home to bed and make love to him.

But we don't wait. Tearing our clothes off it happens right here on the bed of buttercups and daisies, my body soaring with excitement and climaxing fast.

'I love you,' he says afterwards, looking at me with his so-familiar grey eyes.

'I love you too,' I reply and in that moment it's the only truth that matters.

34

The rest of the day is spent drawing a plan of the treehouse we're going to build and pottering round the garden. In the evening we flop in front of the tv to watch a Netflix series called *Prison Break*.

Instead of going back to his mum's Jay stays the night. We make love and talk because there's so much to catch up on, until tiredness beats against our eyelids towing us under, our sweaty limbs entwined.

It's early when I wake, the birds are in full chorus. The sun is streaming into the bedroom, another glorious day awaits. How long will this spectacular weather continue? I want to make the most of each day while it lasts. I turn over and watch Jay sleeping hardly able to believe how things have changed in the last twenty-four hours.

The landline rings and Jay stirs. I stroke his head before stumbling out of bed.

'Dee, Tracy.' She sounds flustered. Something's wrong. I have a bad feeling. 'Andrew's been rushed to hospital. Yesterday evening he could hardly breath and he was dripping in sweat. I didn't hesitate when he said he thought he was dying, I called

999. The paramedics arrived, gave him an ECG but they said while his respiration wasn't great his oxygen levels were okay, so they didn't take him in. But in the middle of the night he woke with earache and a rapid heart rate. We rang 999 again and his heart rate was three times the normal resting rate. He said he had a pain in his chest like he'd been stabbed. He's in what they call the 'Red Zone' - the designated ward for Covid-19 sufferers. He's having a blood test to check he's not suffered a heart attack. Dee, I'm scared, what if he dies?'

'All you can do is wait. They won't let you into the hospital. Was the same with Dad. Makes you feel helpless. Oh Tracy, what are we going to do?'

'I'll ring you later. Got to keep the line clear.'

'Of course.'

Putting the phone back on the cradle I'm aware of Jay's naked body behind me. He pulls me into his arms. 'You okay? What's happened?'

'It's Andrew, he was rushed to hospital in the night.'

'Fudging Nora. Not Covid, surely?'

'He was coughing the other day, but he seemed okay. I should have phoned him. Shit why didn't I?'

'Because of us? Our minds have been preoccupied and I guess you've been trying to switch off after the dramas with your dad.'

'What if he ends up on a ventilator, Jay? The chances of him surviving would be slim.'

'Does he have any conditions? Diabetes?'

'No, he's fit and healthy.' I let out a sob. 'I can't lose my brother. He's the only family I've got.'

Jay pulls me into his arms. His back feels sweaty and my face brushes against the bristles on his chin. 'You've got me. But Andrew's going to be okay.' He looks me in the eyes. 'I just know he is. You've gotta believe it.'

'But I haven't really got you. Yesterday was nice, but you're heading back to New York when this is all over. And I'm... I don't know what I'm doing.'

'So yesterday meant nothing to you?' His facial muscles tighten and he pulls away from me.

'Jay, I love you, but we haven't seen each other in such a long time. We've got new lives.'

'But now I've found you I want you back in my life. You don't trust me, do you? I don't blame you. But I want you and I won't ever let you down again.' He sweeps one hand through his hair. 'I want us to make a go of things. Start over. Time's healed both of us.'

The past day has been so wonderful, I'm choked with tears. 'I can't lose you twice. The pain would be unbearable.'

He takes my face in his hands. 'I'm here and I'm going to do whatever it takes to make it work.' He plants a kiss on my forehead. 'I'm committed to you, Dee, I know right now it doesn't feel like it, but please just give me this one chance.'

'Let's not be rash and go making plans, just enjoy each day and see what happens. This is like a new relationship. It's as fragile as a spider's web.'

'You don't believe me and why should you?'

'You say that time's healed us. So you're basically saying that you couldn't bear to be with the broken me all those years ago but now that you assume I've healed it's safe to come back. How insulting is that.' I turn away from him. It feels as if my heart's breaking all over again.

From behind he grabs my shoulders and pulls me round to look at him. 'No, Dee, it's not like that at all. I love you. I'm committed. Losing you was the biggest regret of my life.'

JAY GOES HOME to his mum's soon after breakfast, leaving me to sit in the garden and reflect on everything that's happened between Jay and me and piece it all together. Did it really happen? The easy conversation, the swim in the river and feeling slightly mad, the unexpected exuberance between us and the wine and feeling lighter and less inhibited. The familiarity of his body, the smell of his skin, the passion. Even after so long, that hadn't changed. And the humour. I smile. I remember now how we'd always laughed our way through sex. That was a funny line of his last night when he'd slipped his fingers inside me. What was it? Oh yeah. He'd said I'd been wetter than a wet market in Wuhan. I stare up at the sky and chuckle to myself. What was it he used to say all those years ago? That I was wetter than a wet weekend in Whitby. And how much did we drink? I sigh. Oh God, what the hell am I going to do? My brain is trying hard to make sense of it all.

After a long walk round the fields with Pippin, I can't make any decisions, but I try to focus on the implications of what we'd done. I tell myself it was just one day, one night. It doesn't add up to a new beginning, a fresh start. What a stupid mess I've got myself into. But no matter how hard I try to dismiss what happened, I feel as though I might explode with the joyous madness sitting in the centre of my heart.

Jay insists on coming round for dinner in the evening, bringing with him delicious steak-and-ale pies ordered from the pub's takeaway menu. I know I shouldn't be seeing him again, especially so soon, but there's a large part of me that wants to see him. Because we had such fun yesterday. With trays balanced on our laps we're finishing off the pies when Andrew rings.

'Andrew...Thank God, bro, you're okay. They didn't keep you in long.'

His breathing is laboured and his voice is hoarse. 'I've just got to get plenty of rest. I can't walk far, or stand for long, this has really knocked me for six. Tracy had to wheel me in a chair to the car. Last night...' He breaks off gasping for breath.

'You don't need to tell me the full story now. Right now you should just rest.'

He's wheezing but is determined to carry on. 'I was slicked with sweat and it felt as if there were iron bands around my rib cage. I thought shit, Andy, your time's up, mate. I'm still here, sis. I'm hanging in there. Covid 19 hasn't beaten me.'

Returning to the sitting room I sink into Jay's arms with relief. 'He's home. I thought he'd end up on a ventilator and die.'

'That is good news.' Always Jay's stock answer but it makes me smile. Such a simple and familiar phrase but makes me realise how comforting his little phrases are.

'This pandemic has made me question so much. I may have had some fantastic times in Australia, but twenty-five years is such a long time. I missed my nieces growing up and took it for granted that Mum and Dad would always be here. Time's flown by. Life is precious. Shit I could have lost my brother. As soon as we can I want to go and visit him, there's so much catching up to do.'

'That's why I don't want to waste another moment. I want us to start again. I've pined for you for long enough.'

'Get away with you,' I say playfully. 'You've enjoyed your life without me.'

He shrugs and I don't know whether he is agreeing with me or not.

35

'What?' I ask.

It's mid-morning, a few days after we built the treehouse. Jay is languishing in bed naked, reading something on his phone and chuckling to himself. I'm standing next to the bed, also naked, drying myself after showering.

'Just some crackpot's post on Facebook. Some people have got some daft ideas about this virus.'

'Go on...' I lean towards him, rubbing my hair dry.

'This guy thinks coronavirus was planned, to usher in a new world order. He says it's not a pandemic, but a plandemic with a dark purpose to create a world totalitarian government. He doesn't care how the virus got here or how serious it is. He simply believes, and a lot of others do too, that it's part of a plan to control us all and take our freedoms away.'

'I bet there are a lot of daft theories spinning round the internet. Christians probably think that the Book of Revelations is coming true and it's a war against the anti-Christ. I'm not into conspiracy theories. The government have made mistakes, sure, but they've been faced with a really tough challenge and it's been a steep learning curve on how to deal with a public emergency. Anyway, put your phone down, I want to get back into bed and snuggle into you.'

He puts his phone on the bedside table and gives me a smutty grin. 'I'd like to do more than cuddle you. I want to devour you, kiss you all over, slip inside you and stay there forever.'

'Erm.' I get into bed.

'You smell divine and I'm all sweaty and sticky. Give me a sec,' he says, getting up and planting a kiss on my forehead. He smiles at me. 'Let me jump in the shower and make myself clean and presentable for you. I don't want you accusing me of being a smelly old runt.'

'I don't mind you dirty and stinky - but gift-wrapped is much more appealing.'

I watch him slink over to the ensuite, his dick half-erect. We've been sleeping in Mum and Dad's old bedroom for the past few nights. It felt odd to sleep in their marital bed to begin with, but I'm getting used to it now. While I wait for Jay, I prop a pillow against the headboard and make myself comfortable. I hear Jay turn the shower on and the cubicle door creak as he opens it to step inside. Smiling to myself as I listen to him sing a tune as he washes, a text pings through on his phone. I lean towards the bedside table and out of curiosity I pick up his phone to see who it's from, even though I know I wouldn't like it if he did the same to me. It feels as if I'm snooping on him, but I don't know much about his life. Why haven't I asked more questions? I've been caught up in the moment. Everything's happened so fast. A few weeks ago I hated him. He was my ex. But now look at the pair of us. We're in lockdown together. Living together. A married couple again. It's completely bizarre.

The name Jeanette is on his phone screen. My heart jolts as I read the message. *I wish you were here in bed with me. I wish you could get a plane. I'm missing you. Xxxx*

It feels as if a hurricane has blown through me. This can't be happening. I stare at the bathroom door. I don't know Jay at all. My gut instinct was right all along. I can't trust him. He's a waste of space, weak and pathetic. Why have I been fooling myself these past few days, thinking we can start over again, thinking it can work? What an idiot I've been. How could I allow myself to be lured in?

The shower stops. Shit, what am I going to say to him? He'll be out any moment. I hear the tap turning on, he's brushing his teeth. Then he swills mouthwash. He's really making an effort this morning. Now he's spraying his armpits with deodorant, getting himself spruced for the shag that won't now be happening. I put the phone back on the table and lean over the bed, grabbing my nightie, hastily putting it on before he emerges from the bathroom, a dirty grin on his face, swinging his thing in an exaggerated way as a precursor to lovemaking.

'Oh, why have you put your nightie back on.' He stops at the foot of the bed, frowning.

'Who's Jeanette?' I ask in a dry tone looking at him coolly before turning to pick my clothes up from the floor ready to dress.

'What are you doing looking at my phone?' I hate it when people do this, throw the guilt back at the other person and I don't like the tone he's using.

'Who is she?'

'You don't trust me.' There's a fierce look on his face.

'Jay, what the fuck,' I scream. 'You should read the God-damn message. You're in a relationship. You're playing with me, passing time till you can go back to her, to New York. How could you treat me like this?'

He sits on the edge of the bed and a strong smell of Lynx wafts towards me. The manly smell would have turned me on but now it makes me feel sick, revolted at the thought of him and his hidden life.

He raises his hand towards me, I don't know why. Maybe he's going to stroke me or put his hand on my shoulder, but I stand up before he has the chance to touch me.

'Please, Dee, don't get angry with me. I've got a lot of explaining to do. I'll show you all the texts to Jeanette.'

'Do you know what, I'm through with your bloody explanations. I'm going to call a solicitor today. I'm going to get on with that divorce.'

Jay doesn't respond but emits a deep sigh. With heart hammering in my chest I put my knickers and bra on, then pull my trousers and top on. I need to get away from him, go downstairs. He's not moving, I want him gone, out of this house, out of my life. I'm done with cheating, lying men. I deserve better than this. But before I have the chance to reach for the door handle, Jay grabs me from behind, pushes me onto the bed, my head flinging onto the pillow. He pins me down with one hand and straddles over me gripping my thighs with his knees.

'Get off me.' I wriggle but can't free myself. His right hand is on my chest and he's kneeling over me.

'No, not till you've heard me out.' He reaches for his phone with his left hand and deftly taps the message with his thumb, keying in the passcode and scrolling through the messages. 'Will you please read these.'

'Not until you take your hand off me, you're hurting me.'

He clambers off me and I sit up, pulling me knees to my chin and hugging them. I'm shaking and suddenly feel cold.

'Here, take it,' he says offering me the phone. 'Read the bloody messages.'

I take the phone from him and scroll through their conversation, their break-up messages, his revelations to her about me, his insistence that it's over between them, his laboured apologies. *I'm so sorry. Yes of course I loved you. No, you haven't done anything wrong. I want to get back with my wife. This is where I'm supposed to be, with her. No, I didn't plan any of this.*

Despite reading their conversation I feel wounded. The memory of what happened with Glen is still fresh in my mind. Something doesn't add up. Why would she have sent her latest text, *I wish you were here in bed with me. I wish you could get a plane. I'm missing you. Xxxx.* He hasn't got through to her, he can't have.

'Have you had a conversation on the phone with her, made it up with her, because why would she send that last message?'

He looks stressed, sweeps his hand through his hair. 'I don't know, Dee. Maybe she's deluded.' He takes his phone from me and clicks on call history, pointing the screen at me. 'See, she's not phoned.'

'She might have phoned on your mum's landline.'

He throws the phone onto the carpet and in a stern voice says, 'Shall we forget this whole thing between us. This guy, Glen, has obviously messed you up and given you trust issues.'

'If that's what you want,' I say in a sulky voice.

'No, it's not what I want.'

'Well what do you want?'

'I want you, I want us.'

'But where do we go from here? You live in New York, you've got a job there, a life there.'

'I can live anywhere, Dee. Anywhere you want. Just name the place. Australia? Here, in this village, till you've sold the house? We've got all the time in the world to discuss all this, but bottom line I love you and I don't want to lose you again. We're meant to be together.'

I'm still shaken and can't speak. I stare at my toes trying to digest it all. Is he really that committed to me? I look over at him and he puts his hand on my cheek. Gently tracing his finger across my forehead, moving my hair aside, he kisses me. I find myself weakening under his gaze. His grey eyes are a magnet drawing me in, triggering something inside me and as I look into them, I can't help but feel a strong longing for him. I realise I want to drown in the love and happiness we've experienced these past weeks. I want to hope of better days to come. I want to believe in us. But I also need to use my head and not let my heart rule me.

'Why didn't you tell me about her?'

'It was difficult. I wanted you back.'

'I don't want us to have any secrets. I want complete transparency, okay? I want us to share any problems we have, work things out together. I loathe men who lie. It's an insult to my intelligence, because I will find out you know.'

'You've got to trust me. No snooping.'

'A single lie discovered is enough to create doubt in every aspect of a relationship.'

'That's way too deep for me. Why have you got your clothes on?' He puts his hand on my zip and yanks at it and as he does so my eyes linger on his face. He looks so handsome, rugged and athletic. 'Hey, you look almost scared of me,' he says.

I smile. 'It's just... I feel nervous about the future, but excited too.'

Our lips touch and I hear my breath, shaky and shallow, feel my body trembling uncontrollably as his hand moves down my neck, his finger finding my nipple making my body tingle.

When we make love it's almost brutal, affirmative, tasting every drop of pleasure purging the years of loss and the many misunderstandings between us.

36

Taking a lungful of linen-fresh air I look up at the cobalt sky scribbled with white wispy lines, drawn like musical staves. It's a perfect day for a public holiday. It's Friday 8th May and today marks the 75th anniversary of Victory in Europe Day, or VE Day, the end of the Second World War in Europe.

The welcoming arms of early summer reach out as Pippin and I make our way over the fields towards the village. It's going to be a long weekend of commemorative events across the country and Jay's mother has invited me to the street party she's helped to organise. Jay is already there helping out. It will be the first time I've seen her in twenty-five years and I'm not sure how I feel about that - strange, nostalgic, unsure of how we will be with each other and what she'll look like after all this time. I saw her a few times before I left for Australia asking her to pass on messages to Jay and to find out if he'd been in touch. She was always kind to me but vague when I asked about Jay. She took my side though because what he'd done horrified her. 'I don't know what's got into him, love,' she'd say and, 'I'm ashamed to call him my son, leaving you like that.' She was disappointed in Jay, I always saw it in her eyes and saddened that he'd walked out, not only on me, but his whole family. When I went to Australia, letting go of Jay's family was nearly as hard as letting go of my own family. They were part of my day-to-day life.

I stop to look at the view over the fields, so many thoughts swirling through my head. These past few weeks have forced everybody, not just Jay and me, to take three paces back from our lives seeing ourselves and our lives from a distance. I think the whole nation feels the same way, collectively we've had an out-of-body experience looking at our lives from the outside and determined to change how we do things for the better, reassessing who we are and how we want to spend our lives. But will we skip back into our old ways once lockdown lifts running ourselves ragged seeking again what divides us rather than unites us? I hope not.

Andrew is on the slow road to recovery. He doesn't know how he contracted Coronavirus. He was religious to a fault about lockdown, social distancing and handwashing. Yet in spite of it all he was infected. He was very ill for about a fortnight with pain in every limb, brain fog, exhaustion and headaches. I hope he recovers completely; it's been a worrying time. As soon as we are able to, we will visit him.

I think about the future. Beyond the easing of lockdown there are likely to be restrictions in place covering every area of life for many months ahead until a vaccine is ready and let's hope that vaccine will come. If it wasn't for the lockdown Jay and I might never have rekindled our love for each other. He would have gone straight back to New York after his niece's wedding and I might have headed back to Oz after Dad's passing. But I'm glad we've had this second chance. The past weeks have been about healing and forgiveness and moving on. Jay and I are living in our own bubble, rediscovering each other all over again. We're over the peak of this dreadful virus but there's a lot of talk about a second wave over the winter months. We're in our own second wave - of love and hope and renewed marriage vows. We don't know what the future holds, we're not at the stage of making any plans, but for now we're living in Dad's house until we are able to sell it. Dad's house is on the market, and people who have got a firm offer on their own houses are able to view online only.

I resume my walk. Reaching the cottage-lined hill leading down to the river bridge, every dwelling is draped in Union bunting and trestle tables brim with cakes and sandwiches. There's a cute bicycle with a basket of flowers leaning against the walls. An elderly couple are pouring tea from an art deco teapot. I wave to a mother and her small daughter dressed in blue and red and a Pug with a silver crown on its head barks and bounds over. A child plays hopscotch on a path and another child is hitting a tennis ball against the side of the house. It's a great slice of nostalgia, this could easily be 1977, the Silver Jubilee.

While large-scale public events are not able to go ahead today, I observe patriotic neighbours making the best of the situation taking inspiration from wartime spirit and finding a reason to party in the new norm - socially distancing. This might be the last weekend in lockdown as Boris Johnson, the Prime Minister, mulls over what easing of restrictions he'll announce on Sunday.

Outside the pub, Jules and his new mates - a gaggle of homeless men now residing there during lockdown, raise their beer glasses as I pass. I stop to chat. Jules is having a blast, but it won't last, he'll be out on his ear when lockdown lifts, wondering where to go next. He's tried ringing his girlfriend Mandy, the mother of his little daughter, but he thinks she's blocked his number because it goes straight to answerphone.

I head towards the primary school and down Summer Lane to the house where Jay grew up and where his mum still lives.

There are seven houses in a row built in the Edwardian period, providing council housing for the poorest agricultural workers of the village. When Jay was a young boy, they didn't have a bathroom and there was no inside toilet. The other day sitting in our treehouse he reminisced about bathing in an old metal tub by the fire and nipping to the 'lav' in the garden in the middle of the night.

There are tables in every garden and bunting adorning the picket fencing. The road is a dead end with fields either side. The back gardens overlook a steep hill where the children of the village sledge when it snows. With no-through traffic the children are playing in the lane, whizzing round on bikes and setting up games like skittles in the lane and again I have flashbacks to life in the 1970s.

Jay's mum smiles at me and I have the overwhelming urge to hug her, but I can't. 'You haven't changed one bit, dear,' she says. But I'm astonished at how much she's aged. She must have been around my age when I last saw her and now she's an old lady with thin grey hair and a wrinkly face, bringing into focus just how long I've been away. But behind this façade is the person I once knew, kind and sincere, what some would call the salt of the earth and warm memories run through my mind. As we chat a fuzzy feeling comes over me, it's as if she's waited all these years for our return. A powerful emotion washes over me - I'm home and this is where I belong.

It's hard to know where to begin after such a long gap so I ask her how she's finding lockdown.

'It's kiddies I feel for. Not being able to see their school friends. I've got ten grandkiddies, not seen 'em in weeks. One of them had a party on the computer. Mel set it up for me. Peculiar idea. The children looked like postage stamps on the screen.' She breaks off to laugh at her own joke. 'And the little girl next door, Amy, well she had what her mammy called a drive-by party. Bit American if you ask me. Like in one o' them old movies. Amy stood at the door while cars decorated with balloons stopped outside the house, littluns waving madly out of windows, dumping presents at gate.'

Sitting next to Jay's mum in the garden is Jay's sister Samantha and his brother John. Mel, Jay's niece, is doing most of the work, back and forward to the kitchen with trays of food which she passes round to the family and the neighbours. There are no bowls of crisps or peanuts or fingers to dip in and contaminate food. Everything has been carefully planned and prepared. There are bags of crisps and portions of food are individually wrapped. Bottles of hand sanitiser have been placed on the tables and children are nagged to wash their hands before they eat. Social distancing and limiting contact with others has become the new norm and everybody is trying their best to keep everyone safe. In years to come we'll look back at the photographs wondering why we're all standing at a distance from each other rather than as a huddled group.

I'm enjoying chatting to the neighbours. A few of the families have been in Summer Lane for decades but I barely remember them. The immediate neighbour is a lady in her nineties.

'How have you found the lockdown?' I ask her.

'Everyone's been very kind to me doing my weekly shop and getting my tablets from the chemist. But I still like going into the shop once a week to catch up with folk.'

'The idea is that you avoid going to the shop.' I chuckle at the madness of her going out anyway. 'Has it been a tough time?'

'No, dear, not really. I was born in the Great Depression. When I was a little girl my parents couldn't afford to buy me shoes. That's what I call tough. I've lived through polio, diptheria and a world war. I learned a long time ago not to see the world through the printed headlines but the people that surround me. I write my own headlines. If I wake up and I'm still alive to live another day, that's my headline.'

She's right. It's about counting one's blessings. I have Jay back in my life. That's all I want, and when I come to think of it, possibly all I've ever wanted.

Hours later Jay and I are cuddled up together watching the Queen address the nation followed by Katherine Jenkins singing outside Buckingham Palace the great song by Vera Lynn, *We'll Meet Again*. I'm struck by the poignancy of the words. Many people have been separated from loved ones because of the lockdown, but for Jay and me the lockdown brought us back together.

THE END

Thank you for reading 'Don't Blame Me.' If you enjoyed the story, I would greatly appreciate a short review on Amazon. Reviews are the lifeblood of authors.

To find other books by Joanna Warrington please go to my Amazon page:
https://www.amazon.co.uk/Joanna-Warrington/e/B00RH4XPI6%3Fref=dbs_a_mng_rwt_scns_share
Or to my website:
https://joannawarringtonauthor-allthingsd.co.uk

Other books in this series:
HOLIDAY My Book
Lyn wakes on her 50th birthday with no man and middle age staring her in the face.

"For readers who enjoy British humour." Readers Favorite.

Determined to change her sad trajectory Lyn books a surprise road trip for herself and her three children through the American Southwest and Yellowstone. Before they even get on the plane, the trip hits a major snag. An uninvited guest joins them at the airport turning their dream trip into a nightmare.

Amid the mountain vistas, secrets will be revealed and a hurtful betrayal confronted.

This book is more than an amusing family saga. It will also appeal to those interested in American scenery, history and culture.

A TIME TO REFLECT
My Book

How many people out there have been let down by their parents?

Having gambled all his life a father risks losing the one thing more precious to him than money; his daughter. Can he win back her love and trust or is it lost forever?
 A trip of a lifetime could be the perfect opportunity for Jules to put things right with his daughter, Ellie and sister, Pandora and heal old wounds but will the holiday uncover more unsavoury secrets? As long-simmering resentments rise to the surface and tensions reach breaking point, can the family ties prove strong enough to keep them together?

Will his family ever understand what drove his destructive addiction?

A gripping contemporary family saga, with beautiful travel descriptions of Cape Cod and Bostonwoven through, this is a story which highlights the dangers of gambling addiction and the pressures of modern life. For fans of Patricia Dixon, Josephine Cox, Callie Langridge & Joanna Trollope.

Previously published as 'Gambling Broke Us'

Every Parent's Fear series

My Book

The greatest fear in pregnancy is that something will go wrong.

We put our faith in the professionals, but they are not beyond making tragic and major errors of judgement.

Based on real events, this is the dramatic story of two lives intertwined by an unbelievable error.

A night in a Brighton hotel leads to grave and far-reaching consequences for Sandy and Jasper.

And Rona finds an unexpected partner in crime when she pushes the boundaries of professionalism to satisfy her intense desire for a child.

This story was inspired by the thalidomide scandal.

Printed in Great Britain
by Amazon